Also in the Gin & Tonic series

Doghouse
Fixed
Collared

CLAWED

A GIN & TONIC MYSTERY

L.A. KORNETSKY

POCKET BOOKS

New York   London   Toronto   Sydney   New Delhi

Pocket Books
A Division of Simon & Schuster, Inc.
1230 Avenue of the Americas
New York, NY 10020

This book is a work of fiction. Any references to historical events, real people, or real places are used fictitiously. Other names, characters, places, and events are products of the author's imagination, and any resemblance to actual events or places or persons, living or dead, is entirely coincidental.

First Pocket Books paperback edition June 2015

POCKET and colophon are registered trademarks of Simon & Schuster, Inc.

For information about special discounts for bulk purchases, please contact Simon & Schuster Special Sales at 1-866-506-1949 or business@simonandschuster.com.

The Simon & Schuster Speakers Bureau can bring authors to your live event. For more information or to book an event, contact the Simon & Schuster Speakers Bureau at 1-866-248-3049 or visit our website at www.simonspeakers.com.

Manufactured in the United States of America

10 9 8 7 6 5 4 3 2 1

ISBN 978-1-4767-5008-8
ISBN 978-1-4767-5013-2 (ebook)

For Shana, Indy, and Pandora, Mei-Chan, Boomer, and Cas.
Because these books couldn't have been written without them.

1

D on't be like that, babe."

His voice sounded the same, his face looked the same, everything was exactly the same as before except for his hands on her hips, his body too close to hers. She went still, the urge to fight warring with the need to disappear, for this to not be happening to her.

His hand stroked through her hair, obscenely gentle. She could scream, kick, shove him away, but the packet on the chair just behind him mocked her. If she did that, would he refuse to give it to her? Would he make trouble?

He kissed her, and it wasn't so bad, but then his hand slipped up, cupping her breast, and she shoved on instinct, moving him back hard enough to knock against the table.

Whatever he was going to say was interrupted by a sharp knock on the front door. He turned as though he could see who it was, and she took the chance to grab the packet, tucking it under her arm as though daring him to take it back. It was hers; she'd paid for it.

He shot her a look, as much exasperation as anger, and left the room, clearly going to see who was at the door. Not willing to stay there, she followed him, thinking to slide out the door while he was occupied with the newcomer.

"Why are you here?" He didn't seem pleased to see the woman standing outside, and sounded ruder than she'd ever heard him.

"We need to talk." The woman glanced at her, then took a longer look, making her uncomfortable enough to shift her feet, gripping the package tighter.

"You okay, sweetheart?" the woman asked.

"I . . . Yes. I'm fine." She didn't want to talk to anyone, she just wanted to go home. He looked like he was going to argue as she slipped past him, out onto the porch, but the woman took his attention again. "Leave the girl alone," she said. "We have business to discuss."

He really didn't look happy, but nodded, letting the woman in and closing the door behind them, but not before he gave her one last long stare.

She fled down the steps, and didn't look back.

Going sixty miles an hour was no time to suddenly feel someone licking the side of your face. The little car swerved slightly in its lane, and the driver used her right elbow to shove her passenger back down. "Georgie, sit. Sit!"

Her elbow barely dented the forty-plus pounds of muscle, but Georgie sighed mournfully, settled herself on the backseat again, and rested her wrinkled muzzle on her paws. Large brown eyes rolled upward as though she were the most put-upon dog in the universe.

"You spend half your life crammed into the back of Teddy's car without complaint. Put you in the backseat of a nice rental sedan, and suddenly you can't get comfortable?" Ginny shifted gears, checked the mirror, and then reached back to rub Georgie's tawny head with her free hand. "We're almost there, kiddo. And don't sigh like that at me. If I'd left you home you would have been even more miserable, and driven Mrs. Olson nuts."

Their next-door neighbor was willing to take the dog for a daily walk when Ginny couldn't be home in time, but the retiree was too old to get down on her knees and romp, and even though Georgie wasn't a puppy anymore, she still needed a lot of personal affection. The shar-pei had sulked for the entire three days Ginny had left her with Mrs. Olson, making the older woman think the dog was sick, and involving a panicked—and expensive—emergency vet visit.

"So it's your own fault that you're stuck back there. Sorry, girl."

The shar-pei sighed heavily, again, but otherwise behaved herself.

It wasn't entirely Georgie's fault, Ginny knew. Ginny was more agitated than usual—certainly more than she was comfortable with—and the dog was probably picking some of that up, and in her own doggy way trying to help.

"Everything's going to be fine," she said out loud, trying to reassure them both.

Being your own boss usually meant that every day was take-your-dog-to-work day. Even when she moved location to Mary's, either to meet with Tonica or just take a break, she was able to bring Georgie with her. Going out of town overnight? Not so much.

But this was her first meeting with an out-of-town client—hell, it was her first out-of-town client, period. And she couldn't focus if she was worried all the time about what Georgie was up to, either moping with a sitter, or moping in a kennel. So Ginny had rented a car instead of taking Amtrak from Seattle to Portland, and found a pet-friendly hotel that wasn't wildly expensive, and they'd see what happened.

"If nothing else, kid, you being able to handle a longer car ride would mean I could actually take you on long weekend trips. That's be nice, huh?" Not that there had been many of those recently, or were likely to be in the immediate future. Things had gone cold with her boyfriend—pretty much ex-boyfriend, she admitted, although they hadn't said the words to each other yet—and her reaction to relationships ending was always to throw herself into more work, but having pet-friendly options that didn't involve boarding Georgie at the vet in the future would be good.

"Maybe I could make you my silent partner," she said to the dog. "Mallard and Canine: Six Legs to Run Your Errands." There was more to being a private concierge than legwork, but she couldn't think of anything snappy that would fit on a business card. She took Georgie's soft snort as a complaint, and laughed. "You are not getting top billing. Deal with it."

The traffic was flowing nicely, and Georgie had settled

down again, so Ginny let her mind wander to a future where she had clients all the way down to San Francisco, letting the road run under her wheels, until her phone trilled, a familiar name coming up on the dashboard display. She fumbled for the phone plugged into the dashboard, managing to hit ACCEPT without taking her eyes off the road or accidentally hanging up on the person calling.

"Hey, Ginny." The connection was staticky, but Tonica's voice was clear. "You there yet?"

"Almost. Coming up on the bridge. Traffic was pretty good."

There was a clink of glassware in the background, and a low voice saying something she couldn't quite make out. She could almost imagine Tonica leaning against the bar, one hand on the phone, one eye watching Stacy or Seth setting up for the day. Then she frowned, checking the dash clock. It was too early for Tonica to be at Mary's—they didn't open until after noon on weekdays, and it was barely ten now.

"Why're you in so early?" And why was he calling her, she thought. They were friends, yeah, but not the call-and-hang-out-on-the-phone kind of friends.

"Delivery," he said with a sigh. "And I'm still the only one who can sign for anything,"

"I can!" Stacy's voice called out, clear for a moment, and Ginny laughed. She could only imagine his expression in reaction to the waitress-turned-bartender suggesting that she could forge his signature. "You don't really look the part," he said dryly, off-mic. "But thanks for playing."

In the backseat, Georgie had picked her head up at the sound of the familiar voices coming out of the phone, and now she whined a little, as though wondering where Tonica and Stacy were.

Tonica must have heard the noise, because he asked, "And how's Herself doing?"

Ginny looked at Georgie in the rearview mirror. "So far so good. A little twitchy, but that's understandable."

"And no projectile carsickness?"

Ginny was offended on her dog's behalf. "She's never once thrown up in your car. Why do you think she'd have problems now?"

"Because for all the jaunting around town we've done, we've never driven her three hours all at once. And because we both know that she's a delicate flower."

The fact that her occasional business partner—an avowed not-a-pet-person-damn-it-Mallard—now used "we" when talking about Georgie never failed to crack Ginny up. He was so totally owned, both by her dog, and Penny, the little tabby cat that had adopted him.

"Delicate flower my ass. She's tougher than you are, Tonica." She looked back at Georgie again. "You're not going to york in the car, are you, baby??"

Georgie remained noncommittal.

Ginny adjusted the rearview mirror again and returned her attention to the phone call. "Did you call just to check on her, or was there something you actually needed to ask me?"

"Yeah. While I'm stuck here waiting, I'm finishing up the paperwork on the Grabien case, and was trying to remember the name of the tow company. You paid for it, so I don't have a receipt."

She frowned in thought. That had been two weeks ago, and she'd been busy since then. "Mackenzie. Maybe? Something Scottish. And Sons? I don't remember. It was a bright yellow truck."

There was silence on the other end of the line. "Yeah, *that's* gonna help so much, thanks."

She could definitely see his expression this time: slightly irritated, eyes squinted, the phone pressed to his ear because he hated wearing a Bluetooth when he was working, running a hand over the top of his head, like the Marine-style haircut he had could get rumpled. Tonica—Theodore Tonica, full-time bartender at and manager of Mary's Bar, and her partner in their part-time and occasional, totally off-the-books "researchtigations" business, could do bitch-face like nobody's business.

Especially when it came to paperwork. It was a source of never-ending, if quiet, amusement that he'd let himself get talked into what was basically a management position the year before. For a man who claimed to not want responsibilities . . .

"Sorry." She sped up to pass a truck in the left lane, watching nervously as the lumber stacked on the long bed shifted as the truck moved. She hated sharing the road with logging trucks. "You're going to have to wait until I get home. Or you're going to have to go over to my apartment and sort through the receipts. They're in the blue folder on the left-hand side of my desk."

"Yeah, in my copious spare time I'll go rummage through your office, and have you glare at me for a week afterward because I messed up your filing system. Pass. It'll wait."

"I'll check it as soon as I get home. Might want to email me a reminder, though. Anything else?"

"No, looks like all the tees are dotted and the eyes are crossed."

She gave that joke the laugh it deserved, and even Georgie groaned, although the dog was prone to grunts and heavy exhales on an understood-only-to-dogs basis.

"Anyway, everything else is quiet down here, for the moment, although having said that I'm sure something's about to go horrible wrong. You really had to go down tonight? You're going to miss Trivia Night. Again."

"Yeah, I know." Trivia Night was a big deal at Mary's, and once upon a time she'd been a fierce member of her team. But truthfully, if only admitted to herself, since the two of them had started solving actual mysteries she hadn't felt quite the same competitive urge. Answering questions about literary quotations, or random scientific facts just didn't seem . . . challenging enough anymore.

And anyway, making money trumped trivia. This new client wasn't paying much, but she was the first in a new city, and if Ginny did well, it could open up a lot of new doors. Or at least the occasional lucrative one.

"Just think of it as your team's chance to finally win," she told him. "I'll be back in a few days. Tell Seth to take the tuna salad off the menu before I get back."

"Yeah, 'cause he listens to anything I say," Tonica groused, and then hung up.

"They can't function without us," Ginny told Georgie, who thumped her slender, twisted tail once—a move that involved more of her hindquarters than actual tail—as though to agree. Ginny didn't have any official connection to Mary's, but the past two years she was pretty sure she'd spent as much time there as in her own apartment, so much so that they'd threatened to put her name on one of the bar stools.

"It's not even the nicest place in town," she told Georgie now. "And their wine selection is seriously subpar. Why do we keep going back there again?"

Well, she knew why Georgie went: because Penny was there. Whoever'd coined the phrase "fights like cats and dogs" had never seen Georgie and Penny hanging out together. She and Tonica might have become friends as well as part-time partners, but Georgie and Penny were besties.

And Ginny went back because it had become her second home, as clichéd as that sounded. The Trivia Nights, packed to the walls and noisy. The quiet afternoons, kicking back and talking with Stacy and Tonica, with Seth muttering in the background, the nearly perfect martinis Tonica made, and the fact that her friends knew that they could find her there, either at the third bar stool down, or the table by the window . . .

"Oh God, I've become a cliché," she said, laughing at herself. "Georgie, we need an intervention, stat, or we're going to become a sitcom."

Then Georgie made an unfortunate, unhappy noise, and Ginny was too busy trying to find a spot to pull over to think more about Mary's.

"No, no, sweetie—just hang on a minute more . . ."

"That Ginny on the phone?" The question came from down the other end of the bar, where his waitress/occasional bartender/*aide de folie* was prepping the bar for open.

"Yeah." Teddy inspected the glassware that had come out of the machine and decided that they passed muster, sliding them into the rack under the counter. "She's running down to Portland on business."

Stacy paused in the act of moving a full bottle behind a half-empty one on the shelf and turned to look at him. "Her business, or . . . ?"

"Her own."

"Good." Stacy finished adjusting the whiskey, and turned her attention to the bottles of vodka. Her ponytail twitched as she moved, and Penny, in her usual perch above the shelves, reached down a paw as though to snag it. Fortunately for them both, Stacy was a few inches too short, and the cat couldn't quite reach. "Not that I don't have a lot of fun when you guys poke into other people's business, where 'fun' means potentially getting beaten up or robbed or puppy-sitting, but her tab needs paying."

"Oh, that's not fair," he said, then paused. Actually, that was a pretty accurate summation of the past year or so. Well, almost. They had gotten threatened, and robbed, and there had been a puppy here briefly, but Ginny hardly ran an ex-treme tab here, especially since they tended to "forget" to charge her for refills. "I do approve of the mercenary way you're thinking, though. Excellent progress, young Padawan."

Stacy made a rude gesture in his direction. She was about twice as mercenary as he was on a good day, and they both knew it. He was a bartender because he liked people, not because he liked profit.

Of course, when it came to mercenary urges, Ginny could and would eat them both for lunch. Her drive and focus, and his people skills: that was what made them such a good team. It was a good mix. "Gin and Tonica Investiga-tions," one of the wags at the bar had dubbed them. It was a terrible pun, but it had stuck, at least with the crowd at Mary's. Outside, they didn't advertise. This was still a side-line, a part-time gig neither of them had planned on taking on, much less keeping.

He'd had doubts at first. And, all right, at second and third, too. This "researchtigations" gig had seemed doomed to crash and burn, and possibly take them both down with it. But Teddy was honest enough to admit that he was hooked on the satisfaction of a successful case, on helping people out of tough spots. And, ideally, not getting hit, beat up, or otherwise busted in the process.

That thought made him look at the paperwork on the bar in front of him, still needing to be finished, and he winced. They hadn't gotten hit that time, but his classic Saab had. And trying to explain why a little old lady had taken a hammer to his front hood . . .

"Hey, we got a couple of requests to put those grilled cheese sandwiches back on the menu," Stacy said. "You want to tell Seth?"

"Not particularly." He might be the manager of the bar, and the final say—short of the owner—on what happened there, but the tiny kitchen was Seth's domain, and the only thing the ex-boxer disliked more than Teddy telling him what to do was a *customer* telling him.

But it was a more appealing job than trying to fill in the accident report paperwork, and thinking about the damage that had been done to his beloved coupe during their *last* case. So he shoved them aside and left Stacy to the bar prep—and Penny to manage in his absence—while he bearded their inevitably surly cook in his kitchen.

His life was busy enough, and Ginny was busy enough. He shouldn't be wishing another researchtigations job would show up.

But he was.

2

Ginny wasn't familiar with Portland, so it took them another hour to navigate the surface roads, and find their destination, even with GPS.

"Good afternoon, Ms. Mallard. Welcome to the Pines." The hotel she'd booked online and sight unseen ended up being a pleasant if bland four-story building just east of Portland's city limits. It was a little run-down at the edges, but the older man at the check-in desk had a smile and a biscuit for Georgie, and the room was ready, so she could forgive things like beige-on-beige decorating and barely audible Muzak. Ginny approved. If she started getting more clients outside of Seattle, this could become a regular arrangement.

Assuming that Georgie could handle being left alone in a strange place, anyway. Ginny really hoped she could, and not just because the security deposit wasn't refundable in case of damage or unfortunate incidents.

Georgie was clearly glad to be out of the car, sniffing everything from the lobby to the elevator to the hotel room from corner to corner, paying particular attention to the rug under the small writing desk.

The room, as promised, was clean and large enough for Georgie's crate to be set up in a corner of the room and not block access to the bathroom or closet. And it didn't smell—to her nose, anyway—of any other dogs who might have stayed there before.

"You going to be okay staying here, girl?" Ginny asked, setting up the travel crate, letting the dog sniff at it as well, until she was reassured that it smelled familiar and, yes, was her own. "Momma has to go to work for a few hours, but I'll be back in time to walk you, promise."

When they were working a case, visiting sites, or questioning potential witnesses, Ginny and Tonica often brought Georgie: for all that she was a marshmallow personality-wise, her blunt-shaped head, strong legs, and broad chest gave her an intimidating appearance that could quell potential problems. Adding to that a strong protective streak, coupled with enough training that she wouldn't do more than growl at someone unless given the command, Georgie was an effective problem-deterrent. But a wheelchair-bound woman in her seventies seemed unlikely to cause problems Ginny couldn't handle by herself, with one hand tied behind her back and a pebble in her shoe.

The crate approved, Georgie wandered into the bathroom, where Ginny could hear her lapping up some water from the bowl Ginny had set up, then the dog padded back out and curled up on her fleece bed in the crate, showing no aftereffects from her roadside upchuck. Ginny took out the new chew toy she had brought along as a bribe, and Georgie took it with her usual enthusiasm, settling back down to add some saliva and tooth marks to make it perfect.

"Yeah, you're not worried about being left alone in a strange place at all, are you? Tough girl, takes down bad guys and pals around with a pussycat, this is nothing." Shar-peis, she had learned, were remarkably unflappable dogs. She couldn't have chosen a better companion if she'd planned it, instead of unexpectedly falling in love at a sidewalk shelter display. "Maybe if the client's a dog person, I'll bring you along tomorrow, huh?"

The thought made her slap herself, mentally, because she should have asked the client, when they were exchanging emails. Having a dog—especially one as unusual-looking as Georgie, with her loose folds of skin and piglet tail—was an excellent icebreaker. People seemed to relax around dogs—and if they didn't, that told her something about them, too. But the information she and her new client had exchanged had been job focused, talking about what the woman wanted, and Ginny's rates, and then arranging this visit to meet in person. Saying, "Hey, do you like dogs? Mind if I bring mine along?" hadn't even occurred to Ginny.

"Maybe I should put a photo of you up on the website," she said now. "Would you like that, huh?"

Georgie's stump of a tail wagged now, as though she understood what Ginny was asking, but otherwise she seemed perfectly content to be where she was, barely even looking up when Ginny packed up her briefcase, gave her one final scratch, and left the room.

In the elevator, Ginny checked the time—cutting it closer than she'd wanted, but still good—and then checked her briefcase again to make sure that she had everything she needed: tablet, cell phone, folder with brochures and flyers from places the client might want to consider for her party, and the printouts of the emails she and Mrs. Adaowsky had exchanged in case the unthinkable happened and her tablet ran out of charge. She was—as always—organized to a fare-thee-well. But not having Georgie's familiar, comforting bulk leaning against her leg was weirdly . . . discomforting.

"You don't need a guard dog, Mallard; the woman's hiring you to arrange an old girls' reunion, not a gunrunner's weekender." That was her specialty: arranging things for people who didn't have the time, energy, or interest in doing for themselves, from family vacations to baby showers to the one client who'd wanted her to organize his rather complicated dating schedule. Ginny grimaced at the memory: she'd charged extra for that one, on the "annoying client penalty" scale.

But Mrs. Adaowsky sounded, at least via her emails, like a proverbial peach. Seventy-two, a retired teacher, who wanted to get her surviving college friends together for one last, as her email put it, "sedate hoo-rah."

Normally Ginny met her clients in a neutral third-party location—a coffee shop or café—or via a Skype or phone call. But her new client was hard of hearing, and had wanted to have a personal contact, at least for this first meeting. Which was fine—especially since the client was covering her travel costs, as an apology for the last-minute nature of the job.

If Mrs. Adaowsky was a peach, then this job was a piece of cake, and Ginny almost felt bad about how much she was charging the woman. Almost. She got in the car, humming under her breath. Odds were, the worst thing that would go wrong was that the GPS screwed up again, she got lost in an unfamiliar neighborhood, and was late to the meeting.

The GPS behaved itself perfectly. Ginny's inability to shift lanes in time to hit her exit, though, cost her nearly ten minutes of backtracking. But there was on-street parking on the block she'd been directed to, and ten minutes late wasn't too bad. Hopefully, the client wasn't the sort to twitch over every minute like it was carved out of gold.

"I'm terribly sorry—I completely missed the exit," she said, practicing her apology out loud as she got out of the car, locked it, and looked for her destination.

The address she'd been given turned out to be a pretty little house in a distinctly suburban neighborhood filled with pretty little houses, most of them single-story, with porches and tiny but tidy lawns. Old houses, she thought. Prewar, certainly; you could tell from something about the windows and doors. She liked architecture, but more in a "that's pretty, that's awkward" way, not being able to identify a particular style or decade.

She found the right house number, and stepped up onto the porch, ringing the doorbell. It echoed inside the house, a warm tone loud enough that an older, deafer woman could hear it. But nobody answered.

Maybe it took a while for her to get around, in a wheelchair. Ginny pressed the bell again after a few minutes, and for good measure used the heavy door knocker, too.

"Hello?"

She was late, but here. But her client wasn't. Or at least, she wasn't coming to the door.

Ginny looked at the number on the door, then double-checked the address in her tablet. Right street name, right street number. She rang the doorbell a third time, and waited, then went back down the stairs to look at the house, hoping to see a curtain twitch, or some other sign of life.

Nothing.

"Great." She reached into her pocket for her phone, and stopped, looking at the house again. "Wheelchair." Mrs. Adaowsky had said she was in a wheelchair; that was why they had to meet here, because it was too difficult for her to get around. But there was no ramp to the front stairs, not even one of those temporary ones they used when someone had an accident.

"Maybe there's one around back?" It didn't seem to make much sense to her, but she lived in a relatively new elevator building that had to conform to Americans with Disabilities Act standards—what did she know about adapting hundred-year-old houses? This was the right address . . . surely the woman had given her the right information!

Maybe Mrs. Adaowsky had forgotten? Or she was somewhere she couldn't hear the bell? Ginny called the phone number she'd been given, and waited. It rang three times, and on the third time she thought she heard an echo coming from the house.

So she had the right location. But where was Mrs. Adaowsky? Ginny climbed the steps again and this time in addition to ringing the bell, she tried the door handle.

It turned, and the door opened under her surprised hand. Huh.

The phone was still ringing, somewhere in the house, and she pressed the END tab on her phone. Silence.

"Hello? Mrs. Adaowsky?"

She took a step in, and waited. Nothing stirred inside the house. The air was still and warm; if there was air-conditioning, it wasn't turned on. "Hello?"

No response.

"Well, I was invited," she said out loud, as though convincing a companion. "And the door was unlocked. Maybe she's injured, needs my help?" That was a loophole the cops could use, wasn't it? If they thought someone was in need of help? So it would probably cover her ass, too. . . .

Why was she even thinking about cops? Paranoid, she was totally getting paranoid. The old woman might be in the bathroom, or taking a nap.

"Hello?" Third time was the charm. She took another step into the house, looking around as she did. The décor was totally not what she'd expected, from the correspondence she'd had with the woman. She'd thought the house would be little-old-lady chic, full of overstuffed furniture and doilies, and fake flowers. Ginny knew that was a total

stereotype but based on memories of her own grandmoth-
ers, not unfounded. Instead, the walls were painted a bland
white, with a few framed photographs on the wall, and the
floor was covered in wall-to-wall carpeting of a vague pale
brown, the furniture obviously Ikea specials right out of
the flatpack.

In fact, she thought, it looked like every rental apartment
she'd ever seen, not like an older woman's well-lived-in
home. Although—on closer look—the photographs were
beautiful: scenes of mountains and vineyards, and busy
city streets, all professionally framed. Mrs. Adaowsky had
good taste. And maybe she'd had to refurnish everything
to make room for a wheelchair. Ginny nodded. That made
sense. Better to stay in your own home and get rid of some
furniture than have to go into assisted living. That fit with
the tone of the emails, too. Mrs. Adaowsky probably took
no shit, and didn't care what anyone else thought about her
choices.

The living room/dining area was one large open space,
with the sofa and coffee table, plus a few chairs at one
end and a long wooden table at the other. But instead of a
table runner and fake flowers, or whatever she'd thought
little old ladies left on their dining room tables, there were
four laptops plugged into a power strip, and a massive,
professional-quality color printer in the corner of the room,
as though someone had decided to start a small business at
home.

Well, maybe she had. Maybe Mrs. Adaowsky was a total
senior citizen start-up machine, and the furniture was

gone not because of infirmity but activity. More power to her if so, and Ginny would feel better about working for someone with an actual income, rather than depending on Social Security and an iffy pension.

But then where was Granny Go-Getter? Maybe those ten minutes Ginny was late had pissed the older woman off, and she'd gone for a stroll—a roll—to cool off? Or something else had gone wrong. . . .

"Hello?" she called out again, all her previous doubts pushing against her wishful thinking. Her fingers twitched, and she rubbed them against the side of her skirt, nervously. This really didn't feel good.

She probably should leave. Instead, Ginny moved toward the back of the house, thinking that most household accidents happen in the kitchen or bathroom, trying not to think about the odds of encountering a little old lady facedown in the bathtub.

A set of swinging wooden doors led her into the kitchen, a large, well-lit space that had made only token adaption to the twenty-first century. Ginny was pretty sure that the stove was older than she was, although everything was spotless. The refrigerator had a handful of takeout menus tacked to the side, and there was an impressive, industrial-looking coffeemaker on the counter, next to an electric teakettle, and several boxes of tea. It seemed more like an office kitchenette than a home kitchen. Maybe Mrs. Adaowsky didn't like to cook, or her being in a wheelchair meant she wasn't able to, or . . .

Or this was the wrong house, despite her having the address written down and double-checked. Despite the fact that the phone number she'd been given rang here.

The smart thing at this point—probably ten minutes ago, Ginny acknowledged—would be to backtrack, leave the house, go back to the hotel, and wait for the client to call her with an explanation and an apology for running late. That would be the smart thing to do.

Instead, she kept going. A narrow door led to a cramped half bathroom, nothing but a plain toilet and a tiny sink. At the other end of the kitchen, a slightly wider door opened into what might have been a maid's room at one point, maybe, but now looked like it had been repurposed into a photography studio.

She blinked, and then looked again, but that first impression held. The space was painted entirely white, a sort of bland, nonreflective color, with a beige cloth covering the far wall. There was a single window, but it was covered with a blind the same muted white as the walls, making it appear almost invisible. There was a black metal cabinet against one wall, and a chair at the other, in front of the beige drape. That was the only furniture in the room. Curious, she bent down to see what was in the cabinet. The door opened easily, revealing a camera, lenses, and a tripod, all neatly put away on the bottom shelf, and on the top, a long, narrow plastic box. She knew she shouldn't, but curiosity drove her to open it, revealing a stack of cards made of flexible white plastic, and a smaller stack next to it, with printing on them.

"Huh." She reached up to look at the smaller stack more

closely, then frowned and went down the line, checking each one.

When she'd been in college, someone down the hall had pulled in decent money making fake IDs for underage drinkers. He'd set up an oversized replica of a driver's license, and the person buying it would stand in front of the display and have their photo taken, then he'd downsize the entire thing and laminate it. A quick glance by a bartender or bouncer wouldn't have seen anything fake about it.

These looked about a thousand times more sophisticated, but were pretty clearly fake. Unless the DMV in Oregon worked out of residential homes. "I know we're outsourcing everything these days," she said, "but that's a bit extreme."

The sound of her voice echoed in the enclosed space, reminding her that she was poking around in a stranger's house, and while making fake IDs might be amusing in college, it was still illegal. Whoever was involved probably would not be happy about finding her in there. And it was pretty clear by now that Mrs. Adaowsky was not at home, and odds were, this wasn't her home at all.

Right now, she was *hoping* the latter.

Ginny replaced the card in the box and wiped her hand against the fabric of her skirt, then retreated back into the kitchen, turning off the light as she went. Her nerves were prickling now, and the need to be out of the house overwhelmed her worry about her missing client. She would call again once she was in the car, and see if she'd misread their meeting place somehow.

The bright lime-green paint of the kitchen seemed unbearably gaudy after the dimmer white of the smaller room, and Ginny squinted instinctively, turning to push open the swinging door back into the living room, when her entire body froze.

She was almost a hundred percent certain that the body hadn't been there before.

3

She'd never had to call 911 before. The dispatcher took her information, confirmed her number and location because she was using her cell phone with a Seattle address, then told her to go wait outside, and not to touch anything.

She sat on the front porch, wishing Georgie was with her, for nearly half an hour before the ambulance arrived, a cop car hot on its wheels. To be fair, Ginny admitted it wasn't as though the person inside was going to mind waiting, and she wasn't sure she could have stood up steadily before then. The sirens drew a few people outside, staring at the house, and Ginny suspected there were a bunch of curtains being pulled aside in other houses. This might be the most excitement this block had seen in years.

The paramedics pushed past her with their gear, followed by one of the cops. The other walked up to Ginny and—after identifying her—gave her a thorough once-over and motioned for her to come down off the porch. "You okay?"

"For not-okay versions of okay, yeah," she managed to say, and his mouth twisted a little in what she thought might have been a smile. He was middle-aged, with an odd mole next to his left eye, and an attitude that said he'd been on the job a few years too long, but his voice was gentle when he had her run through everything she'd seen and done that morning.

He wrote down everything Ginny said, then glanced back at the house and asked her again, "And you didn't touch anything?"

"No. I . . . I saw it, and then I came outside, and I called it in. And I waited here until you arrived." She had told him this already, same as she'd told the dispatcher, but she knew they'd ask again, and probably again, as though she were going to change her story. At least they hadn't made her go back inside: the sight of the body shoved under the kitchen table, its limbs curled around itself, neck at an angle that *said* it was broken, even though she'd never seen anything like that before . . .

"All right, wait here." And he walked off, she guessed to see what was going on inside, although he didn't actually go inside the house, just checked in via radio. Was he watching her? Or keeping an eye on the people who were clumping on the sidewalk across the street? Probably both, Ginny decided.

This made the second dead body Ginny had ever seen up close and personal, but somehow it was so much worse. Because she hadn't been expecting it? Because it was so obviously a violent death, not prettied up to seem like natural causes, or an accident?

Or because it was the body not of the elderly handicapped woman she'd been expecting to meet, but a man probably—from the quick look she'd had—about her own age? In the still coldly rational part of her brain that was observing everything that was going on, Ginny suspected it was the latter: that she was not shocked that there had been a dead body, but that it hadn't been who she was expecting.

That wasn't a particularly good thing to realize about herself.

She waited another fifteen minutes while things happened out of sight inside the house, resisting the urge to check her phone or tablet in case that was a no-no she hadn't been warned about, feeling the itch for information like a thousand mosquitos all at once. The crowd across the street had grown to about fifteen people, not counting the curtain-twitchers, and she wondered if they were coming in from other neighborhoods as word spread.

Eventually, the cop who'd been inside came out again and met up with her partner, just as an unmarked sedan that screamed "cop" pulled up to the curb. A white news van pulled up behind that. She wasn't sure if she should be surprised someone sent a crew to cover this, or insulted that they hadn't gotten there earlier. Wasn't her murder important enough?

Both cops turned and frowned at her, as though they'd heard that last thought. She lifted her hands and widened her eyes in a "what? I'm just standing here like you told me" response. Snark might not be the best response, but she was pretty sure that she hadn't done anything wrong—other than walking in the house, but she'd thought she was meeting someone there!—and they were still giving her dirty looks.

The cops came back to her, the woman scowling. "And what were you doing inside, again?"

She had explained that to them already, too. Twice. So might as well go for three. "I had made an appointment to meet with a potential client." She'd given the first cop her business card, showed him the information in her schedule, and the call log on her phone that connected to the landline inside. "When she didn't respond, but the door was unlocked, I went inside to see if she was in need of assistance."

So far, nobody had mentioned illegal entry, so she was probably right about some Good Samaritan law covering her ass. Or they were waiting for her to say something incriminating. "I've told you three times already: I thought I was meeting a woman named Amanda Adaowsky, for a business meeting."

She didn't mention poking around in the studio, was thankful that she'd had the presence of mind—or the paranoia—to wipe where she'd touched the cabinet door, hoping to make her fingerprints unreadable. Whoever that guy was, and whyever he'd been killed and shoved under the table, she just wanted to be the poor woman who'd found him, not someone of interest.

The problem was, one of the first things she'd learned during their very first job was that if the cops were looking at you, you were already in trouble. And the fact that she claimed to be here to meet someone who—according to the first cop's terse comment—didn't live here? Yeah, she was already on their radar. She should just give her statement and get the hell out of Dodge. But her curiosity was warring with her desire to disappear, and curiosity was winning. As usual.

"So what happened?"

The second cop was still scowling, shooting a glance over to where a woman with short, graying hear, wearing a Portland Police Department windbreaker and cap, but with no obvious gun, was standing, looking at the house. She must've arrived in the second car. "And you have no idea who the individual inside might be?" the female cop asked again, ignoring Ginny's question.

Ginny shook her head, feeling the once-smooth knot of hair at the back of her head start to fall apart, curls brushing against the back of her neck. She didn't even bother to try to tuck them back in: nobody was going to be impressed by her professional appearance at this point. "No. Mrs. Adaowsky"—except that there was no Mrs. Adaowsky here, it seemed—"didn't mention having a son or a care-taker, so no. Is he, was he . . ."

Of course he was: you didn't end up shoved under the kitchen table accidentally, not like that, not without any signs of an accident, but she had to ask, anyway.

"That's still under investigation, ma'am." Deadpan stonewall. "You'll be staying locally, in case we need to speak with you again?"

They didn't tell her not to leave town, but it was implicit in the tone. The fact that she'd come here to see some-one who didn't seem to live here at all, and found a dead body . . . Yeah, she wouldn't let her leave town, either. Ginny smiled politely and told them again where she was staying, and watched them write it down again. The advantage to telling the truth, the whole truth, and nothing but the truth was that it was a lot harder for someone to catch you out in a lie. But it got boring, repeating it over and over again.

She glanced at the activity on the front porch of the house, then at the small crowd of rubberneckers, trying to decide if they were more interested in the activity on the porch or the two local news teams now covering the activity, then looked at her watch again.

"May I go now? I left my dog at the hotel, and she'll need to be walked soon. . . ." Georgie would probably be fine for another hour or two, but as reasons to go it seemed like one cops couldn't give her grief about.

The first cop flapped his hand at her, which she took to mean "yeah, go on, get out of my face." They were taking the body away now, a covered gurney, and Ginny hesitated a moment, then shook her head. She wasn't involved, she didn't need to linger—especially since if one of the news crews saw she was off the cop's leash, they might try to corner her for an interview. She really didn't want to talk to anyone right then: she just wanted to get back to her hotel, walk Georgie, and let everything that had happened today shake down into some kind of sense.

Of course, she was too flustered to pay attention to where she was going, missed a turn, and got lost on her way back to the hotel. By the time she let herself into the room, enough time had gone by that her excuse was true: Georgie was nearly frantic with the need to go for a walk, although she'd been a good girl and not done anything that would have required apologizing to the housekeeping staff.

Despite the worry and chaos that was tangling her thinking, Ginny smiled at the dog's exuberance, all other thoughts put aside for a few seconds. "Hey, girl, you were a good girl, weren't you?" A blue-black tongue washed her face, paws pushing against her legs as she knelt down to say hello. "Yeah, okay, hang on a minute."

The act of clicking the leash onto Georgie's collar and shoving a few poo bags into her jacket pocket was familiar enough to be soothing, as was watching her dog's simple pleasure at the smell of the air outside, the feel of grass under her paws, and the relief of being able to pee. The shar-pei dragged her from one end of the designated dog walking area to the other, sniffing at everything, and occasionally remembering what she'd come out here to do in the first place.

The physical act of walking the dog let Ginny's brain focus on the day's events with a little more composure, pushing aside the mildly emotional weebling and focusing on the facts.

Fact one: her client had not been at the house.

Fact two: her client did not, by all appearances, live at that house.

Fact three: someone probably not her client had been, by all appearances, running a fake ID shop out of that house.

Fact four: someone—probably someone who did live in

that house, or maybe worked there, or was just a random stranger, although she thought that was unlikely—had been killed there.

She had the where, and could guess at the how, but the who and the why were still unanswered. The cops would be able to get the who pretty quickly, but the *why* . . .

"People are complicated, Georgie," she said. "We lie, we cheat, we steal, we do things that require fake ID, and then we kill people and shove them under tables. What's with that, anyway? What in that guy's life made him worth killing? Was it the fake IDs?" She shook her head, having trouble imagining that. "Who gets murderous over fake driver's licenses?"

Her dog, finished with her rounds, bumped her head against Ginny's leg and aimed deep brown eyes up at her owner with a quiet plea.

"I'd rather be a dog, I think. You've got all the basics covered, don't you?" Ginny said, giving Georgie the expected treat from her pocket. "Food, shelter, belly rubs . . ."

Georgie took the treat gracefully, then whined as though to say, "Well, yes, and where *are* my belly rubs?" and flopped over on the pavement, wiggling happily against the rough surface. Ginny laughed and bent down to oblige, one hand scratching the plush fawn-colored fur on the dog's stomach.

"Not my circus, not my monkeys, isn't that the saying?" She should just walk away, leave it be, leave town as soon as the cops gave her the all clear, which hopefully would be today, or tomorrow at the latest.

"It is weird, though," she went on, still rubbing Georgie's belly. "Not the dead guy, because sadly that's not weird at all, I've discovered." Even before she'd started looking into people's uglier secrets, she'd not been an idealist about human behavior—she'd worked in too many offices for that. "I mean, Mrs. Adaowsky. She contacts me, hires me, pays my retainer, which, okay, isn't huge but it's not chump change, either, and then gives me the wrong address, the wrong phone number? And it just happens, hey, to be a murder scene?" Ginny frowned, staring across the parking lot without really seeing anything, still petting Georgie's belly. "Which raises the question of, if Mrs. A actually calls me back, do I *want* to take the call? Or do I tell her that her retainer bought my trip down here, but her games cost her the rest of me?

"What do you think, baby? Maybe I should call Tonica, get his take on this?"

Georgie whined again, but that could have been requesting harder scritches, not telling her to call her sometimes-partner.

"No," Ginny decided, pushing back to her feet. "This is weird, and my serious bad luck in getting caught up in any of it, but we're done. Whatever the hell is going on, this one's for the cops to figure out, not us. And Mrs. Adaowsky can whistle for me—I'm done." Ginny worked with a wide range of divas—that being the personality type who hired private concierges, as a rule—but she wasn't a docile lapdog they could ignore and scoop up at whim. She demanded respect from her clients, as well as a respectable fee—it was the only way to get the job done. And giving her the runaround was not respectful.

"And neither is dumping a dead body on me," she said out loud. "I need to add that to the website's FAQ. If you have a dead body, you have to say that right up front."

So what now? The job was a bust, but she'd already paid for the night's stay. The hotel wasn't going to give her a refund just because her client turned out to be a no-show. And while she didn't think the cops would really give her shit about going back to Seattle—they could find her there easily enough, and there was the technological marvel of the phone, if they had anything else they wanted to ask her—wanting her own bed didn't trump the probable annoyance of having to call the police station and tell them she'd changed her mind, she was going home.

But sitting in the hotel room with nothing to do except wonder about a dead body she shouldn't even know about wasn't going to do her any good. Might as well try to get some positive out of this trip. . . .

Fortunately, Portland wasn't without friendlies. She pulled her phone out of her jacket pocket and dialed a number from memory, waiting for the other person to pick up. "Ron, hi, it's Ginny again. Thanks for the advice on the rental car, it's as solid as you said. But it looks like my job fell through so I'm free for dinner tonight after all. You still—all right, yeah, that sounds good. Just tell me where." She listened to Ron yelling to someone else, then giving her an address.

"McMenamins Kennedy School, seven o'clock. No,

s'okay, I can find it. I have been to Portland before, you know." He said something and she made a face but, in light of her mishaps this afternoon, couldn't really argue. "I have GPS on my tablet, thank you very much."

Seven o'clock. That gave her two hours to kill before she'd have to leave, even allowing time to get lost. "C'mon, Georgie, back inside. Momma needs to fire up the laptop."

She'd said she was done with her would-be client, but the fact that the phone had rung in the house that the woman didn't live in bothered Ginny. And by "bothered" she meant "was starting to piss her off."

Once she had Georgie settled down with her dinner, Ginny sat cross-legged on the bed and flipped open her laptop. She'd almost not brought it, thinking the tablet would be enough for a two-day trip, but at the last minute she'd thrown it in the bag, mostly out of habit. She was thankful now: she could run searches on her tablet, but it was easier to work with a full keyboard.

She flexed her fingers and called up her browser, common sense warring with curiosity. The dead body was a matter for the cops. She wasn't going to mess with that, not when she'd been the one to find the body—she'd watched enough TV and movies to know how badly that could go. And anyway, she didn't even have a name to start with— "random dead white guy in Portland" might be enough for professionals, but Ginny knew her limits—even if she didn't always admit to them.

"Pull the threads you can see first," she told herself. "Amanda Adaowsky."

Ginny had done a basic search on her would-be client when the woman first approached her, but that had been an "is there something negative about this person I need to know before I accept?" search, not a "does this person even exist?" dig, because who thought to do that?

Ginny didn't like wasting time, but she really hated being played for an idiot.

"Fool me once, shame on you. And I won't get fooled twice," she told the screen grimly, entering in the search parameters. "Every new client's going to get a full scrub-down, from here on in." Too late for that now, on this job. But if there *was* an Amanda Adaowsky anywhere in the contiguous forty-eight, the two external states, or Canada, she'd know by dinnertime. After that . . . well, she'd see where that thread led her.

Tuesday afternoons at Mary's were usually quiet, as though gathering strength for the chaos that generally erupted once Trivia Night began. Once a week, people came in from all over the city, filling the bar for two hours of heated smarter-than-you gamesmanship. And drinking. Teddy both hated it and loved it. Usually more the former than the latter, by the time he kicked the last person out and could close up.

But it was routine, honed to perfection over the past few years. He had woken up around eleven, gone for his morning run, then showered and headed into work to open the bar for Stacy before heading out again to run some errands and coming back for his own shift. A perfectly ordinary day, no urgent phone calls or sudden disasters, nothing at all odd about it . . .

Except there had been a niggling sense of something missing, something out of order. He gave the bar a quick once-over but found nothing that could explain it. He hadn't turned the stove on that morning, so he couldn't have left it on, and his coffeemaker was timed to shut off on its own.

It wasn't until he'd stumbled over doing his receipts that he'd realized what was missing: Ginny. And Georgie. Not that it was unusual for her to go a day or two without coming by, but Tuesdays had been sacred for as long as he'd known her. She was slightly fanatical about her team—a little competitive, was Ginny Mallard.

Except she hadn't been quite so into it the past few months, had she?

Shaking his head, he told himself that he should be glad if Ginny was losing interest in trivia, because it meant his team could win more often. Not that, as manager, he played often anymore . . . When you had to keep an eye on everything both in front of and behind the bar, it was tough to focus on the questions.

He finished pouring the current round of orders and took a thirty-second breather to check the action. Trivia Night wouldn't start for another four hours, at nine o'clock, but someone had already pulled three of the smaller tables together, although there were only two people at it right now. He made a mental note that there would be a larger group hitting soon. Most of the other tables had bodies at them, but only half the bar stools were taken. It was normal enough business for an afternoon, not like Thursdays or Fridays, when people were starting to let off steam for the weekend.

Not that anyone ever let off too much steam here, thankfully. He'd worked all kind of places over the years, from trendy clubs to dives, and Mary's was his favorite—a neighborhood joint, warm but not flashy, where you took someone you'd already kissed, and liked kissing, and planned to kiss again.

Or—he raised a hand to greet newcomers, already reaching for the pint glass, knowing what they would order—where you went and ordered the same thing every single time, and expected the bartender to know that . . . because he did.

"I'm working in a sitcom," he muttered, and the woman waiting for her drink grinned at him. "Not Norm!"

"You're *all* Norm," he shot back, to the confusion of the twenty-somethings waiting their turn. And for a moment, just a moment, the sense of something being out of place subsided.

"Hey, boss, Seth says we're out of bread because, and I quote, we have two-legged locusts, end quote, and should he run out and buy more bread or just tell 'em the kitchen's closed?" Stacy widened her eyes at him, waiting for an answer, even as she loaded the three waiting beers onto her tray.

"Jesus, it's barely seven, the kitchen just opened." He'd

accuse Seth of tossing perfectly usable bread because he didn't want to make more sandwiches, except the older man might take a swing at him. Or quit. He'd come back after Teddy groveled a little but that was an extra argh he really didn't need this week. Any week. They'd hired a second waitress last month, but it wasn't enough. They needed more people, and they needed people who would *stick around.*

Once upon a time, he'd just been lead bartender: no responsibilities, no obligations, no need to mediate. A lot fewer headaches. Where had it all gone wrong?

"Tell him to keep the kitchen open and roll the meat and cheese in the lettuce, then stick it with a toothpick. Call it, hell, I don't know, 'No-Carbwiches' or something."

"Boss, you're occasionally brilliant." Stacy took her tray and disappeared into the back to pass the news on to Seth. The old man liked her; he wouldn't growl at her too much for bringing bad news.

Grabbing a piece of chalk from the speed rail, Teddy turned to change the chalkboard with the night's offerings. If the orders actually went *up,* they'd put it on the regular rotation, no matter how much Seth moaned about trendy food and idiot hipsters. The old man had been on a steady tear about hipsters for a month now, ever since they'd gotten a write-up in one of the little community newspapers.

"You didn't want hipsters, you shoulda moved to Cleveland, not Seattle," Teddy said, as though the old man could hear him through the wall and over the noise of the bar, and could hear the disgusted snort he was likely to get in return, if the old man *had* heard him. Personally, Teddy shared that opinion about hipsters, but while he might not be as gung ho as Patrick, the bar's owner, to expand their clientele, he liked seeing the place busy, and hipster money was as good as anyone else's. And they caused less trouble overall than both college students and middle-aged happy-hour habitués.

At that moment, the red-painted front door swung open, and a large group of twenty-somethings came in, making the noise level rise noticeably for a moment. Teddy watched them head for the tables that had been pushed together, making a mental note to keep an eye on them, and leaned forward to better hear what the couple at the bar were ordering. Thankfully, they stuck to basics; it was too early for someone to order a Fuzzy Pink Marsupial, or otherwise try to play stump-the-bartender.

"Where's Ginny?" The question was directed at him, and he shrugged. "Do I look like her keeper?"

"Yes?" the other man said, and his companion laughed.

"You want me to spit in your beer, Mac? Keep it up. . . ." Teddy shook his head and passed the beers across the bar. "She's out of town on a job," he said. "That's all I know."

And that reminded him that he hadn't heard from her how the client meeting went. It was good that this place kept him busy, both hands and brains, because it kept him from checking his phone for a text message or voice mail, just then, and for a while after. Not that there was any reason for her to check in—like he'd said to Stacy, she was working her own gig, not one of theirs. No reason for her to check in, nope. Just because they'd gotten into the habit of talking over the day like an old married couple, her coming in for a drink most afternoons he worked before the crush hit, didn't mean it was a thing they *always* had to do. And he'd talked to her just a couple of hours before, so he knew she was all right. . . .

Just because he had a niggling sense of empty where she usually sat didn't mean he had to indulge it.

"Too many sisters already; I don't need another one," he muttered to himself. "She's a big girl, more than capable of driving out of town on her own and doing her job without falling into trouble. Get a grip."

Above him, Mistress Penny-Drops woke from her doze, stretching her body along the cabinet and flexing her claws slightly, just to feel them stretch and retract. It was almost too warm atop the bar shelves, and the noise made her ears flatten against her head in annoyance, but the view of the room was too good to abandon. She liked being able to keep track of everyone with a swift glance. Plus, Theodore was just below her, behind the counter, close enough that a single well-timed leap could land her on his shoulders.

If she were to do that, she knew from experience, she would be dumped onto the floor. Penny didn't resent that: her claws were sharp, and human shoulders were unsteady; it was natural to dig in to make sure you kept your balance. But she tried not to do that unless Theodore was wearing a jacket, to give him extra padding. Generally, when she decided to grace him with her presence, she leapt down to the bartop. It was a longer leap, but an easier landing. But tonight, she was content to sit, and watch.

And, watching, she could tell that Theodore was worried. Humans worried about so many things, all the time; one of the reasons she enjoyed his company was that he didn't do that, didn't have the wound-up energy that made other humans difficult to sit near. Except when they were actively sniffing something out, of course. But that was different. Hunting was different. But he wasn't sniffing anything out now—was he? He didn't do that without Georgie's human, Ginny, and neither Georgie nor Ginny had been in today. Or yesterday.

Penny's whiskers twitched as she tried to remember the last time she'd seen Georgie. It had been not-long-ago, but not-recent, and her whiskers twitched again, even as her ears flattened slightly. Georgie liked to think she was rough-and-tumble, but the dog needed Penny to explain things to her, keep her focused. What was she doing, without Penny?

And why was the new woman who had come to work at the Busy Place doing that? She tracked the woman's hands for a moment, puzzled, then was distracted by the conversation below her.

"She's out of town on a job. That's all I know." Theodore's voice was smooth, but she could hear it cut through the clatter as he spoke to the humans who approached the bar, his hands moving quickly, surely, as he passed bottles and mixed drinks. "Two Dead Guy ales and a Holy Spirit, check. You going to run a tab?"

The people laughed; he had said something amusing, although she didn't understand what. Those were people who were often with Ginny; had Ginny come in with them? No, she hadn't, and no Georgie, either. Was that the she he'd mentioned? Out of town where? Why hadn't Georgie told her they were leaving?

Her tail lashed once, before she got it under control. She needed more information. But Theodore was busy serving other people now, his hands moving surely, without speaking. Stacy? No, the other human was too far away to hear, even if she'd been saying anything of interest.

It had gotten more crowded in the bar since she had last looked around. Humans were so noisy. Penny much preferred the afternoons, when only a few people were here, talking in low voices. When Theodore moved more slowly, and looked up when he spoke to her, and Georgie was sprawled on the floor, making a perfect cat bed. But it was night and busy, and even if Georgie were here, they wouldn't be allowed on the floor, she would have to be in the back room, or outside if the weather was good, and then Penny wouldn't be able to keep an eye on everything.

Penny settled back down on the cabinet, feeling the urge to sulk. Her humans were too busy to pay attention to her. And Georgie wasn't here, and neither was her human. Penny's tail twitched again, and her whiskers quivered. Why weren't they here? Where were they? Why hadn't Georgie told her, if they were going away?

Penny was a creature of order. She did not like it when things weren't in the right place, people where she could see them.

She didn't trust them not to get in trouble without her.

4

I f she had to get stiffed by a client, Ginny thought,
then this was the way to deal with it: dinner with an
old friend, and no worries. The restaurant Ron had
suggested was nice—some sort of gastropub where they'd
actually considered acoustics, so they could hear each other
talk, but not also have to listen in to the conversations
happening at the tables around them. She dug into her
cheeseburger—locally sourced, the menu informed her—
with a ferocity that made her companion laugh.

"Shut up," she said. "I haven't eaten anything since . . .
God, since this morning, I think." She'd had a protein bar
during the drive down, but nothing else since breakfast in
her apartment in Seattle. There had been an honor bar in her
room, but she'd taken one look at the prices and blanched.

"Being on the most-wanted list builds an appetite, huh?"

Ginny shook her head. "Don't even joke about that."
She'd told him about what had happened, and how the
cops had questioned her, but then had asked that they go
on to less stressful topics, like politics.

Ron stopped laughing, giving her a long look. "It's bothering you, huh?"

She put down her hamburger and stared at him. "It wouldn't bother you?"

He shrugged. "Not particularly, no. But then I'm a jaded bastard used to getting the stink-eye from cops of all descriptions."

She laughed, because it was true—he'd grown up on the proverbial wrong side of the tracks, and stayed there, professionally. "Yeah well, I'm still new to that." Then she sobered, picking at her fries without eating one. "And yeah . . . yeah, it's bothering me. Not just finding the body—I wish it were that, but I guess I've gotten jaded enough that once the shock was gone it was just sad. And it's not just because they're side-eyeing me, because I'm not only innocent, because I can pull up an airtight alibi of being somewhere else at the time, assuming the guy was killed more than twenty minutes before I got there. But that's it, you know? I was sent there, Ron. And that's . . ." That was eating at her, sending her thoughts around in tighter and tighter circles, even as she tried not to think about it. "Someone might have set me up, and I don't know who, or why. Wouldn't that bother you, just a little?"

Ron smiled at her response. "I was born with the need to dig up answers, Virginia." Then he leaned forward, looking up over his glasses to study her expression. "You want me to see what's going on?"

She did. She really did. "Can you do that?"

"I can do many things, my dear." The leer he sent her was so at odds with his appearance—a narrow man with a narrow face fringed with long graying hair and wide, impossibly innocent blue eyes behind those horn-rimmed glasses—that she laughed. They'd been friends for nearly a decade, after fighting on the same side of a local zoning issue just after she got out of college, when he'd still been working in Seattle, and he'd never once hit on her. Then again, he'd never hit on anyone she knew, male or female, and if he'd been dating anyone in all that time he'd never said. He was either incredibly discreet or happily asexual.

But one thing she knew was that Ronald O'Riley *could* do many things. Her friend was a wizard, although instead of a wand he carried a little black book. An actual little book, full of names and secrets, coded in case it fell into the wrong hands. After twenty-seven years as a reporter, Ron knew everyone who was worth knowing in the Pacific North-west, and probably down into California, too. It wouldn't surprise her at all if he had a half dozen local cops on speed dial, even though his normal beat was politics, not crime.

Although, when she thought about it, there probably was a lot of overlap between the two.

"All right, do your worst to set my mind at ease," she said, smiling as though she were joking. They both knew she wasn't. He patted her hand once, avuncular, and got up to make a few phone calls out in the hallway, where fewer people might overhear.

While she was waiting, Ginny checked her own messages—nothing urgent, and nothing from Tonica—and ordered them another round of drinks. Just as the waiter brought them over, Ron returned. But the expression on his face was no longer amused. "Kid, you got a problem."

"What?" That had not been what she expected to hear. "Holy shit, Ron, don't tell me they really think I did it?" She was making a joke, but the look on his face, if anything, got gloomier.

"Your alleged client? No such person. Anywhere."

"Yeah, I was beginning to suspect as much." She'd been able to find a baby-sized footprint online in that first search, but once she went deeper, it was clear that everything had been created within the past year, and none of it went down another layer—no comments on any forum she'd been able to find, no reviews left anywhere, and no photos or references kicked back by any of her search engines. And no email associated with that name beyond a freebie account . . . Who had only one email these days? But she'd been waiting to get home before she dug deeper—there was only so much she could do from the road, without her own little book of people to call. "But that just means I got punked, that's all. There's nothing to tie me—"

Interrupting her—something he would never do, normally—Ron went on, "And your name and phone number were found in the dead guy's pocket."

Ginny walked into her hotel room, closed the door behind her, leaned against the door, and said, "Today has, without a doubt, sucked."

Georgie looked up from where she'd been sleeping on the bed, the hotel room too small for her to have the usual "hear Mom at the door, run to greet her" reaction time. Her tail wagged once, and her jaw dropped open slightly, as though to say, "But I'm here; you got me!"

Ginny dropped her coat on the floor, toed off her shoes, and slid the door's security locks into place before sitting down heavily next to the dog on the bed. She rubbed the top of Georgie's head with her knuckles the way the shar-pei liked and managed a smile. "Yeah, I got you, kid, and that's no small thing. Dogs are awesome."

Ron had paid the bill and sent her home, warning her to go directly back to the hotel and stay close to her room, where she'd told the cops she would be. "I'm not saying there's going to be trouble, but there's already trouble and you don't want to be making it worse."

She really didn't. Ginny had spent the entire drive back telling herself that this wasn't anything she should get her fingers into, that every indication pointed to the fact that she'd been baited and hooked and left to swing, and she should let professionals sort it out. That anything she did would just piss off those professionals and possibly make things worse.

Contrary to her parents' opinion, she did have a head full of common sense, and contrary to the opinions of certain other people, she didn't actually *enjoy* being hip-deep in trouble.

But—a little voice had been saying, counterpoint to the very sensible voice—she made a living getting her hands dirty fixing other people's problems. And she was good at it. So how could she just sit back and ignore her own? And didn't she have experience solving crime? She did. Well, she did, with help. Ginny looked at the digital time display on the television. A little after nine thirty. She sighed, imagining what Mary's looked like right now. Probably a madhouse, with the trivia game about to start and everyone getting their drink orders in. Even if she'd been there, she wouldn't have been able to get Tonica's attention. Anything short of a siren going off on his phone would be ignored.

But sitting here doing nothing was going to drive her mad. She needed to bounce this off someone, and Georgie, loving as she was, gave terrible advice.

With one last scritch between Georgie's ear for luck, Ginny pulled her phone out of her jacket pocket and sent a text message to her partner. "Call when can. Trouble."

A few minutes later, she got a response: "Watering the savages. Skype in twenty?"

Cell phone reception in the back office was crap, unless you stood at exactly the right angle and sacrificed a chicken. She'd installed Skype on the office computer and taught Tonica how to use it—under protest—but this was the first time they'd be using it for an actual conversation, rather than a test drive.

Thankfully, she'd paid for high-speed connectivity when she did her Net search earlier, justifying it as a business expense. "Okay."

Twenty minutes was enough time to take Georgie for a quick walk in the hotel's doggie "recreation area" again— it was just off the parking lot, which should be in clear enough view for the cops if they'd decided to keep active tabs on her, or quizzed the night clerk later about her behavior.

"It's not paranoia if they really do have you under surveillance," she told Georgie, who seemed pleased to be going outside, even if people were watching.

There were two other people walking their dogs: an older woman with a tiny dog that was all hair, and a younger woman with an overenthusiastic hound puppy. They nodded to each other, the way people did when their dogs passed on the street, but nobody seemed to be in the mood for conversation. Ginny wondered, briefly, if one of them was an undercover cop, tried to imagine the pocket pup as a K-9 officer, and had to force herself not to break into a bad case of the giggles.

"C'mon, Georgie, do your thing," she said to the dog, flicking the leash lightly. "Before I become one of those moms and embarrass you in public."

Ginny didn't believe that Georgie actually understood more than five words, total, and most of those had to do with "walk" or "dinner," but the shar-pei was pretty good at picking up moods. She did her business quickly after that, and was willing to go back upstairs a few minutes later, despite the appearance of a midsized collie and its owner, who looked like they wanted to make friends.

"Night," the desk clerk called to them, and Ginny raised her hand in acknowledgment, herding Georgie back into the elevator. "Wonder if he's a cop," she said to the dog as the doors closed in front of them. "Or a snitch. More likely a snitch, supplementing his salary with payoffs when someone suspicious checks in. Because this is a very shady place full of suspected criminals, don't you think?"

Georgie had no opinion on the subject, sitting down and waiting patiently the way she'd been trained to do when in moving boxes. "Good girl," Ginny said.

Ron had said—trying to be reassuring—that as seriously as he wanted her to take the situation, it was probably nothing, that it was the kind of thing cops were trained to sort out, especially since she did have an alibi for where she was and what she was doing for twenty-four hours beforehand, thanks to security cameras and tolls. Even if they couldn't figure out how her details got into the dead guy's pocket, if it didn't lead anywhere useful, they'd probably just put her in a back drawer, evidentially speaking.

But being put in the back drawer wasn't the same as not being under suspicion.

Ginny realized that she was clenching her jaw, and sucked her cheeks in to force her jaw to relax. The expression that reflected back at her from the elevator's control panel made her sigh instead of laugh, though. Then she felt forty-plus pounds of solid muscle lean against her leg as the elevator took them back to their floor, and some of the tension faded. "I'm glad you're here with me, too, kid," she said, reaching down to ruffle Georgie's ears affectionately.

Back inside, Georgie went into her crate, turning around several times until the bedding was to her comfort, and then settling in for the night. Ginny moved her laptop from the desk back to the bed, and leaned against the headrest, then opened the Skype program to wait for Tonica's call.

When Ginny finished recounting the day's misadventures, Teddy shook his head, although he wasn't sure if it was in disbelief or awe. Or both. Only Ginny Mallard could get into that much of a mess in less than twelve hours, without doing a thing. "That's either the most massive coincidence in the history or, or somebody's set you up, Gin."

Ginny nodded, moving slightly out of frame, then moving back in as she readjusted the laptop. He could see the beige-on-beige wallpaper behind her, and what looked like a modernish padded headboard behind her, so he assumed that she was sitting on the bed, not at the hotel room's desk. He didn't see Georgie so he assumed she was, as usual, sleeping at her owner's feet.

"Yeah. You know how I feel about coincidences," Ginny was saying. "And the fact that my alleged client doesn't actually exist, far as I can tell, prior to this year . . ." She made a face. "But even so, a coincidence makes more sense than someone trying to set me up for murder, doesn't it?"

"There's coincidence, and then there's whole lotta coincidence, Gin. A client accidentally giving you the address of a house where there just happened to be a murder, okay, wild but potentially a coincidence. That, plus your client going AWOL and probably being bogus? Shades of a made-for-TV Lifetime mystery. The dead body having your contact info?" He shook his head. "You probably should be bracing yourself for Bogart to show up in a sharp-cut suit."

He could hear Ginny's sigh all the way back in Seattle, even without the connection. "Bogie wasn't the one in the—okay, noir movie education can wait. And yeah, all right. You're right, Ron's right, my gut instinct is right, we're all right: something is rotten in the state of Denmark. But, I mean . . . why? Why me, why this, why drag me all the way down here just to find a body? I'm pretty sure I haven't pissed anyone off *that* much."

But she stopped to think about it. So did Teddy: they'd been sticking their noses into some dangerous things lately—as Seth never tired of reminding them—and maybe someone had decided to stick back?

"No, you're right," he said, "that doesn't make sense. It's too . . . lumpy."

"Lumpy?"

"Badly designed. Not smooth." It had made more sense in his head. "Like the entire thing was stitched together out of a bunch of separate parts, by someone who couldn't actually sew?"

"Like Frankenstein's monster? A Frankenstein frame-up?"

"Yes. Kinda. Maybe?" He shook his head and tried to vocalize his thoughts better. "Okay, let's look at this logically, from the start." That was usually Ginny's job; he was the one who worked with hunches and people-reading. "You got called down for a consult with a client in another city. Which, yay, good on you, expanding the base, all that. But where did she hear about you?"

Ginny looked up at the ceiling, thinking. "She said she'd gotten my name from a relative of Mrs. Kern. The one with the twins' birthday parties?"

"Right." He had a vague memory of horror stories about that client. "But not directly from the client herself?"

"No. And I didn't call to confirm, because there was no way in hell I wanted to talk to Mrs. Kern again. She—the alleged Mrs. Adaowsky—said in her original email that a relative had raved about how smoothly everything had gone off, and how calm Mrs. Kern had been. Mainly because she was tipped up with Xanax the entire time, but anyway, Mrs. Adaowsky—the alleged Mrs. Adaowsky," she repeated, "said that she wanted someone who could keep their cool no matter what happened, because, and I quote this, 'I love my friends but they're prone to hysterics if someone uses the wrong fork.'"

"Huh. And she couldn't have found someone a little more local who came as highly recommended?"

Ginny made That Face at him, clear even through the webcam. She had that expression down cold: Are you implying that I am not as awesome as my credentials suggest?

He kept his expression serious, but he was pretty sure she knew he was holding back a snicker. He didn't think needling her would ever get old, although they'd stopped keeping track of points awhile ago. Triple-digit numbers got unwieldy without an actual scorecard. "Cool your jets, woman. I'm just saying. Bringing someone down from another city? That's expense above and beyond, isn't it?" Mallard's services didn't come cheaply, he knew that.

"Maybe she could have hired a party planner," Ginny said. "But there's a difference between party planning and what I do. A personal concierge handles *everything*, even the unexpected bumps and disasters. Which means we have a lot more control over the situation, without having to get everything okayed on a micromanager scale. They hire me because they trust me. It's like having a personal assistant, for a set time, the length of the project."

He knew that, mostly, but talking it out, or hearing it talked out, helped him think.

"And, let's be honest, there aren't that many people doing this—and most of them prefer long-term clients, not one-offs."

"So for an older woman who didn't want the bother, only the result, and probably prefers personal recommendations rather than doing an Internet search, you'd be the perfect choice."

"Exactly."

And, he thought but knew better than to say out loud, Ginny's ego would assume that of course her reputation was spreading, and not look too much further. "So you get a call from this woman, haul down there, and oh, hey, no woman but a dead body?"

She sighed. "Dead body, in a house that didn't look like it belonged to an older woman, and what looked like the setup of a small, probably illegal business," she said. "Unless the local DMV is seriously outsourcing their workload . . ."

"Yeah, no. Oregon's a little crunchy-granola, but I don't think so."

"Neither did I."

"So yeah, this is either the world's largest convocation of coincidences, and cause for a hairy eyeball if you ask me—which you did—but then the dead guy's got your contact info on him? Sorry, Gin. At the risk of repeating myself, that's not coincidence. Either the dead guy was the one who contacted you, pretending to be an old lady, or someone stashed the paper in his pocket, probably after killing him. Either way, it's not good."

"Yes, but why? I mean, either scenario? It's one thing to build a conspiracy theory, but why would there even be a conspiracy? Why would someone *want* me involved in this? Let's not forget that she—someone—paid my retainer to start. So they were willing to sink a thousand dollars into this, plus the cost of my rental car and hotel. And yes, the check cleared," she said before he could ask. "It was PayPal, though, so tough to look into that without a court order."

"And the possibility of that happening would be . . . ?"

"Low to none," she said. "The cops didn't seem interested in anything other than why I was in the house, and if I touched anything or saw anything—they're treating my mystery nonclient as irrelevant."

"Or they don't believe there was a client at all."

They looked at each other through the screen, both frowning.

"I told them. I showed them the email. I told them I'd gotten a retainer." And they'd written it all down, and then asked her again, as though they were expecting her answer to change. "Shit."

"You need to pass on that bit about the PayPal, so they can establish someone did pay you to come down there. Pronto. Just, you know, in case." He was being paranoid, but he wasn't going to apologize for it.

"Right." She leaned out of frame to do something—probably, if he knew her, to start a list of things to do on her tablet.

Teddy leaned back in his chair, trying to think of what else Ginny should do, to keep her nose clean, and looked up to see Penny on the shelf over the desk, washing her paw calmly, as though she'd been there all night. "And when did you come in, missy?" he asked her.

"What?"

"Nothing, just Penny escaping the noise out front. Look, the not-a-client is a mystery, yeah, but in and of itself we could assume someone was pranking you, maybe. Even the dead guy—that could just be bad luck he got dead, maybe someone else he'd pranked having no sense of humor. Or, hell, maybe the guy is your client's nephew and he was trying to do something nice for his auntie, or maybe he was there to meet you because auntie was in the hospital."

"And auntie doesn't seem to exist, online?"

"I know this will come as a shock to you, Mallard, but some people don't. Especially older people." He'd only started paying bills online recently himself, mainly because Ginny had gotten on his case about it.

"But with your contact info in his pocket and him dead by violence, and you being the one to find him dead by violence? Your friend's right, that's when it gets serious."

"Thank you, Captain Obvious," she said.

"I'm just laying the pieces out on the board, Mallard; don't snipe at me."

She made another face, then nodded once. "Yeah, sorry. Go on."

"Your friend's also right that the cops might dismiss it out of hand because like you said, you've got an alibi, and odds are he was dead before you even hit town. But they might not—especially if they don't have anyone else to look at. Unexplained murders in quiet neighborhoods, especially white neighborhoods, makes for a really bad time in the mayor's office."

She laughed at that, a little. "And you call me the cynic?"

"I only wish that were cynicism. The most obvious thing could be, he's the guy who called you down there, for whatever arcane reason, and someone killed him before you got there. It's bad timing all around, but if the cops find another lead, you're in the clear, and worst-case ending is that we'll never know why he pulled the scam."

"When that's the simple answer, my life has taken a seriously wrong turn," she said dryly.

"Oh, a long time ago," he agreed. "But there's also the chance that the cops can't pin it on someone else, and you're *not* in the clear, not immediately, anyway. I wish we knew who the dead guy *was*. Any chance of getting that information out of the cops?"

Ginny tilted her head at him, her expression slipping from irritated to curious. "Tonica . . . are we investigating this? Officially?"

He stared back at her. "Um."

"Because that would be really, really dumb."

"It's a fool who has himself for a client." He thought Abraham Lincoln had said that, but college was far back enough that he wasn't going to cite it, in case he was wrong. Not that Ginny would correct him—who was he kidding, of course she would.

But she didn't counter-quote, proof that she was a lot more distressed about this than she was letting on.

"Right. Investigating this ourselves would be stupid. We're just trying to get perspective on what might happen." That almost sounded believable.

"I think—" There was a noise, and Ginny shifted, then suddenly Georgie's head filled the screen. "Georgie!" her owner yelped, and there was a slight tussle as Ginny tried to reclaim control of the laptop from the curious canine.

"Having some technical difficulties there, Mallard?"

Her hand, one finger upraised, filled the screen, and he laughed, the tension not gone, but broken a little. He felt something nudge his elbow and looked down to see Penny's head shoving her way through, coming to settle on his lap. "Well, hello there," he said in surprise. Penny wasn't an unaffectionate cat, but she was more of the "pause for petting" type than prone to laps or snuggling. Now she seemed intent on sniffing the computer monitor, as though trying to tell who was on the other side.

"Hey there, Mistress Penny," Ginny said, reappearing in front of the screen, having apparently come to a compromise with her dog. "Come to join the discussion, or did you just want to say hi to Georgie?"

The cat let out a faint mrrowr—also unusual for her, since she wasn't much of a talker—and settled back into Teddy's lap, her tail curled primly around her hindquarters, her gaze on the screen, as though to say that the conference could now proceed. Despite the seriousness of the matter, Teddy had to chuckle. Well, every PI had a sidekick, right? They had two. And Georgie at least earned her keep, playing guard dog and conversation starter, as needed.

"So we're not going to investigate this ourselves," Ginny said, going back to their pre-interruption discussion. "Not in any kind of official or semi-official capacity. Because that would be foolish. And also dumb, getting in the cops' way. Right?"

"Right. We're just . . . looking into things, in case there's something we can figure out, that we can pass along to help clear you of suspicion. Then the cops can go do their part of the job, and catch the actual killer instead of side-eyeing you, and you can get back to work without this hanging over your shoulder annoyingly."

"Right." Ginny nodded again. They were in complete agreement. "So, first step is . . . what? Find out who actually owned the house, and if the dead guy was the owner, or renter, or happened to be passing through in time to get killed?"

Penny mrrowed, louder this time, and Georgie answered her with a snort, settling back down into Ginny's lap. "Shush, kids," Ginny said, knuckling the top of the dog's head affectionately.

"Finding the owners will take you ten minutes of digging, and you'll do it before you go to bed," Teddy said. He was actually surprised she hadn't done it already, but being side-eyed for a murder could throw anyone off their game, even Ginny. "I think the first thing you need to do tomorrow is Operation Neighborhood Walk."

"I suck at Operation Neighborhood Walk," she said glumly. "You're better at it."

"Yah well, I'm here and you're there. Suck it up, Gin. It's not like you're doing the hard work, anyway. Georgie is."

She opened her mouth to protest, then made a "yeah, you're right" face, and nodded.

Penny purred, gently kneading her front claws into Theodore's leg, while her ears twitched back and forth, picking up Georgie's voice under the humans' speaking.

"She didn't let me go with her," Georgie was complaining. "I had to stay in this room all day!"

"Make her take you tomorrow," Penny said. "Soil the carpet if you have to."

"I couldn't do that!"

"You'd rather be left behind?"

Georgie grumbled, and licked Ginny's hand as though to apologize ahead of time.

"Just . . . She likes taking you places. Be enthusiastic. Suck up to her, make her think you don't like being left alone."

"I don't!"

Penny sighed. She was fond of Georgie, but some days she just wanted to bat the dog's ears, hard. "Then it should be easy, right?

You need to do this, Georgie. I'm here; I can't do everything this time."

Georgie settled back into her human's lap and rested her nose on the edge of the keyboard, so all Penny could see was the top of her head. "All right. But I don't like it. And if she's mad at me, I'm blaming you."

Penny's tail twitched, the only sign she gave that she was amused. "Fair enough."

5

She was chasing after a large orange bird with plastic wings that couldn't quite get it off the ground but kept it just out of reach, and Georgie was no help, sitting on the sideline with her tongue hanging out, laughing at her owner's efforts.

"Don't use your hands, use your nose," the dog suggested, and Ginny has just enough time to consider that before she realized how absurd the whole thing was, and the alarm on her phone went off.

Ginny managed to grab at the offending noise without having to look. Turning it off, though, required actually opening her eyes. When the alarm shut off, she closed her eyes again and took internal inventory. Still incredibly tired, check. Body aching from a too-soft bed, check. In dire need of caffeine, double check. She opened her eyes again, and the brown-eyed, wrinkled face peering over the edge of the bed at her held a familiar expression: Georgie needed to be walked, check.

"Ugh. Right." She dragged herself out of bed and pulled a sweatshirt over the sweatpants and T-shirt she'd slept in, then shoved her sneakers on bare feet and grabbed

Georgie's leash off the desk, where she'd coiled it the night before. "C'mon, kid. Your bladder waits for no woman."

She managed to remember her room key before locking herself out, and exchanged a sleepy smile with another guest, who was coming out of the elevator with a terrier mix in his arms.

"They have coffee in the lobby," he told her. "Free."

"Oh, thank God," she said, and he laughed.

The coffee was hot and strong, even if it lacked in the taste department. She dumped two sugars into the paper cup and let Georgie drag her outside. There were two other guests walking their dogs that morning, and Ginny, holding her coffee in one hand and the leash in the other, watched them with a little more interest than she'd been able to muster the night before. The tall black man, already dapper in a suit, had two puppies that looked like some kind of shepherd mix tumbling at his heels. He was talking into a cell phone, softly enough that she couldn't hear what he was saying, and occasionally glancing down to make sure that the puppies were staying out of trouble. She appreciated that kind of multitasking. The other guest was an older man, with a staid, graying black standard poodle that perfectly matched his own hair. Georgie and the poodle ignored each other, but she sniffed at the puppies—missing their abandoned pup Parsifal, maybe. They'd finally gotten Parsy a new home with one of Stacy's friends, who lived in Kirkland and had room for an ungainly, overenergetic puppy to run around.

Neither human attempted to speak to her as they strolled

the length of the dog run, and while normally Ginny liked talking to other dog owners, this morning she was thankful for their preoccupation. She had gotten a full seven hours of sleep, but somehow it felt earlier than 6 a.m. The sun was up, though, and the sky was a grayish blue, and there were birds singing in a nearby tree, making Ginny feel like a slacker for not being more cheerful.

Then again, she decided sourly, having a job go south was enough to ruin your mood—knowing that you were stuck here until the cops said you could go pretty much trampled it into the ground. If she had to extend her stay here . . .

"At least I brought the laptop," she said, not quite loud enough for the dog to hear. "Being stuck here without would have driven *me* to kill someone." And then she looked around guiltily, as though a cop would be standing there writing down her words as a confession.

Once Georgie had taken care of her basic needs and Ginny had finished her coffee, they went back upstairs and Ginny took care of her own morning maintenance. The water pressure in the shower was mediocre, but there was enough hot water that she finally started to feel alert—and a little less paranoid.

She came out of the bathroom dressed in a pair of jeans and a sweatshirt, about as far from the smart-but-approachable suit she'd been wearing yesterday as her suitcase could manage. She let her hair dry naturally and studied herself in the mirror. Her normal look was Professionally Tough, No Bullshit Taken. But if she left her hair down, and didn't wear makeup?

Her curls framed her face in a haphazard way that might be able to pass for innocently tousled, and her skin seemed reasonably clear, no more than normal shadows under her eyes, despite how tired she felt. She widened her hazel eyes at her reflection and tried to project Trustworthy Girl Next Door vibes.

"Tonica's so much better at this," she told her reflection. "He could be dressed like a Goth IRS agent and people would still trust him." It was his body language, making his strong build seem comforting rather than threatening, his expression inviting rather than forbidding.

Oh well. She was honestly interested in what people had to say, especially when it was on a topic that she had a vested interest in solving. That was going to have to be enough.

"C'mon, kid," she called to Georgie, who had curled up in the corner while she took her shower, and seemed to be napping. "Time to go to work."

Operation Neighborhood Walk was Tonica's term for it. Ginny preferred the simpler "take Georgie for a walk and see what falls out." But it came down to the same thing: drive to the area they wanted to check out, snap on Georgie's leash, and wander along the sidewalks until someone came up to talk to them.

Someone always did. No matter who was holding the leash, Georgie's wrinkled skin and sweet brown eyes drew people to her, exactly the same way she'd first drawn

Ginny to her at the sidewalk shelter adoption display. Shar-peis were a blend of odd and adorable, and Georgie's one drooping ear, the off-breed inheritance, made her even more appealing. Strangers would approach cautiously, looking at Georgie then flicking their gaze up to the human with her, turning sideways, and offering their hand for Georgie to sniff at the same time they were asking if it was okay to approach the dog. Ginny thought it would be smarter to ask before putting your hand out, but people couldn't seem to help themselves. She wasn't much better, with other people's dogs.

People *wanted* to believe that dogs were friendly, for the most part.

As they drove back to the house where she'd found the body yesterday, Ginny felt a familiar nervous tension in her stomach. It wasn't the snooping around that made her uncomfortable—even when they'd started this, she'd been okay with the idea of asking questions and poking her nose into other people's business. That was what she *did*, after all. All right, usually with their permission, and them paying her to do so, but the theory was the same. But returning to the same street, walking past the same house, where she'd been the one to discover a murder victim? When the cops had their eyes on her already?

She gave herself a pep talk. "You're just going to look. And maybe talk to anyone who's out and about." It was just after nine now, so the commute-to-work folk would be gone, and anyone on the street now might be more likely to stop and gossip about all the cops who'd come by the day before. That was the theory behind Neighborhood Walk, anyway, and it had always worked before.

And it was unlikely anyone would connect her with the woman who'd been there the day before, even without the change of clothes and hairstyle. She hadn't talked to anyone other than the cops, hadn't been caught on film—that she was aware of—and hadn't stopped to chat with any of the rubberneckers. Everyone had been focusing on the house and the cops, not the person who'd called in the scene.

Normally, she'd be upset to be so overlooked, but in this instance, Ginny was thankful. Plus, she had Georgie now. People remembered the dog, not the owner. She was guilty of that herself, too.

Just to be on the safer side, though, she parked the rental car a block away, and the two of them ambled in the direction of the house slowly, ready to abort the mission if she saw even a hint of a cop car. But whatever investigating the police had done, they seemed to be done. When she looked down the street, she could see that there was the usual yellow tape on the door, but no sign of anything else.

Maybe they were treating it as an accidental death, despite what Ron had said. Maybe she was panicked for no reason at all.

Then Ginny remembered the way the body had been crammed under the table, the torn clothing and bloodied hands, and shook her head. Even the most inept or corrupt TV cop would have to investigate that, even if they overlooked or ignored what was in the small studio, or—

she presumed—on the computers lined up in the living room.

"They'd have to have looked at the computers, whatever was on them. Wouldn't they?" she asked Georgie, who was busy sniffing the base of the stop sign at the corner.

Georgie had no opinion.

"Some help you are, partner," she grumbled, but gave Georgie a treat anyway. It wasn't the dog's fault she didn't know enough about actual police procedure. She should learn. Except the cops she knew back in Seattle would be more likely to tell her to back off than to actually tell her anything. . . . Maybe there was a website with that kind of info? There was always a website.

"Oh, isn't he a beauty," a voice said, and Ginny looked up to see an older woman walking down the street, a tiny black fluff of a dog at the end of her leash. "Is that a shar-pei?"

"Mostly," Ginny said. "And she's good with little dogs, don't worry," even as the fluff spotted Georgie and strained at the leash, wanting to go meet the newcomer. Georgie looked at the strange dog and wuffed once, then turned her head to look at Ginny, asking if this was all right.

"Play, Georgie," she said, and let the leash go slack enough that Georgie had room to move forward and sniff noses, then butts, before the black fluff tried to put its paws on Georgie's head, indicating it was time to play.

"Little dogs always think they're so fierce," the woman said fondly. "Mika firmly believes that she's a Great Dane."

"Hey, Mika," Ginny said. "Is she a Pom?"

"Mostly. And a little Jack Russell, I think."

Ginny's eyes widened. "That must make for . . ."

The other woman laughed. "A very energetic dog, oh yes."

Mika's owner had to be in her late sixties or early seventies, and Ginny only hoped that she was up to that kind of energy at that age. "You must have to walk her a lot?"

"Three times a day, minimum." They paused a moment to untangle the leashes, as the dogs circled each other, sniffing noses, then tails. "I have a yard where she can run around, but it's good for her to have the discipline of a leash, too."

Ginny had the suspicion that the woman had been a teacher at one point. "I know that feeling," she said with sincerity. "Georgie's getting full-on training, because if she decided to take off I'm pretty sure she'd take my arm with me. Not that she ever would, she's a sweetheart, but, well, things can startle even the best dog." It was a lousy opening, but Ginny took it anyway. "And you never know what's going to happen these days, do you? Were you out when the cops showed up yesterday? I only heard about it after the fact. . . ." Technically true: He was dead when she got there, so that was after the fact, right?

"Oh my, yes, such a shame." The woman made a face, the kind you make when you talk about a tragedy that doesn't really affect you directly: slightly too concerned, too interested. "Not that I knew the boy who lived there—he seemed to keep rather odd hours, and spent his time with much younger people than me, obviously—but you don't ever want to think about someone dying in such an awful fashion."

The dogs had graduated to mock-leaping at each other, and their owners had to keep adjusting leashes while they talked, handling the reins like seasoned pros to keep them from becoming hopelessly tangled. "Signs have already gone up; we're going to have a neighborhood watch meeting at the end of the week, with the local police in to talk about safety precautions we can take."

"They think it was a break-in?"

"Oh my, dear, what else could it have been?"

"That's terrible. . . . I'd hoped maybe he just fell, or . . ."

"Oh no, it was definitely murder."

The woman didn't lower her voice or look either wide-eyed or nervous saying the word: definitely a teacher, Ginny decided. Or ex-military.

"Someone bashed his head in, and left him to die. I can't imagine that was anything but a crime of passion, can you? I mean, a planned death wouldn't be so . . . sudden?"

"Maybe he was actually one of those so-quiet types who turn out to be mass murderers, and he was killed by an escaping victim?" Ginny couldn't help herself; the woman seemed so fascinated by the ghoulish turn of the conversation.

"Oh." The woman's eyes widened. "Oh dear, the property values of the neighborhood would *never* recover if they start finding bodies in the basement. . . ."

They looked at each other, and there was a moment before they both started giggling, slightly ashamed of themselves.

"Oh dear." The woman's expression eased a little, true regret there now. "A man is dead; we should not be so . . . But I suppose there are only a few ways to respond to death, and gruesome humor always seemed healthier to me than the others, if you didn't actually know the victim. . . ." She shook her head, and then suddenly seemed to recall her manners. "I'm Daisy."

"Virginia." Fake names were pointless trouble. A limited truth's easier to keep track of, and gives you plausible deniability if you happen to know people in common. "And that's Georgie."

"Do you live in the area, Virginia? I'm sure I would have noticed Georgie before."

"No, I'm down from Seattle on business. Georgie came with me, since it was only a car ride."

"Oh, that's nice." From ghoulish to grandmotherly in .002 seconds. "Business trips can be awful; it's nice to have company. She's good in a car?"

"Surprisingly so," Ginny said.

At that point, Mika decided she'd had enough, and started tugging at her leash again, indicating she wanted to get a move on.

"Well, I hope you enjoy the rest of your stay in Portland," Daisy said.

"And I hope they catch whoever did that, soon," Ginny said, bending down to pet Georgie, who looked forlorn to lose a playmate. "Sorry, kid," she said as Daisy and Mika moved away. "That's how business meetings go." Bless Daisy. She might not have been the most informative informant, but it was an excellent starting point. The victim *had* lived in the house, and kept, quote unquote, "odd hours."

Maybe someone else down the block might know more.

What she discovered, though, was that the cops weren't quite done with the scene yet. As they strolled closer to the house, a cop was visible, not so much standing guard as lounging against what looked like an unmarked squad car: a too-boring dark blue sedan with slightly tinted windows. As they came closer, the woman straightened and turned toward them, clearly asking Ginny to stop, and raising an eyebrow as though to ask what Ginny was doing walking her dog near a crime scene.

All right, she might be getting paranoid again, but the probably-a-cop definitely took notice of them.

"May I help you?" Definitely a cop: her voice was regulation dealing-with-the-public pleasant, but there was an undertone that suggested that the right answer would be "no thank you, just moving along."

"I'm sorry, was the street closed? I didn't see any signs. . . ." Ginny had an excellent Innocent Civilian voice, but about three seconds in, the cop's expression changed, and Ginny knew she'd been busted.

"Ma'am? May I see some identification, please?"

Ginny sighed, and pulled her wallet out of the bag slung over her shoulder, opening it and handing it to the nice officer in proper fashion, photo identification clearly visible.

"You have a reason for being here, Ms. Mallard?" Had they seriously passed her name along as a person of interest, or whatever term the real cops actually used? She felt a tremor of panic. But even if they had, that wasn't enough for the cop to be eyeing her like that, was it? She hadn't done anything wrong, just being here. . . . Or had they run her name through their computers, found out she'd been involved in murders before? But if so, they'd know she'd never been a suspect in any of them, right? Or was just being around dead bodies too many times cause for suspicion?

No, it couldn't be, otherwise Miss Marple would have been cooling her sensible heels in prison for years, right?

"I'm banned from the entire street?" She kept her tone surprised, not amused, or anything else that might possibly read as snark to someone with a gun. "I promised not to leave town, so that limits where I can walk Georgie," and never mind that she was staying at a hotel in another neighborhood entirely; if the cop didn't ask, she didn't have to volunteer that information.

The cop glanced down—she'd given Georgie a once-over as she approached, and apparently dismissed her as not-a-threat, but was now able to give her proper notice. "And you're Georgie, I take it, huh? Hi there."

Ginny blessed the money she'd spent on getting Georgie properly trained, because the shar-pei glanced at her for approval, then dropped onto her haunches and leaned her squared-off head into the cop's hand, accepting the ear-scritch as her just due.

"Looks tough, but melts like butter, huh?"

"Pretty much," Ginny admitted. "But she has to be walked on a regular basis, no matter what—or if momma's on the most-wanted list."

"Yeah, I get that. A dog's gotta pee when a dog's gotta pee." The cop had a sense of humor, thank God. "I was just coming to take the tape down, actually. You're fine, so long as you don't actually go near the house itself."

Ginny shuddered, and it wasn't entirely an act. "Believe me, I have no desire whatsoever to go near that house ever again." She might be an investigator, but she wasn't a ghoul. And it wasn't even a lie: desire and need had nothing to do with each other in this case.

"So just cross the street and I'll pretend I never saw you."

Ginny knew that was a lie: she wasn't as good at reading people as Tonica, not even close, but this cop wasn't going to "forget" that the only witness and a possible suspect happened to wander down the street the day after, not when they hammer into everyone's skull that killers sometimes return to the scene of their crime. But hopefully she wouldn't bother to tell anyone until the end of her shift, and by the time anyone followed up on it, they'd have a real suspect to go after. . . .

Ginny crossed the street anyway, and only looked back once.

Georgie was confused.

She had been uncertain about getting in the unfamiliar car the first time, but trusted Ginny, because she always trusted Ginny.

She had been willing to stay in the strange room, because Ginny said to stay, and there were enough things there that smelled like Ginny to reassure her. And walks were always good, and meeting new dogs and smelling new smells was always good, but it was all too much of a newness. She had trusted Penny, who told her to make sure she went with Ginny, and she had asked the little dog, who hadn't known anything, but Ginny had spoken with the other humans, who maybe knew something, so that was good.

But even though Ginny said the human who was petting her was safe, Georgie wasn't convinced. The scritches were good, the hand was firm and warm, and the human smelled of coffee and soap, and those were all good things, safe things, pleasant things, but there was something else there, too, that Georgie didn't like. Something cold and hard and bitter.

But the scritches were good, and Ginny said it was all right, so Georgie allowed it.

But as they crossed the street, Georgie suddenly, violently, wanted her own den, her own streets with the familiar smells. She wanted to go to the Noisy Place and have the girl give her treats, and have Penny there to groom her ears and explain the things she didn't understand.

She wanted to go home, away from whatever it was that was making Ginny smell uneasy under her soft words. Away from this place that wasn't Home.

But Penny had told her to look, and listen, and report back. To find out what was making Ginny unhappy, so Penny could solve it. So Georgie would.

Stopping to smell a particularly interesting tree root—there were three alpha dogs on this street, which made her uneasy, too, but that wouldn't be what was bothering Ginny—she turned her head so that she could see the second human standing across the street. She was watching them, too.

The human was carrying something that smelled like metal and burning, like humans did sometimes. Ginny was always upset around people who did that, although her voice never showed it. And they almost always gave good scritches, so they couldn't be bad people, could they? Did bad people scritch right?

Penny would say yes. So maybe that had been a bad person, even though the scritches were good.

The person was still watching them. Instinct rose in her to growl, to show her teeth, even though the human was too far away now, but Ginny would be upset if she did that without a command. So Georgie dropped her head back to the root, and then peed a little, leaving her own mark behind, and kept looking.

She hoped they went home soon. Being on her own was hard.

6

*T*heodore was in his element, pouring drinks and talking to people. Stacy was behind the bar, too, ducking around him gracefully, handling the people he couldn't. The old man was in the back: Penny could faintly hear him clattering and muttering, a familiar, comfortable sound under the muted roar of people talking. The only off note was the new girl. She was doing that thing again, Penny noted. Where she put her hands down on the table and then into her pockets, a gesture smooth enough to almost be invisible, unless you were a cat and accustomed to looking for things that were furtive and smooth.

Penny watched her, darting in and out of the thinning crowd, picking up glassware and smiling at people, the same way Stacy did. She did everything the same way Stacy did, except that, that smooth glide of her hands.

And then she paused at the bar, and did it again, smooth hands over the openmouthed jar, smooth hands over the drawer of the cash register. Did Stacy do that? Penny couldn't remember, and Theodore didn't say anything, but Penny felt her tail tip twitch, anyway.

It happened tonight. It happened the last time the new girl had worked, too. She considered the girl more carefully, the long pale tail of hair swirling around her shoulders, the way she smiled at every-

one, and everyone smiled at her. Penny didn't like her. But Penny admitted she didn't like many people. If Georgie were here, Georgie could tell her . . .

But Georgie wasn't here.

Penny sighed, wrapped her tail over her nose, and let her eyes close to half slits until, if anyone glanced at her, they might think she was asleep. But she was watching.

Wednesday was Teddy's all-day shift: he opened the bar at noon and worked through to close; even with help, it was exhausting, and brain-consuming. Worrying about Ginny and what was going on down in Portland had to take a backseat. Teddy didn't like it, but the truth was that there wasn't anything he could do for her just then, and he had other obligations that wouldn't wait.

The thought made his lip curl as he watched the last reveler stagger out the door, lifting a hand in farewell, and it was just them, Stacy and Seth and himself, their new girl having clocked out already. He'd come to Seattle to get *away* from obligations, not take on more. Some days he thought his life would have been easier if he'd stayed on the family fast track for a law partnership, or gone into DipCorps. And then he remembered that he didn't have the patience for diplomacy *or* negotiation.

A point that the conversation he was about to have was driving home, painfully.

"Seth, look." And Teddy stopped, not sure exactly what he was going to say next. Or, he knew what he was going to say, but just didn't know how to get the older man to *listen* to him. It had been a very long day, and he was pretty much done with everything, including his coworkers. "I saw what happened earlier tonight, so don't give me any bullshit. You're going to try and shove this off and puff your chest and tell me you're as strong as a guy half your age, and you probably are." Seth had been a boxer in his youth, before he decided that concussions weren't a great retirement plan and got out, and his physique was damn good for a guy in his late sixties. Teddy wasn't blowing smoke on that. "But trying to haul forty-pound boxes around is going to throw your back out or blow your knees, and then you're screwed for, what, a month? Maybe longer?"

Seth crossed his arms across his chest and glowered. "I don't need no punk kid doing my job for me."

They'd gone through this before: every time Teddy had hired someone to help Seth out, the older man had run him off within a month, sometimes less. Last week had been pretty epic, though: the kid only lasted one shift. No, not even a full shift. Not that Teddy blamed him.

"No, you need for that shit to not be part of your job. This isn't open for discussion any longer," he went on, when the older man opened his mouth to object. "I talked with Patrick and he agreed. Your job description has officially changed. You can accept it, or you can quit. But I'm not going to be dealing with your job injury paperwork *or* having to retrain someone because you're out on disability."

Teddy hated being "the boss." Usually he could mediate and cajole well enough that it never came down to that. Not today, though.

"Don't push me on this, Seth."

Seth muttered imprecations under his breath, then stomped back into the tiny kitchen where he (still) reigned supreme, but he didn't take off the apron and storm out the back door, so Teddy was going to call it a win.

"I was pretty sure I was going to have to call the paramedics when he stroked out," Stacy said from where she'd been watching behind the bar.

"Shut up," Teddy said reflexively, as though to ward off the possibility of that happening even now. He could admit to himself now that he'd been afraid the old man *would* quit. There were a lot of things that made working at Mary's the best job he'd ever had, and Seth's acerbic presence was part of that. The old man was a pain in the ass, but he always got the job done, without supervision.

And having to explain to Ginny when she got back why her favorite verbal sparring partner was gone was not something he'd been looking forward to.

That thought made him check his phone again, but there were no new texts, and no missed calls. Hardly surprising, since it was after midnight. Ginny did mornings; he didn't. And she turned into a pumpkin around eleven. But at least that meant he wasn't needed to post bail. On the other hand—he'd promised to help, and so far he hadn't done anything.

He stared at the phone, chewing his lower lip, thinking. He knew people in Portland. Not many, not all of them particularly useful, but . . . "Oh, what the hell." He dialed a number and waited for someone to pick up.

"Corky, hey."

Corky said something unprintable about the state of his genitalia, and then added something in Portuguese.

"Always delightful to speak with you, too. Got a minute?"

"Sure, it's not like we're doing anything here 'cept last call; never gets crazy around here then."

"Yeah, I hear you've got a rowdy bunch down there." The Allegheny had started out life as a cop bar, but when Corky and his brother Dean took over, they'd swerved upscale with the foodie revolution in Portland. It was still popular with cops, only now they took their spouses there instead of their partners. "Seriously, you got a minute?"

"It's gotta be now?" A heavy sigh. "Yeah, arright, hang on a sec. Judy!" The last was a bellow, thankfully directed away from the mouthpiece. "Get these bums loaded up and outa here. I gotta take this."

There was the sound of a door being closed, and the background noise dropped considerably. "Arright. What's the favor?"

Teddy didn't bother denying it. "A friend of mine's down in your neck of the woods, and she's run into a bit of a situation."

"This your PI hug-buddy?"

"She's not my . . . Yeah, okay, fine." One little news article—all right, three, but one of them'd been in the local fish-wrapper and shouldn't count—and every bartender in the area knew about him and Ginny working together, because they were worse gossips than a cul-de-sac of 1950s housewives. The half that didn't assume he was sleeping with her had tried to get her phone number from him— and there was probably some overlap in that. Corky knew better and was happily married to the incredibly patient Judy, but that didn't mean he wasn't going to give Teddy grief if the opportunity came up. "Look, this is serious, okay?"

"Arright, my man. What do you need?"

"You got a friend on the force you could get information from, and not have the fact that you'd asked slip into any-one else's ear?"

There was a moment's thoughtful silence, and the sound of Corky sucking his teeth. "Maybe. Depends. You know that shit, Teddy. Tell me what your lady friend needs."

"There was a body found yesterday, dead of suspicious circumstances—those being that his head was bashed in and he was shoved under his kitchen table. Out in the burbs, I don't know what neighborhood."

"Probably not more than two or three of those yester-day. And you want to know, what? Who did it, or who the dead guy was?"

"I want to know anything that we can find out. At this point, mainly I want to know who they like for it." He fig-ured Ginny would have found out anything else, but she wouldn't be able to get that particular tidbit.

There was a snort of laughter from the other end of the line. "You know cops don't really talk like that, right?"

"If I talked the way cops really talk, my mother would get on a plane and fly out here to wash my mouth out with soap. Thanks, Corkster, I owe you."

"Yeah, you do. So when're you coming to work for me?"

Teddy looked up, glancing around the familiar space of Mary's, and smiled. "Never," he said. "Talk to ya soon."

He hung up on Corky's foul-mouthed farewell and slipped the phone back into his pocket. "You done there?" he asked Stacy, who had been doing the bottle recount a second time, trying to pretend that she wasn't eavesdropping.

"Yep. Everything accounted for and set up for tomorrow. Can this be Trisha's job soon, please?"

"Maybe." Probably not. His new hire might be legal to work here, but that didn't mean he was going to trust the twenty-one-year-old with inventory. Not until she'd proven herself.

He sighed, and stretched until he heard something in his back crack. "God, this grown-up shit is . . . shit."

Stacy laughed, and let down her ponytail, running her fingers through the strands with a sigh of her own. "I wouldn't know."

"Brat. Go home, Stace. I don't want to see you until your next shift starts. Seth!" he yelled into the back. "We're done here. You get to lock up!"

Patrick, the owner, would have kittens if he knew Teddy was letting Seth set the alarms, but Patrick could take a long leap off a short pier: he'd made Teddy manager while he ran off to indulge in the new, snazzier bar he was investing in across town, so Teddy would run the place the way he wanted. And hopefully the responsibility would remind Seth that not being able to haul heavy boxes around didn't mean he was useless.

He waited for a grumpy shot of acknowledgment from the back, then walked Stacy to her car—this part of Ballard was reasonably safe, even at nearly two in the morning, but there was no point in taking chances. He waited until she pulled out of the parking lot and flashed her headlights in farewell before turning to his own car, parked next to Seth's banged-up old motorcycle. He wasn't sure what it said about them that the old man drove that while he drove a Saab sedan, even if she *was* a classic. Ginny joked that he was becoming a Seattle cliché . . . maybe so.

A shadow moved by the front tire, tail held erect, and he crouched, extending his hand so that the small tabby could sniff at him. "Didn't see you 'round much tonight," he said to the cat. "Important matters requiring your oversight?"

Penny didn't bother answering him, but when he opened the driver's-side door, she twined around his ankle and leapt into the front seat, picking her way over to the passenger side and sitting down, as prim as a Yankee matron.

He tilted his head and stared at her. "Excuse me?"

She looked at him, and he was pretty sure she was saying "get in and close the door, idiot human, it's cold out there."

"Huh. That's new." He studied her, one hand on the door, the other holding his keys. From the very first moment he'd found her, a half-grown, half-starved kitten, Penny had been a bar cat, not a house cat. She'd never shown any interest in going home with him, or anyone else, for that matter: Mary's was her home, her domain. And he liked it that way. He wasn't a pet person.

More to the point, he had no supplies at home, no litter box or cat food, or any of the things he'd been assured cats needed. Then again, she rarely used the litter box in the back room, either. . . .

Was she lonely? Without Georgie stopping by, he didn't think she had many other animal buddies . . . in fact, he was pretty sure she put her nose up at every other visiting dog.

She meowed once, a long, thin noise, and he threw up his hands in surrender. Teddy had been around Mistress Penny-Drops long enough to accept the inevitable, if that was what she wanted. He supposed even a cat could get lonely, now and again. He could stop at a twenty-four-hour grocery on the way home, pick up the basics. God, Ginny would laugh her ass off if she could see him now. He'd email her when he got home: she could probably use a laugh right about now.

He looked at the cat again, the door still open in case she suddenly changed her mind. "You sure?"

If cats could sigh, that one did. He got in and put on his seat belt, looked over at her again, now curled up on the passenger seat, and drove them home.

The woman was slightly older than those around her, her hair just beginning to silver, and dressed more formally in

dress slacks and a dark blue blouse. One heel rocked back
and forth slightly as she spoke into the phone, the only sign
she gave of impatience.

"Someone's been asking questions."

"The cops?"

"No." She tapped a fingernail against the rim of the
window and shook her head, even though their connection
was voice-only. "I don't know who. But I'm going to find
out."

"Should we put things on hold?"

"No. Stopping now might raise more unpleasant questions. We continue." She paused. "We need to stay entirely
out of this, whatever it takes."

"You'll handle it?"

"Of course." Anything that was a threat to her, she handled. That was why she was successful.

She hung up the phone and checked her watch, then
crossed the space to her destination, her heels a muted tap
on the dented, dull hardwood flooring.

The Portland Cowork Enclave was a grand name for
what was basically an open loft in an old warehouse with
a dozen long tables covered with laptops, coffee mugs, and
random bits of paper, each laptop connected to a human
who was either working furiously, intent on their own
screen and whatever was pumping through their head-
phones, or talking quietly, emphatically, with the person
next to them, either indicating something on a screen or
a sheet of paper. Despite the very late hour—or the early
hour, depending on if you'd gone to sleep that night or

not—the room was full: start-ups and freelancers worked a twenty-four-hour clock, and 3 a.m. made as much sense as 3 p.m., for some of them.

Along the far wall there were a series of glass-walled cubicles. In one of them, two men were taking their seats at a small round conference table. The two at the desk were in their late twenties or early thirties, like those behind her wearing the standard uniform of jeans and T-shirts. They were only just settling themselves when the woman entered, closing the glass door behind her.

"And then we were three. We seem to be one short," one of the men said. "Did Jamie have a hot date or something?"

The other man at the table shook his head, mouth pursed like he tasted something bad. "Yeah, about that. He's dead. Cops called his family to ID him. Someone broke his neck."

"What?" The first man seemed more surprised than shocked, shooting a look at the third figure before lowering his voice slightly, uselessly. "And you didn't think to tell me?"

"Hey, I just found out, too. Told you that little bird in the police department would come in handy."

The woman's chin lifted a little, her heel stilling and her mouth tightening, but she showed no other reaction to the news. That seemed to reassure the first man, who leaned back in his chair and stared up at the ceiling. "Huh. That's unfortunate. Still, he could have called—what?"

The other man had made a noise that might have been a muffled protest.

"You expect me to shed a tear? C'mon, Ben. The man might have been talented as hell, but otherwise he was a waste of blood and bone."

"I'm not going to argue that," Ben said. "But he was also part of this organization."

"Organization." The other man laughed. "That's a good one. You make it sound like we have a flowchart and shareholders or something."

"We do have shareholders—people we are obligated to, people it's in our best interests to keep happy." He shot a glance at the standing woman's back, and raised his eyebrows significantly. "And part of keeping them happy involves keeping our system humming along happily, and our noses clean. Police investigations don't lend to either of those things."

His companion glanced at the woman as well, but rolled his eyes immediately afterward, as though to show that he wasn't intimidated by her presence. "His nose, if you're going to use that metaphor, was filthy. You want to keep our people"—and he made quote marks with his fingers around those words—" 'happy'? Forget about him, like he never existed. Let his waste sink to the sewer, where it belongs, and leave us alone."

"Christ, Dave, you're cold."

"I'm practical. And no, I never liked the guy. You didn't, either, so stop being a hypocrite. If he hadn't been useful we'd have cut him out of the loop months ago. So now he's dead. We'll find someone less problematic to do the job. Okay?"

Ben sank into his chair, raising his hands in a gesture of surrender. "Yeah. Yeah, you're right."

The woman turned and glanced from one to the other, then spoke for the first time. "While I applaud your ability to adapt to sudden changes, considering the manner of death and your known association with him, do you think that dismissing the police as a threat is all that wise?"

"You know our structure, that's why you liked us in the first place: everything's compartmentalized. No links back to us—or you, which is what you're really worried about." The older woman raised an eyebrow, but didn't disagree. "Ben and me, we've got a legit side company to run," and he gestured at the design logos on the table in front of them, the alleged reason for their meeting. "You're a client. That's all anyone sees, all anyone ever will see. Besides, once Jamie's other hobbies come to light they're going to bark up that tree. And that's probably why he got killed anyway, so more power to them." Dave made an "are we done here?" gesture with his hands. "Now can we get back to business?"

The woman studied the two of them for a long moment, causing them both to fidget slightly, then nodded. "Agreed." She relaxed her posture, but did not take a seat at the table, instead standing in front of them like a teacher in front of a classroom. "Before we discuss any further business, where do you stand on current projects?"

"Everything's good," Ben said. He didn't seem thrilled about reporting to the woman, but Dave gave him a "go on" gesture, so he did. "We're going to lose whatever was in the house, but the drop was made Sunday night, same as ever, so we're talking a day, max. And it's not like anyone's going to come howling for a refund."

They didn't hold on to the fake IDs for more than twenty-four hours, usually: quick in and quick out had been their business model from the start. The larger projects the woman dangled in front of them required that kind of agility, so he wasn't going to admit to any slow-down, even if there was one.

"And with Jamie out of the picture? Will there be a problem?"

His blood ran a little cold at the lack of inflection in her voice: threats were easier to deal with than her dispassion-ate efficiency. "I put in a few calls when I got the news; we'll drum up a replacement in a day or two. He might've been brilliant, but there are others who are nearly as good, and a lot less trouble. We won't have any real delay to worry about."

"Excellent." The woman almost smiled. "I had been concerned, during our test runs, about your partner's po-tentiality as a weak link. But now that that seems to have sorted itself, if you two are interested, I have a new client for you. One that should bring you to the next rung you've been aiming for—an international one."

Ben and Dave exchanged glances across the table, a mix of guilt and relief and anticipation, then gave her their full attention.

7

Ginny spent her second night in Portland holed up in her hotel room, the television showing a Spanish teledrama, on mute for undistracting company, while Georgie chewed on a toy under the desk and she sat cross-legged on the bed with her laptop, debris from a local fast-food chain shoved to the side.

Despite there being a news van on the scene, the murder hadn't gotten any real air time, which said something about the local news. She'd had better luck with print, but only just. The only thing she'd discovered was that the dead man's name was Jamie Penalta, and that he'd lived in the house for two years, buying it at a significant decrease from the previous sale—that last bit coming from a real estate site, not the news. He was thirty-seven, single, a graduate of the Kingsbridge School of Fine Art, and made his living as a freelance photographer, specializing in making awkward, pimply teens look less awkward and pimply. From the brief look at his portfolio, he wasn't half bad at it. Also, it wasn't much of a living, but he seemed to be paying his bills in a timely manner—again, that bit coming not from newspapers, but a little under-the-hood researchtigating.

Ginny considered the cost of living out here, and the mortgage payments on that house, and thought that fake IDs must pay better than she'd thought.

Around eleven, her eyes started to burn, so she shut down the computer, took Georgie for one last walk, and crawled into bed, hoping that tomorrow would turn up something more useful.

The next thing she knew, there was a voice in her ear. "Gin. Gin?"

"Mmmmm?" She had a phone in her hand. She had answered her cell phone while she was still asleep. She was awake now. The thoughts parsed themselves, slowly focusing in her brain. "Tonica?"

"No, it's the Easter Bunny. If I'm awake at this ungodly hour, you'd damn well better be, Mallard."

Her eyes opened enough to see the blurry numbers on the clock on the nightstand: 7:10. "Oh God, Georgie?"

She sat up in bed, her eyes focusing to find the dog. Who was sitting in the corner by her crate, looking both sheepish and judgmental.

"Oh damn. Baby, I'm sorry. No, not you, Tonica. Can I call you back? Thanks." She hung up before he could answer, and went to clean up the mess Georgie had made—thankfully on the bathroom tile, not the carpet. "Mom's sorry, baby, I don't know why I overslept."

It was the first time since she'd brought Georgie home, an awkward bundle of fawn-colored wrinkles, that she'd not woken up in time to take the dog for her morning walk. And she had no excuse for it—she'd gone to bed at a reasonable hour, hadn't had anything to drink, hadn't . . .

"Nightmares." She remembered them vaguely now, remembered waking up in the small hours of the morning, unable to get back to sleep until, apparently, she had. And then slept like the dead.

She winced. Bad choice of words.

Ginny shoved her feet into her shoes, snapped Georgie's leash to the collar, and the two of them headed downstairs, in case Georgie had any more business to conduct.

Slept like the dead, though, was an apt phrase, no matter how tacky. Had she dreamed about dead bodies? Death chasing her? Guilt over not being able to solve the mystery with a snap of her fingers? Ginny admitted that any of those was a possibility, but it could also have been the squirrel nightmare again.

"Sorry, baby," she said again to Georgie, as the shar-pei sniffed at the grass outside and left a brief message against a rock, seemingly more out of habit than any great need to relieve herself again.

Squirrels aside, as a rule, she didn't have nightmares—if something was bothering her, she worked it out while she was awake, unpicking the details in her psyche the same way she would a job, taking it down to basics and then figuring out how to deal with it. A dead body, by itself, wasn't enough to jolt that. The guy under the table hadn't been the first dead body she'd ever seen. It hadn't even been the first dead-by-violent-causes body she'd seen.

It had been the first one she hadn't *expected* to see, though. So maybe that was why this was upsetting her.

Or maybe, and more likely, it wasn't the body or even finding the body that was messing with her. For all her brave words about slipping alongside the letter of the law, all her love of the hard-boiled detectives who did the right things and damn the cost, Ginny knew that she was disgustingly law-abiding. She might drive above the speed limit, and justify breaking and entering in a good cause, but that was as far as it went. And now she was a murder suspect.

Ginny stared at the sky, the cloudy blue bright enough to remind her she was nearly an hour off schedule. "You've had the cops side-eye you before," she said out loud. "Why's it bothering you so much now?"

She knew the answer to that the moment she asked: because Tonic wasn't getting side-eyed with her.

"It's easier to get into trouble if you've got a partner," she said. "Huh." Not that it was any shocking discovery, really, but learning something new about herself was always interesting. It also explained why she was only now discovering her relatively wild side: because she had a wingman. Her mother would be *so* pleased.

That reminded her that she'd promised to call Tonica back, and the question of why he was awake at seven in the morning, when he usually slept until eleven after a late-night shift, drove her to gather Georgie and head back up to the room, pausing only long enough to grab a cup of lobby coffee. It was crap, but it was free, and it was already made. Those were two strong points in its favor.

She picked up the phone and dialed while she was getting Georgie's breakfast ready and refilling her water bowl. "Hey. Sorry. What's up?"

Tonica sounded as groggy as she'd expect with only a few hours of sleep under him, but she didn't apologize: he'd been the one to call her, after all. "Last night . . . this morning, whatever, I called in a favor on your behalf."

His network of contacts was equal to, if completely different from her own. That was part of what made them so effective together. She made sure Georgie was set, then sat down on the bed and reached for her laptop, opening up a new file and resting her fingers on the keyboard. "Talk to me."

He yawned, an audible snapping of his jaw. "Sorry. Friend of mine's a bartender down there, hangs with a bunch of cops. So I asked him if there'd been any gossip around your dead body."

"Not my body," she protested automatically, and he snorted. "Yeah, okay, sorry, *the* body."

"And?" He wouldn't have called her if something hadn't come up.

"And I thought it would take him longer than a few hours to find anything out, but I guess nobody sleeps down there. Gin, word is the guy you found? Wasn't just making fake IDs. Rumor mill has it that he was part of a national identity theft ring the cops were this close to busting."

She stilled her fingers on the keyboard, blinking at the screen thoughtfully. "Well, that explains how he's making enough money to afford that house," she said, reaching for the coffee cup. She took a sip and winced at the horribleness of it, then took another sip. "That pays a hell of a lot better than a sideline in fake driver's licenses for underage drinkers."

"One would think, yes," Tonica agreed. "And you stumbled into their investigation at a really awkward moment, when one of their targets gets knocked off. Congratulations on that, by the way."

"No wonder they side-eyed me," she muttered. "Great."

"Yeah, but get this," he went on. "This is why I called. Corky says they've already determined that the guy was dead at most six hours before you even hit town. You have proof of when you hit town, right?"

"I checked into the hotel first, so they know when I arrived, yeah," she said. "Although I could have—no, I stopped for coffee just after I left Seattle, and paid by debit card, so they have a record of that. And I took money out at an ATM, so their security camera would have me time-stamped." She nodded, for once pleased by her hyperawareness of security cameras. "Proof I was a couple of hours away at the time, or near enough to make it unlikely I was also in Portland that morning."

"So you're off the hook. Mostly. Or at least, no longer a prime suspect. So you can unclench everything you've been clenching."

She thought about objecting to his phrasing, thought about her unremembered nightmares, and said nothing. It was hard to argue when he was totally right.

"So you think I'm probably off house arrest? I can come home now?"

"I'd wait until they give you an official all clear, but yeah, I'd think so. Miss us?"

She pursed her lips, although he couldn't see her. "I don't know, there's a nice little brewpub in town. . . ."

"Mallard. Have you been drinking around on us?"

He managed just the right amount of horrified hurt, and she bit her lips to keep from laughing. None of this was funny, not even a little bit. "I hate this. I mean, great that they can't try to pin the death on me, but I still don't know why the dead guy called me down here. Or even if it *was* him who made up the fake name and hired me. And it's going to bug me forever, you know that. Short of hacking into the PayPal account . . ."

"Not recommended," Tonica said, all humor gone from his voice.

"I'm not even close to good enough and I wouldn't ask anyone else to do it," she said. "Even if it wouldn't bring attention right back to me, where I don't want it to be. We're going to have to wait for the cops to untangle that, which they probably won't bother to. But I still want to know, why me?" Her voice might have been a slight wail: across the room, Georgie lifted her head and whined, as though to ask what was wrong.

"It's okay, Georgie," she reassured the dog. "Mom's just having a slight meltdown here."

"Maybe we should let the cops figure that out, too?" It wasn't a question: he was telling her to put it down and back away slowly. She felt a burn of frustration: Where was his curiosity?

"Yeah, right. They're going to find out who killed the guy . . . maybe. Murder gets priority, especially in a nice neighborhood like that, especially if the guy was already on their radar. But once they drop me from suspect status, hopefully right about now, they're not going to care about a fake client where there wasn't actually any fraud done. I mean, maybe they'll care about the fake identity, but let's be real: if this scam is nationwide, they've got bigger fish to fry. And he's probably done worse than hire a private concierge for a party that never happened."

She stopped, thought for a second. "And if I go to the cops about it, if the money came from an illegal source, a made-up person's credit card, I might have to give the retainer fee back."

There was silence on the other end. A very telling silence.

"Tonica, that was two thousand dollars!" And, she realized, she couldn't exactly submit the receipt for the hotel room, as planned. So if she returned the money she was seriously in the hole for all this.

"All right, untwist your knickers, Mallard. So you want to know why you got dragged into this, but not bad enough to risk your ill-gotten paycheck?"

"If someone demands it back, because the money was stolen or something, of course I'll give it back." She was offended that he thought otherwise. "But we don't know for certain the dead guy was the one who hired me"—

although that seemed the Occam's razor reality—"and far as I know right now that was honest money, even if they did use an assumed name to hire me under."

"Gin . . ."

"But yes, I would like to know why I'm here, and why someone wanted me to go to the house of some guy who was running a fake ID business out of his living room. Even if it costs me the retainer." She hated herself for it, but there it was. "Don't you want to know, too?"

At the other end of the line, Tonica hrmmed, and she felt a flash of satisfaction. He *did* want to know, he just—still—didn't want to admit he was hooked.

"Maybe it wasn't a scam so much as a roundabout?" he suggested. "Maybe the dead guy was going to blow the whistle on his coworkers, and wanted us to help him? There was that crazy-ass blog post about us last month. . . ."

A blogger down in Vancouver had gotten hold of some press about one of their cases and gone totally off the rails with it, making them out to be the Batman and Robin of Emerald City, or something. That would just have been slightly embarrassing, but her parents had found it, somehow, and she'd had to spend an entire evening convincing them that no, she wasn't running around righting all wrongs for free. Nor, she had added before her father could ask, was she wearing Spandex.

Ginny rolled her eyes at the memory, and the suggestion. "Oh yeah, an identity scam in Portland needs pseudo-PIs in Seattle to help them take down their own system.

That makes a *lot* of sense. Especially if the local cops were already breathing down their necks."

"Maybe he didn't trust the local cops?" Tonica was always willing to assume someone was on the take; she'd always blamed that on his being from Boston.

"And then someone else killed him for hiring me? And my info was on him when he died, as the person he was going to squeal to? Great." Her stomach went sour, and she couldn't blame that entirely on the cheap coffee. "I'm packing up and heading back to Seattle now. Screw this."

"And never know who hired you, and why?" He was flipping her own argument on her: she hated when he did that.

"Easy for you to say: nobody's gunning for you. Come down here and help me!" She paused, thinking. "And why aren't they, anyway? Gunning for you, I mean. If someone hired us in that capacity, why didn't they hire *us*?"

From the silence at the other end of the line, she assumed he didn't have an answer for that.

"No, much as it would be nice to think we'd been called in to save the day, I think someone was just screwing with me, and this is totally unrelated to him getting killed. Maybe there really was a job, if not the job he actually told me about, and he just didn't want it traced back to him. . . ."

That actually made sense, the kind of sense she could understand and work with. Something he wanted arranged, that he didn't want to be associated with? It didn't have to be illegal—maybe he wanted to do something nice for someone but not have it traced back; she'd arranged that sort of thing before. "So yeah, maybe he wanted me to manage something, and used that as a way to get me down here, and then maybe, I don't know, hire a woman to play the client? Or fess up and try to hire me for whatever . . ." She shook her head. "No. That doesn't make sense, either."

No matter how she tried to twist it, she couldn't find a good—or even a non-bad—reason why someone would have hired her using a fake name and false pretense. And an older woman, that wouldn't raise her suspicions the way a younger male client might, asking her to meet at his home.

"Or maybe someone wanted me out of the way so they could burgle my house. I mean, if we're going to go wide-scale paranoia."

"The most expensive thing in your apartment is a two-year-old laptop," Tonica said. "Unless you have diamonds stashed somewhere?"

"Yeah, right. Tucked away right next to the Rousseau and the T-bills."

"So." There was silence from his end of the phone. "How much will it kill you to never know what really happened?"

She already knew that: it would bug her the entire ride back to Seattle, and probably for weeks afterward, and she'd already cleared her schedule for the next two weeks for the job that wasn't, so it's not as though she had anything she had to race back to and distract herself with. "I've gotta know, Teddy."

She rarely used his first name, a habit she'd fallen into when they first became friends.

"Okay then." And as simple as that, he was on board.

"So, are we taking ourselves for a client now? Because we've agreed that's a dumb move."

"Nope," he said. "We're not a client if we aren't paying. This is . . . making sure that our backs are covered. Or your back, anyway, since mine doesn't seem to be hanging in the breeze."

"I can feel the support all the way down here, Tonica."

He laughed, and suddenly she felt better. He might not have gotten side-eyed along with her, but he was there. Well, he was there, but he was *here*, too.

"Okay, assuming the cops tell me I can go today—or tomorrow, more likely—I've got one more day I can poke around down here, but then I need to return the rental car, or shell out more money to extend it." She'd figured she would keep it to run errands when she was back in town, so long as the client had been paying. Without a client . . . "That gives me two days, at least, to poke around on-site. So what's the next step in operation 'Why Am I Here?'"

She'd no sooner asked the question than Georgie's head lifted and the dog looked toward the entrance, just seconds before someone rapped sharply on the door.

Ginny glanced down at the dog, then at the door. "Georgie, did you order room service again without checking on me?"

"What?" That was Tonica, not Georgie.

"Someone's at the door," she said, still watching it as though it might suddenly bust open on its own.

"You ordered breakfast?"

"No."

She could imagine his expression: those wide-set eyes alert, but his face gone still, the way it did when he thought trouble was coming and wasn't going to give a hint of what he was going to do; what she called his bouncer face.

There was another rap at the door, this time more obviously impatient. "Ms. Mallard. Open the damned door."

A woman's voice, and familiar in the way that had Ginny getting off the bed and heading for the door, phone still in her hand, without questioning.

"Gin?"

"Hang on," she told her partner, but kept the line open. If this suddenly went bad, he was too far away to do anything but he could tell the cops what he'd heard, anyway. Which was morbid as hell, but—

She unlatched the safety locks and opened the door, aware that Georgie had gotten up and was pressing against her leg, as though to say "you've got me here, too, Mom."

"About time. Here, I brought coffee."

Ginny took the offered coffee automatically, staring as the tall, dark-haired woman moved past her into the hotel room, pausing only to give Georgie a passing scrub on the head. "I figured you'd bring her, so I checked the dog-friendly hotels in the area first. You just can't stay out of trouble, can you?"

"I'll call you back," Ginny said into the phone, and hung up.

8

"Mallard? Mallard!" Teddy stared at the phone in his hand in disbelief. But no matter how much he glared, the screen told him the same thing: she'd hung up on him. "All right, I'm going to assume that wasn't a mass murderer or the cops coming to haul your backside down to jail, and if was the cops, don't be calling me for bail money after that." He could put up with a lot, but being hung up on was a serious do-not-push-the-red-button thing, and Mallard knew that.

Then again, she *had* said she'd call him back, which suggested that whoever had come to the door wasn't an immediate threat. Unless she'd said that to tell whoever it was at the door that someone would be waiting for her to call?

"Damn it, Mallard. . . ."

No, her voice had been surprised, and maybe a touch annoyed, but not worried or scared. He'd heard her voice when she was scared: it tightened up, and her vowels flattened.

The only thing he could think of, other than a highly dubious morning booty call, was that someone had come by with information about the case, and they didn't want

her to share it with the unknown person on the other end
of the line. It didn't make him feel any better, but short of
annoying her—and possibly scaring off whoever it was—
by calling back until she answered, he was shit out of luck.
It wasn't as though he could call the local cops and say, "I
think my partner is being menaced by someone having
to do with the case of yours we're poking our noses into,
sorry about that."

Not unless he was sure there was a real threat, anyway.

"So I guess that's my cue, too. Time to get to work.
Coffee, then work." He'd been woken up by the early
morning call that made him in turn call Ginny, and now
that the mental adrenaline was running down, he could
feel the caffeine craving kicking in. He checked the time,
and considered if he had time for a run before work, or if
today was going to be one of Those Days.

There was a soft thud, and a slight dip in the mattress
next to him, alerting him that he wasn't alone any longer. He looked to his left, to see Penny picking her way
across the bed toward him, her tail held erect, her ears
forward. He hadn't even thought about telling Mallard
about the cat demanding to come home with him the
night before. She would have gotten a laugh out of it,
and God knows it sounded like she needed a laugh now.
Well, when she called back.

"And good morning to you, too," he said now as the cat
settled herself on his pillow as though he'd bought it just
for her. "Did you have a good snooze?"

The tabby had hung around long enough last night to

sniff at the food he'd picked up, then turned her nose up at it and disappeared. How a cat could disappear in a six-hundred-square-foot studio apartment he didn't know, but she'd managed it.

"Clearly you didn't want to come home with me for my company. Or the tuna."

Penny meowed once, sharply, and he laughed.

"Okay, maybe it was the tuna." He'd put it back in the fridge when she didn't seem interested, figuring she'd be hungry in the morning. Looked like he was right. "Coming right up, your highness."

Penny followed Theodore to the kitchenette, where he busied himself making coffee, and putting food on a plate, then placing the plate on the floor next to her. It still smelled strange to her, but it looked like that was her only choice, and since she didn't know how to get outside to hunt and her stomach was starting to grumble, she tucked into the strange food without further delay. She hadn't gone without food in years, not since Theodore had picked her up off the street and taken her indoors, but she still remembered the panic of hunger.

"So, looks like we have another job," Theo said to her, his hands busy with something on the counter out of sight. "Ginny got herself into trouble."

Penny knew this: she'd been listening. But Theo forgot that, sometimes. That was all right; she liked it when he talked to her— he knew things she didn't, sometimes. But she already knew that Ginny and Georgie were somewhere else, and that they'd found a dead body, and someone thought Ginny was responsible.

Penny sniffed at that again. She knew what violence smelled like, and there was none of that on Georgie's human. She was the kind to release a mouse, not eat it.

She didn't know where Ginny and Georgie were, though, or when they were coming back, or how she was supposed to figure out a solution, stuck here. So she meowed, encouraging her human to keep talking.

"Ginny's going to poke around, see what she can find out. Normally I'd be running interference with the in-person interviews, because she's still not as good as she thinks she is at finding someone's sweet spot, but, well, can't do that, stuck up here." Theo had a mug in his hands now, the bitter smell of coffee making her whiskers twitch. He moved away from the counter to sit at the table by the window, and she abandoned the rest of the tuna and went to sit on the windowsill, grooming her tail to encourage him to continue. "So she's on her own, God help us all. Although she's gotten better at listening, rather than trying to talk her way to an answer. But that means the only thing I can help with right now is research." He laughed. "And you know Ginny's shuddering at the thought. She doesn't think I can even order food online, much less dig for information, just because it's easier to let her do it. All right, I'm nowhere in her class when it comes to digital research, true, but let's see what fact-finding magic I can work."

He reached across the table and pulled a thin book from the top of a pile of papers. "Papa's Little Black Book to the rescue. Portland, fake IDs, prank-hiring. Who do we know who might be able to help with that?" He stared at the book, then opened it and riffled through the pages. "No, no, no . . . God, I need to update their address at some point, no, maybe . . . huh." He stopped and stared at the page, then tilted his head and looked at Penny, who stopped washing her tail and looked back at him with grave courtesy.

"You think Becky's forgiven me yet?"

Penny had no idea who Becky was or what he'd done, but she had confidence in her human's ability to charm anyone into anything.

"Yeah, she'd know if anything shady was going on down there. A little too early to call her out of the blue, though. Especially if she's still pissed. Email would be better. And while I'm at it, I should probably run through the news accounts, see if anything's been written up about our dead body that might have an angle we've missed . . . look for news stories about identity theft, maybe, instead of murder investigations?"

He sighed, and reached out to rub behind Penny's ear. "Yeah, so much for a run this morning. And we're gonna need more coffee."

He pushed the book aside and got up from the table, grabbing something off a counter and coming back to the table with it. "I probably should upgrade my computer, if I'm going to get stuck doing this," he said. "God knows Mallard would love to take me computer shopping. No, scratch that, she'd just go out and buy me something and then I'd spend the next year trying to figure out how to do anything. Never mind."

Penny had no interest in the screens that so fascinated Ginny: what was displayed there was a meaningless blur to her, unless there were pictures, and even then it was hard to tell what was happening unless there was also sound. How humans communicated without smell, she'd never been able to understand. But she liked it when there were people on the other side of the screen, like the night before. She wanted Theodore to do more of that, so she could talk to Geor-

gie, and find out what was going on on the dog's side of things, even if she couldn't nose it out herself.

But he was typing and there were no pictures, and he wasn't talking to her now, so she jumped down from the windowsill and went to finish the food still on the plate. No wise cat ever left food for the taking; you never knew when you might get the chance to eat again.

While she ate, Penny pinned what she knew under one paw.

Someone had died, and someone else thought Ginny might be involved.

Ginny was somewhere not-here.

Georgie was with Ginny, wherever that was, where the action was.

She was stuck here, dependent on Theodore to tell her things.

He didn't always remember to tell her things.

She needed to be where Georgie was. Or find some way to get them back on the screen so she could find out what was going on.

Short of learning how to turn it on herself, she was going to have to rely on Theodore to do that.

Penny finished the last scrap of tuna and cleaned her whiskers. She didn't know how she'd manage that, but she would. Otherwise they'd never figure this out, and Ginny and Georgie wouldn't come home.

Ginny stepped back from the door as the woman walked in, dropping her phone as unobtrusively as possible on the desk. "Agent Asuri. This is a surprise." That was putting it mildly. Special Agent Elizabeth Asuri hadn't been all that keen on their "playing detective" the last time they'd met, and had, in point of fact, told them to cut it out. Certainly she hadn't expected the other woman to make a point of looking her up—unless it was to arrest her, but why would she have brought coffee, then?

"Be glad it was me, and not someone else," the federal agent said dryly, still petting Georgie's ears. She was wearing a pair of dark slacks and a button-down shirt that had clearly been tailored to her frame, and Ginny would bet good money that there was a matching blazer in her car. No visible gun or holster, though. That was good. Wasn't it? Did federal agents carry, off duty?

"I beg your pardon?" Being polite never hurt anyone, her mom claimed. And it would probably do her more good than "what the hell are you doing here and what do you mean, 'someone else'?"

"I happened to be on the wire when your name and description came in yesterday, and told my boss I'd take this visit. And you should be thankful for that. Trying to explain your continuing idiocy to someone less informed as to your hobbies would have taken up most of your morning and probably would have gotten you at the very least a hard slap on the wrist."

"Okay, first of all, none of this is my fault," Ginny said indignantly. "If you know what's been going on, you know that. I came down here on what I thought was a perfectly normal, ordinary, boring life-management job."

"Life management?" Asuri looked amused, like she'd just seen a kitten do something particularly adorable. "Is that what you're calling it now?"

"You know, you seriously piss me off." Probably not the smoothest thing to say to a federal agent, and her mother was sighing loud enough to hear all the way from Edmonds, but Ginny figured the woman had barged into *her* hotel room, never mind that she'd brought coffee—one taste proved that it was more of the free coffee from the lobby—and now she dared make snide comments about Ginny's job? Both of her jobs?

"And that fact has truly ruined my morning," Asuri said, dry as bone. Ginny had forgotten that about the woman: she might look like a hard-ass fed on the outside, but on the inside she was a hard-ass *snarky* fed. "Look, Mallard. I warned you two over a year ago that this hobby of yours was going to get you in trouble, and now it has."

"It's not a hobby, and I wasn't here to investigate!" Ginny raised the hand not holding the coffee, and then modulated her voice when Georgie pulled away from Asuri's hand and gave her a considering look, clearly wondering if the command to "hold" or "guard" was about to be given. That's all she needed, for Georgie to attack a government employee. "I told you. I've told *everyone*. I was hired by—"

"By a little old lady who didn't exist. Yes, I read the report."

Of course she had. Asuri was a hard-ass, but she was good at her job, too, from what Ginny had been able to observe. "And you're still giving me grief?"

Asuri shrugged, turning the desk chair around and sitting in it. Taking the authority position, Ginny recognized, and sighed. "If you know all that, then you know that I'm really not in the mood for more games. Or getting my leash yanked. So why are you here, in my hotel room, at oh God early in the o'clock, with or without coffee?"

"I've kept tabs on you two, you know."

Ginny waited, presuming the non sequitur would be explained in due course.

"You've done better than I expected."

That made Ginny laugh. "You mean, you expected us to crash and burn out of the gate."

"True. And you didn't. I am, cautiously, impressed." Asuri didn't look impressed. Then again, she didn't often look anything other than stone-faced. "Have you given any thought to getting proper training and licensing, as I suggested?"

"I've thought about it," Ginny admitted, putting the coffee cup on the end table and sitting cross-legged on the edge of the bed. The hell with trying to play power games; she wanted to be comfortable for this conversation. "But I've been kind of busy."

"And Mr. Tonica has no interest in furthering his education?"

"He's been kind of busy, too." She'd been pretty sure he was going to say no to any more investigations anyway. Until they'd been asked to help out Seth's friend, and after that . . . well, it just seemed to be a done deal. They were good at it, and people needed them, so . . .

"Consider making time," Asuri said. "Because I might have told the story of your first case a few times, and it might have been retold in other offices . . . so you're not as under the wire as you might have thought you were. Having credentials, however minor, could be . . . helpful."

Ginny did not roll her eyes, and was proud of herself for that restraint. "Great, thanks. Warning duly noted." And she'd not tell Tonica about that little detail, at all. He was already paranoid about something coming into conflict with the bar . . . although maybe that would get him more into taking—no, no, better not to tell him.

"So you came here to warn me?" she asked the other woman. "That was nice. A phone call or an email would have done the trick, though, too."

"A warning in person is often better heeded. And I thought, in light of our past history, you might remember something that slipped your mind when you were talking to Portland's Finest."

"Are you accusing me of withholding evidence, Agent Asuri?" If she was, then Ginny was in a serious pile of poo. But if she were, this wouldn't be a friendly, coffee-bearing visit. Would it?

"If I were, there wouldn't be any doubt in the matter," the other woman said calmly, confirming her suspicions. "Stop being so paranoid, Virginia. It doesn't suit you."

Ginny raised an eyebrow at the use of her full name, trying to project an aura of cool unconcern but pretty sure she was failing miserably.

"I know that you would not interfere with a police investigation. And I know that you have at least enough sense to be aware that you're a person of interest by virtue of having discovered the body, in a city you don't live in, visiting a house you have no reason to be in." Asuri held up a hand. Her nails were cut short, polished with a dark red that, on her, looked professional as hell. Ginny was envious. "Yes, I am aware of your claim that you were hired by a person reportedly residing at that address. And I have no reason to think that you'd lie about something that obviously false, and I'm also aware that you have no reason to trust the local police to believe you and so might be contemplating investigating this on your own, to cover your own ass."

Ginny tried to come up with a suitable "never would I ever" response, but came up blank. Because the agent was right, of course. On all counts.

"I am, of course, concerned as to the state of my reputation with Portland's finest," Ginny settled on saying, falling back on her blandest office-speak. "And, yes, the reputation of my company, if it is true that I was hired by a person who does not exist. That . . . tends to reflect badly on someone selling their problem-solving and research skills."

Right now, everything Asuri had said fell under the category of "friendly advice" and "unvoiced warnings." Ginny wasn't going to admit to a damned thing, and she wasn't going to ask Asuri for clarification on her earlier words, either. So long as neither of them said anything definitive, they both had plausible deniability.

"Yes, I can see where that might be an issue, in your professional capacity." There was just the slightest emphasis on "professional." Ouch.

There was something Asuri wasn't telling her—there was probably a lot Asuri wasn't telling her—but Ginny didn't know how to ask about it without digging the hole she was already in even deeper, so she didn't. The two women looked at each other, those unspoken things wandering loudly around the room, bumping into furniture, until Georgie let out a heavy, dramatic sigh, lay down between them, and farted.

"Oh God, Georgie!" Ginny was mortified, but at the same time, she could feel laughter pressing against her chest, as much a reaction to the stress as any actual humor.

"Dogs are . . . refreshingly blunt," Asuri said, but the edges of her lips were curved up, not down. "Although I'm not sure 'refreshingly' was the correct word. But, if you have no further questions—or arguments—then that may be my cue to leave." She stood up, her slacks, of course, falling perfectly back into place without a crease. Ginny wondered if there was some kind of federal anti-muss field in effect. "Ms. Mallard, if you do think of anything . . . please call me."

Back to formality, Ginny noted. Probably everything from here on in was on the record. So she should just keep her mouth shut, but . . . when you had a source, you used it.

"This is a federal case? The fake IDs, I mean." She'd thought fake driver's licenses would be a state thing, but Tonica's contact had said it was national, a nationwide ring . . . and yeah, she could see where they'd call the feds in for that, since post-9/11 any fake identification had to be serious business. It was just that when they'd met, Asuri had seemed more interested in real estate fraud than identity theft—although when Ginny thought about it, that had been kind of identity theft, too, with the building contracts being signed by the wrong person. . . .

"Possessing a false identification is a felony, and a federal crime. As is the making of and the selling of them. Homeland Security takes a keen interest in those things." And didn't that sound like a canned line of bullshit? "My involvement is slightly more tangential, but it may have relevance to a larger case we're working on." Asuri looked as though she'd just thought of something. Ginny didn't believe that for a minute. "I'll tell you what. Since I'm well aware of your disinclination to walk away from any rocks you may have turned over, however innocently . . . "

She paused, as though expecting Ginny to protest. She didn't.

"If you share what you know with me, I'll return the favor. *Not,*" the agent was quick to add, "to include you in the investigation, but simply to satisfy your inevitable curiosity. And, hopefully, keep you out of any further trouble."

In other words, Asuri was offering to bribe her. Or, in more charitable terms, to give her fifty-yard-line seats in exchange for staying off the field. The fact that Asuri seemed to think that Ginny would abide by that was, honestly, kind of adorable.

Then again, the fed had the power to get Ginny arrested if she interfered. So maybe not so adorable. Maybe she should just take the deal and behave herself.

Ginny stood up in turn, smiled politely at Asuri, and offered her hand to shake on it, thinking *yeah, probably not.*

9

After Asuri left, Ginny stared at the closed door for a long moment, wondering what the hell she was supposed to do now. Nothing brilliant came to mind. "I suppose I could just sit here until the cops call to tell me everything's clear, and then go home."

Georgie sneezed, and wagged her tail.

"Was that a yes or a no, Georgie?"

Apparently, it was a "whatever," because the dog just curled up in her crate, rested her muzzle on her paws, and looked up at her owner as though waiting for the next command.

"Some help you are." Ginny headed into the shower, turning the water as hot as she could get it: hot water, she'd long claimed, stimulated problem solving. But by the time she'd gotten out, dried herself off, and gotten dressed, she still didn't know what she was going to do about what Asuri had told her—and what she'd warned her about.

She sat on the edge of the bed, finger-combing her hair and staring at Georgie, who didn't seem like she had come up with any brilliant ideas, either.

"I guess we're back to the original, amazingly vague plan then," she said. "C'mon, kid—back to work."

Georgie grumbled at having to get up again—she was fine with walks, but clearly felt that Ginny was overdoing it on this trip. Still, she let herself be loaded back into the rental car with a minimum of fuss, settling into the back-seat and resting her head on her front paws with a heavy sigh.

Ginny knew that she was pushing it, returning to the scene of the crime yet again, but the fact that she probably wasn't on the suspects list any longer—or at least not in the top five—made her bolder than she might have been, otherwise. Foolhardy, Asuri would probably say.

But not so foolhardy that she didn't call her partner back as soon as she figured he would have gotten his own hot shower and coffee routine finished.

"Look out for cops, will ya, Georgie?" she asked, as she took a hand off the wheel to set up her phone in the holder, then tapped the screen to call Tonica's cell.

"Guess who was at the door," she said when he picked up. "I'll give you a hint: it's Federal Express."

It took him a couple of seconds to figure it out. "Asuri?" His voice through the speakers sounded as surprised as she'd felt. "What's she doing in Portland?"

"Well, excuse me for not asking, and poking my nose further into a federal investigation," she snapped back, splitting her attention between the conversation and trying to catch the street signs: this wasn't like back home, where she could figure out where they were purely by familiarity. In the seat behind her, Georgie shifted restlessly but didn't respond, used to the back-and-forth between them, even if it was broken up by phone speakers now. "I was a little more interested in getting her out of my hotel room before she officially told me to stay out of things."

"You mean, as opposed to unofficially warning you to stay out of things?"

"Exactly." She couldn't help but feel a slight satisfaction from his put-upon sigh. It was almost like having him in the car with her. Although normally he'd be the one driving, and she could have focused on the directions. "Look, nothing she said changed anything we already decided. I'm going to sniff around a little more, see if anything else turns up, and as soon as I get the official free-to-go, we'll work our angle from a safe distance away from the actual murder investigation, so nobody can say we were interfering in an open case. Right?"

He sighed. "Watch your back, Mallard. Georgie, watch your owner's back, okay?"

Georgie lifted her head again and whined at the sound of her name.

"We'll be fine, you worrywart," she said. "I promise, I won't stir up any hornets' nests until I'm back where you can keep an eye on me."

"I'm going to hold you to that," he said. "All right, I need to get going. Check in this afternoon, before shift, and we can compare notes?"

"Will do."

She thumbed the OFF switch on her phone, and there was silence in the car, broken only by Georgie's grumbles, as Ginny spotted the street name she wanted, and turned left. She cruised past the house at a sedate pace, giving it a once-over.

The cop from yesterday was gone, the yellow tape was gone. The cars parked on the street in front weren't police sedans, marked or otherwise. The house was quiet and innocent-looking, as though nothing terrible had ever happened there.

She pulled to the curb at the end of the street, cut the engine, and got out, walking around to open the passenger-side door.

"C'mon, Georgie," she said, waiting while the dog scrambled out, then bending down to attach the leash to her collar. "We're going to see if you've got any bloodhound in you."

This was part of her particularly not-brilliant idea. She didn't want to go back inside the house—and even if she were less freaked out by it, the cops would have gone off with anything that was actually relevant, or even *seemed* relevant. But sometimes five-feet-above-the-ground wasn't the only angle to investigate. Nose-to-ground might kick up something new. Or not, but it didn't cost anything to try.

Admittedly, shar-pei were bred for muscle strength, not for their scent-tracking skills. Still, a dog's sense of smell, even untrained, was sharper than a human's, so who knew what Georgie might find. And Georgie was smart. Not people-smart, but smart about people. She'd have to be the stand-in for Tonica, and Ginny grinned to herself, imagining his reaction to that.

"Is there an eau de killer, Georgie? Or parfum does-not-belong? God, I hope so. Not that I want you to lead me directly to the killer, because yeah, that's totally the cops' job, but if there's something odd, something out of place or terribly interesting in the house . . ."

Georgie let out a soft woof, as though to tell the human that she understood her job, and could they please just get on with it?

"Yeah, okay. Okay."

They walked over to the house, not even pretending to be casual about it, figuring that a direct and confident approach would get fewer looks than someone who was trying to sidle in unobtrusively. They paused just in front of the porch steps, almost as though they'd rehearsed it.

"Please don't pick up a scent that takes us inside, okay?" she said to the dog. Odds were that the front door wasn't still unlocked, and while she'd become a decent hand at basic lock picks, thanks to YouTube and a kit she'd bought off one of Seth's friends who was a professional locksmith—or so he claimed—she hadn't brought her kit with her, and she was pretty sure a nail file and a credit card weren't going to do it. Not at her skill level, anyway.

Ginny stared at the wooden planks of the porch, thinking. While Georgie sniffed around, she thought about the back of the house, the single door that led into the kitchen, and how rickety the steps had looked. Some folk used the back door more often than the front, either to avoid the formality of the front hall or because they didn't want to make a public point of who came to visit. She suspected that the former resident of the house had been more the latter type. But the front door had been unlocked two days ago. Even if the killer hadn't gone in that way, odds were good he'd left that way.

But she didn't want to find the killer. She wanted to find some explanation for why she'd been called in. Maybe, ideally, a scrap of little-old-lady perfume that led to the actual Mrs. Adaowsky, who had been living with her—grandson? Great-nephew? Boy toy?—And had taken off when things got bad?

That was just as possible as anything else, at this point. Of course, it could also just as likely lead her to little-old-lady bones in the cellar. "Oh, great, thank you, brain. We are not going into the root cellar, Georgie. Just FYI."

Georgie pulled at the leash, refocusing Ginny's attention from the front door to the dog.

"You got something?" Ginny admitted to herself that she was surprised; she hadn't really expected any one smell to stand out, at this point. "So how do we do this, girl?" she asked. Hold, stay, fetch, release—those were things Georgie had learned quickly. Guard had come almost naturally. But find was a different thing entirely, especially without any other guidance. So instead, she just jiggled the leash a little, telling Georgie that it was okay to walk forward, and let the dog do what dogs did best: sniff the ground for anything interesting.

At first, Georgie meandered, sniffing here and there in no clear pattern, occasionally leaving a drop or two of urine as a marker, but not showing any real interest in any one direction. Ginny was about to call it quits, when suddenly Georgie pulled against the leash, just hard enough to say that she had something in mind, and wanted to go there now, please.

"Okay, okay," Ginny said, trying to pay attention to the dog's body language, the way their trainer had taught them, as well as keeping an eye on where they were going. Georgie led her around to the back of the house, then back to the front again, and to the sidewalk. Something—or someone—who smelled interesting had circled the house a few times, recently enough that the smell still lingered.

"Where're we going, baby?" Ginny said, not loud enough to distract the dog's attention. "What's got you so focused?"

It was a good thing it hadn't rained recently, she thought. The grass was green, even along the curb, so there'd been enough water lately, but not for a day or two, maybe three? She was pretty sure they'd gotten the same rain as Seattle, three days ago, but would a smell last that long?

Using her free hand, she pulled her tablet out of her bag and pulled up the weather app, checking the past few days. A light rain had passed through two days ago. Was that enough to wash away a scent? She pulled up a search engine and asked it.

Rain pushed a scent down, but humidity trapped it, made it easier to find. Huh. She supposed that made sense, thinking about how things smelled after a few days of dampness. And the air had been seasonably damp, she supposed. Ginny kept reading, caught up for a moment in the new information, then shook her head, and slipped the tablet back into her bag. The problem was, she had no idea what had gotten the dog's attention. Georgie could be fascinated by a squirrel or raccoon's scent, or some other dog that had been by, or . . .

Whatever it was, it was leading Georgie out of the yard. Ginny let her go, the leash taut between them. Georgie's neck was stretched forward, and her stump of a tail was wagging slightly, which meant her entire backside was in motion. Happy, interested dog. They were probably on the scent of a food truck.

Georgie took her down the sidewalk and around the corner, to the south. This street looked the same as the last one, although the houses were on slightly larger lots, and some of them had attached garages. Georgie kept moving until she came to the house two from the edge of the block, a house with dark green paint and white trim, and two teenage girls sitting on the front stoop.

Whatever scent Georgie had been following, it led here. Ginny checked her watch, pretty sure that the girls should have been in school.

Georgie tugged at the leash again, and Ginny pretended to lose hold of it, curious as to what Georgie might do. The dog trotted happily up the walkway to where the girls were sitting, and shoved her nose into one of the girls' hands, causing her to shriek—thankfully with excitement, not fear.

"I'm so sorry." Ginny came up the walk and clapped her hands to get Georgie's attention. "She's usually so good on the leash but sometimes she just wants to make friends. Georgie, sit, girl, play nice."

The girl Georgie had zeroed in on had dark auburn hair in a long ponytail, and dark freckles across pale brown skin. Her companion's hair was blonder, in the same style of ponytail, with blue eyes, but otherwise they could be siblings, dressed in the same uniform of jeans and long-sleeved T-shirts, barefoot and letting bright blue polish dry on their toes.

"No, it's okay," the blond girl said. "She's sweet."

The redhead pulled her toes out of reach, and was petting Georgie cautiously, making the familiar "oh, good doggie" noises she seemed to bring out in people.

"She likes it if you scratch—yeah, right there," Ginny said, as the girl found the spot, and Georgie collapsed onto her back, paws limp with pleasure. "I'm Ginny. That's Georgie."

"I'm Kim," the redhead said.

"Nancy," the blonde offered.

Ginny hesitated, then offered up what she hoped was a Tonica-worthy grin, hoping it came across as willing conspirator rather than interrogator. "Should I even ask why you guys aren't in school?"

They looked at each other, and then at her, and then seemed to decide that she wasn't about to rat them out.

"It was too nice to stay indoors," Nancy said. "And we're seniors."

"Fair enough." She'd cut classes enough times to understand, even if it had been a while ago. She thought about trying for more small talk, then decided she'd better cut to the chase, before they got bored or weirded out talking to a stranger. "So you guys heard there was some excitement in the neighborhood yesterday?"

"Excitement? Here?" Nancy was slightly scornful, but both girls tried to look politely interested, the way you would when someone too old to understand what real excitement might be started talking. Ginny tried not to take it personally.

"Well, for kind of sick levels of excitement, I guess. They found a body a few blocks over."

"A body? Really?" Nancy lit up with vaguely ghoulish interest at that, and Ginny wondered if she was related to Daisy, from yesterday.

"A human body?" Kim was more cautious.

"A human, yeah. In one of the houses over on the Terrace." She waved her hand vaguely over her shoulder in the direction she'd come from. "The pale blue one? There were cops all over the place."

Both girls had gone slightly green when she mentioned the street, and tensed when she described the house. Interesting, although they probably knew enough people in the neighborhood—had they known the victim? He was older, but a slightly older single male could be of interest to teenage girls if he was good-looking. She hadn't looked at his face long enough to see anything other than blood and bone, and she pushed that memory down hard so she could focus on the moment at hand.

"You hear anything about it? Who it was?"

"No," Nancy said, clearly speaking for both of them. "No, we didn't. If you'll excuse us? We promised to meet friends for lunch."

"Of course," Ginny said, picking up Georgie's leash and tugging her away. "Have a nice day, girls."

Georgie hadn't taken her there by accident. They hadn't known about the murder. But they knew who had lived there—now that she thought about it, they were the right age to have gotten fake IDs there, if someone were dealing in the neighborhood. The way they'd reacted, Ginny would put good money on them knowing something, even if it was just a bit of gossip that could be horribly relevant. Should she mention that to Asuri, have the agent follow up on it? No. If they weren't willing to come forward on their own, without any more evidence Ginny wasn't going to force the issue. Not on a federal level, anyway. No teenager needed that in their life, if their only crime was being teenage-level stupid.

If they were clients of the dead man's fake driver's license business, though, that would explain why Georgie picked up Kim's scent: she must have been at the house recently, to get an ID. If so, then her fingerprints were probably inside, too, and the cops might be paying a visit, anyway.

She suspected that neither girl would get the chance to cut school and sit in the sunshine for a while, after that.

Teddy pulled his car into the parking lot at Mary's just before noon on Thursday to find Stacy waiting at the back door. He lifted a hand to say hello to her, then opened the passenger door to let Penny, graceful as a duchess, leap down from the seat to the sidewalk.

His waitress/bartender had gaped, then started laughing. "You are so, so whipped, boss."

"Shut up," he said. "She wanted a change in scenery, okay?" They walked in together, Penny darting ahead to take up her usual position on top of the liquor shelves.

"Seriously?"

"Yes, seriously. She came out with me last night, and got in the car, okay? What was I supposed to do, kick her out?"

"Seriously?" Stacy said again, incredulous. "She went home with you?"

Seth chose that exact moment to walk in the back door, shucking his jacket and hanging it on the employees-only rack. "You got lucky, boy?"

"Shut up, Seth. She's talking about the cat." He glowered at Seth's back, hearing the old man's cackle, then turned and glared at Stacy, who gave him a wide-eyed innocent look that didn't even come close to working. "Thanks for that note of astonishment. Everyone's always telling me she's my cat, or I'm her person, whatever, so why is it so incredible that she decided to come home with me?"

"Because cats are like the original Republicans," Stacy said, pushing a table back into position from where the cleaning crew had moved it. "They don't like change. At all. And Mistress Penny is a bar cat, not an apartment cat. Did she sleep on your bed with you?"

Teddy shook his head. "No. Although she was pretty quick to take over my pillow, once I woke up."

"Huh." Stacy pursed her lips and hrmmed. "Interesting."

"Please. Like you know anything about the psychology of cats?"

"Maybe she's lonely," Stacy said. "Georgie hasn't been in for a week, and Ginny's been gone, what, three days now? Maybe she just wanted to make sure you didn't disappear, either."

Teddy wanted to say that was a crackpot theory, except it was pretty close to what he'd been thinking, too. "Makes as much sense as anything, which is to say, not damn much. Stop psychoanalyzing the cat, and get the tables in back set up."

They'd agreed to host a reading group that afternoon. Or rather, Patrick, Mary's owner, had agreed, and left them to deal with it. It was their second meeting, once a month, and while nobody in the group drank beer, they did do a rousing business in soda and coffee, and they kept it quiet enough that Teddy could get work done at the counter. All in all, it could be worse.

The extra business didn't hurt the bottom line, either, which meant that Patrick was happy, and a happy Patrick meant he left them alone.

And speaking of a happy Patrick . . . Stacy had that look on her face, the one she usually got whenever there was something she needed to say but didn't want to, and that usually happened whenever the owner came around and raised stress levels. Teddy stifled a sigh, wondering how he'd missed that.

"All right, out with it. What did Patrick do this time?"

"What?" The look of surprise on Stacy's face was real. "No, I haven't seen him since . . . last month?"

That was the last time Patrick had come around in person. "So what's up, then? You've got that line between your eyes that says you've got something to say and don't want to say it but if you don't you're going to be fretting all shift, and your tips will go down."

"That's just it." She hesitated, then plunged on, picking up Penny and cuddling her as though for comfort. "The tips are already down."

"Oh?" The regular crowd were decent tippers, usually—everything went into a communal pot at the end of the evening, lion's share to whoever was waitressing, the rest split among the bartenders—and he hadn't noticed any dip in regulars. But he also didn't pay much attention to the tip jar, since he'd become manager and opted for a smaller cut.

"It's probably nothing. I just . . . I'm doing okay, right? I'm not . . ."

"You're doing fine," he assured her. "It's probably that Tricia hasn't gotten up to speed yet, and they're giving her less."

That response didn't sit well with either of them, since the new girl had enough charm to compensate for any newbie gaffes, but it was the only thing he could think of. "Maybe it's just one of those downturns, people feeling pinched. It'll come back up soon enough."

She nodded and put Penny down to go behind the bar and start the day's setup, even as Seth banged around in the kitchen, setting things to order.

Ten minutes later, there was the further sound of muddled cursing, and Seth yelled, "Who's been eating all the damn bread?"

Teddy and Stacy looked at each other, waiting for the follow-up. Sure enough, a minute later Seth came out front, his face creased in a scowl. "Tonica, what's the point in having a cat if she don't eat the damn mice?"

"Is the plastic wrap bitten or torn?" he asked.

"No."

"Then it wasn't mice. Unless you left it out on the counter, unwrapped?"

Seth scowled at him, then turned on his heel and marched back into the kitchen, muttering under his breath.

"Are you making after-hours toast, Stacy?"

"Not me, boss."

He considered the possibility of mice, and then shook his head. They'd done renovations to the kitchen recently, and if there'd been signs of mice then, the workmen would have said something. But he'd lay down some traps, anyway, just in case Seth wasn't eating it himself and then forgetting.

"You want I should go out and get more bread?"

"After you set up, yeah." The book club usually brought their own food, so he wasn't worried about them, but the sandwiches had been popular with the happy hour crowd, and he'd rather feed them that—better alcohol absorption—than having them chow down on the smoked nuts and pretzel chips.

Satisfied that everything else was as under control as Mary's ever got, Teddy finished doing the setup behind the bar, making sure all the taps were ready, the tanks refilled, and the speed rail supplies restocked. After a decade of doing that, it was muscle memory, allowing his mind to go over his conversation with Ginny that morning. The fact that Asuri was there was actually reassuring, he decided. If there was trouble, they could trust the agent to watch their backs, even if she wasn't entirely on their side. He wished he'd gotten better responses from his own outreach, but most of it had turned up dry, or simply not responded. He wasn't good at that, not the way Mallard was; he didn't maintain his contacts, didn't play the favor game as smoothly as she did, and his Internet search skills were, as Ginny had said more than once, laughable.

But not trying to help wasn't an option.

He was running over a handful of theories, based on Asuri's presence, the fake driver's license business, and someone getting beaten to death, and was so caught up in the multiple what-ifs that it took him a minute to realize that Stacy was standing on the other side of the bar, trying to get his attention.

"Oh. Sorry, what?"

"Now it's my turn to ask—boss, are you okay?"

"Yeah, yeah, I'm fine." He looked to the top of the shelves, an ingrained habit now, and reached over his head to tug lightly at the tail dangling behind him. "Just a little distracted, is all. Gin may have stumbled onto a job while she's in Portland"—he wasn't going to give her the details; Stacy was a friend but she was also an employee—"and my brain's kind of working that, too."

"Huh. Sidelined while Ginny's knee-deep in the good stuff, huh? No wonder you're grumpy, stuck here with us."

It was too close to the truth for comfort. "I'm not grumpy. You want to see grumpy? Have those tables not ready by the time the book ladies show up, I'll show you grumpy."

"I'm done!" She waggled her fingers in front of his face, and then pointed one finger toward the back, where the chairs had been rearranged to suit the fifteen or so members, with the tables moved to support positions. "And now I'm going to pick up some lunch before we start, and a couple of loaves of bread, to shut Seth up. You want anything, while I'm gone? Pizza? Alka-Seltzer? Prune juice?"

"Get out," he growled, and she laughed and flipped him off before heading out the door. It closed firmly behind her, and he remembered the days when they used to leave it open except in the very worst weather. Before they'd twice had goons come in and try to wreck someone's face, because of jobs he and Ginny had taken.

"Why do I do this again?" he asked Penny. She poked her head over the shelf, wise cat eyes in a little tabby face, her ears perked forward, whiskers quivering, and blinked slowly at him.

"You're no help at all," he said. "I take back the partnership offer."

She didn't seem all that impressed.

"Oh, you think you could do so much better? I'll bet—shit," and he looked at his watch. "We're late to check in with Herself." He ran his gaze over the counter, determined that everything was ready, and headed for the back office.

Penny blinked again, then leapt lightly down to the floor and followed him.

Theo was already settled at the desk when she entered the room, and the soft sounds of a phone ringing filled the air. She leapt up onto the desk, narrowly missing a glass that had been left there, and wound her way across the desk to step delicately into his lap. He lifted an arm absently to give her access, then rested it on her back, petting her absently. She let a purr rise up, but didn't let herself forget why they were there.

The ringing stopped and the screen changed from a single color to moving imagines. Concentrating, Penny was able to recognize Ginny's face, a second before they heard her voice.

"Hey. You're late."

"Yeah, all of three minutes. Sorry. We were getting ready for the terrorist book club you sicced on us."

"That's a terrible thing to call them. Nea is perfectly nice people."

"Yeah well, I don't trust anyone who carries that many knitting needles in one bag." He stopped petting Penny and she butted at his head until he continued. "So how did it go this morning?"

"I'm not sure. Georgie picked up a scent, and we followed it a few blocks over."

"She's part bloodhound now?"

"You had a better idea, you should have told me beforehand. You want to hear what happened or not?"

"Right, sorry. So Georgie picked up a scent?"

There was a scuffle, and Ginny said "ooof," and Georgie's face was in the middle of the screen.

"Hi, Penny!"

"What did you find, Georgie? And don't hog the screen or she'll make you get down."

"I found a girl!"

Penny's whiskers twitched, and she looked up at Theo, then back at the screen.

"Georgie, down," Ginny said, as Penny had predicted, and pushed the dog out of the screen, so Penny could only see the top of her head and one ear.

"We followed it to a house a few blocks away, and two girls sitting on a porch," Ginny said.

"See!" Georgie said, slightly muffled now. "I found a girl!"

"Shhh, Georgie, just for a minute." She needed to hear what the humans were saying, too.

"They were about sixteen, maybe seventeen. Still in high school, and ditching. I let Georgie soften them up, then asked them about the murder, if they'd heard anything, if they knew who it had been."

"You think teenagers care about someone dying a few blocks over?"

"They did. I'm pretty sure they knew that house, Tonica. I mean, other than the fact that Georgie went straight from the back porch to that front porch, both girls looked a little sick when I said they'd found someone dead there. And they couldn't get away fast enough after that."

Theo scoffed. "You seriously think that two teenage girls killed him?"

"No. Probably not, although with how many sisters and cousins, you should know better than to underestimate a teenage girl."

"Point taken."

"No, I think they bought fake IDs from the dead guy."

"So did half the underage population of Portland, from what you said about the stack of IDs you saw. Which means what?"

"I haven't a clue." Ginny laughed, but it wasn't her usual happy sound, and Penny pricked her ears, wishing she could see better, or smell, or . . .

"Georgie? What does she smell like?" There was only one "she" in Georgie's world, no need to clarify.

"Unhappy," Georgie replied. "She's worried, and unhappy." The shar-pei whined in frustration. "And the girls we met were unhappy, too. Really unhappy. Even when they were petting me, they were unhappy."

Penny considered that, her tail twitching thoughtfully.

The humans were still talking, about police reports and theft, and a friend of Theo's who might be able to help.

"Unhappy sad, or unhappy scared?" she asked Georgie, who cocked her head and whined a little in thought, causing Ginny to rub her head and distract her for a moment.

"Unhappy sad. Unhappy scared. And unhappy . . ." Georgie whined again, not being able to describe it.

"And it came out when Herself asked about the body?"

"It was there to start, but it got stronger then, yeah."

Penny couldn't make out details through the tiny screen, but she could see how mournful Georgie's eyes would be, looking at her as though to ask her to make it all better. "They were so sad, and then they were scared, and I couldn't make them feel better, Penny."

"We will," she promised the dog. "We just need to figure out how."

Penny had an idea, though. Ginny had to sniff some more around those girls. Unhappy-waiting-to-be-yelled-at meant they did something wrong. Humans were like dogs: if you looked at them long enough, they'd admit to every bad thing they'd ever done.

She stretched her front paws up, until they reached the keyboard, and waited.

"I keep thinking about those girls, though," Ginny said, and Penny hit as many keys as she could, trying to make the right thing happen, the keys that made the smiley face appear. She'd seen Theo do it before, when he wanted to encourage the person on the other screen to keep talking. . . .

"What? Sorry, Ginny," Theo said, and erased the gibberish that had appeared on the text screen below her image. "You were saying?"

"How many kids in that neighborhood, in the city maybe, were in and out of that house? If they were actually doing business directly from there, I doubt teenagers were wearing gloves, or thought to wipe their handprints away, and I'm pretty sure they didn't have a cleaner in on a regular basis. So there must be a dozen or more fingerprints in that house."

Penny pressed more keys, and twitched her whiskers in irritation when Theo simply pushed her off, then lifted her and put her on the desk rather than his lap. If she could hit the right key, pictures came up. If she could find a picture of a girl . . .

"Well, if nothing else, a lot of kids are going to lose their fake IDs and be grounded for the rest of their adolescence," Theo said.

"Yeah, I had that same thought. I just . . ."

"What? Spit it out, Gin. Your instincts are pretty good, most of the time."

"Most?"

"Gin . . ."

"I just keep thinking that the girls knew something. Something about why the guy was killed. Why did Georgie go to that particular house, those girls, out of all the scent trails there must have been—there were cops all over the place, and the paramedics? Why was their scent particularly strong?"

"Gin. Finding the killer's not our case, remember? If it doesn't have to do with why you were hired . . ."

"But what if it does? What if it was all tangled together?"

"Okay, how? And why?"

She sighed. "I don't know. He had my contact details on him, in his pocket. So either he was the one who contacted me, or the killer planted the information there, which implies that the killer contacted me." She licked her lips, and looked off-screen. "I think I'm gonna be sick."

"Penny," Georgie whined. "Do something!"

She pushed up into Theo's lap so that the dog could see her, for reassurance. "Shh, Georgie. We've got them on the right track, now I need to figure out what to do next. Just trust me."

Theo sighed, then picked her up off the desk and put her on the floor, not allowing her to get back into his lap. "Down, Penny. The adults are talking."

Disgusted, Penny lifted her tail and flicked it once to indicate

*her displeasure, and stalked out of the office. She'd find high space
somewhere, and think. This would be so much easier if they weren't
separate!*

"Sorry about that. I'm not sure what's gotten into that cat
recently."

"They've both been acting weird. Georgie's never pulled
out of my leash before, not even when there was a squirrel
to chase." Ginny shook her head. "They miss each other, I
guess."

"Yeah, maybe." He thought about Stacy's suggestion,
that the animals were lonely, and shook his head. "But
specific to Georgie, her behavior might have a reason. I
mean, more than her just following a scent and wanting
friendly pettings."

"Like what?"

"Guilt."

Ginny widened her eyes at him, placing a hand to her
chest in mock shock. "Now you think those girls are the
killers? Seriously?"

"Weren't you the one just telling me never to underestimate teenage girls? But no . . . I'm pretty sure not. Or if
they are, then let the cops go after them because teenage
girl catfights look way better on-screen than in person."

"I'm just going to pretend you didn't say that. So what
are you thinking?"

Teddy bit his lip and ran a hand over the top of his head,
thinking that it was almost time for another buzz before

summer hit, for whatever variation of the season Seattle gave them this year. "I don't know. I just keep thinking that if Georgie did that, there's got to be some reason. And if the girls reacted the way you said . . ."

"They did."

"I wasn't doubting you, woman, just thinking out loud. If the girls knew something about the guy who died, that might tie back into why someone tried to connect you to him. And no, I don't know how or why but they're the only possible clue we've got. And it would explain why Georgie picked up the scent—the difference between people going about doing their jobs, and someone who . . . well, strong emotions affect body chemistry, even I know that. And it's not like Georgie hasn't been right about these things before."

He hated to admit it, but the dog's sense about people was almost as good as his. Maybe even better, in some ways. "I think you're going to have to try to talk to them again." He laughed, although it really wasn't funny. "Good thing you were down there, not me. If I tried to approach them a second time, I'd probably get maced."

"Yeah well." Ginny exhaled and shook her head, making her shoulder-length curls—nowhere near as tidy as usual—bounce around her face. It looked amusingly similar to the way Georgie's ears flopped when she shook her head. Teddy wasn't anywhere near punchy enough to say that, though. "I'd rather you were here," she said. "I'm still not good at this, female to female or not."

"Just ask yourself, What Would Teddy Do?"

She snorted at that, but smiled. "Yeah, I'll try, but no promises. Those girls really didn't want to talk to me." She reached down to pet Georgie's ears, her lips pursed in thought. "I think, before I try to corner them, I'm going to check in with the local cops and make sure that I'm cleared to go, and then maybe do one last pass through the neighborhood, see if there's anything else anyone can tell me."

"And then you'll talk to the girls." She was going into avoidance mode, because she didn't think she was capable of handling it. "Assuming the cops don't arrest you beforehand."

"Oh gee, thanks for the support, Tonica." She glared at him, her self-doubt forgotten, and he mentally chalked up a point to himself.

"If the girls won't talk, short of tossing the house for clues, which I'd really rather not do, I think we're beat on this one, Teddy. I'm never going to know why I got dragged into this, or by whom. And now I'm going to be paranoid as hell for *months*."

Years, he thought. He might be able to let go of an unknown, but for Ginny, it would always be this itch she couldn't reach, the question she didn't ask, and it was going to drive her crazy.

And she was going to take him along with her.

10

Normally Ben and Dave would get together once a week, do whatever was needed to keep the surface business running—one client at a time, carefully chosen, bringing in just enough money to make them legit—and then deal with whatever had to be done on their real moneymaker. They both had other jobs, with regular hours, so meeting during the workday normally didn't happen. But this wasn't a normal week—even without scrambling to hire someone to replace Jamie. Ben wasn't happy about changing his schedule, but they'd both known taking the next step would require some changes.

It would be worth it, in the end. And he could smooth things over with his bosses later.

They'd reserved the small conference room again. Ben stared at the clock on the wall, and wished that the glass wall to the main room had drapes, or was one-way glass, something to help with the itchy sensation of being watched. Nobody was paying any attention to them. That was why they met here, because everyone was too self-involved with their own projects to wonder about anyone else, especially if they weren't working on the same sort of projects. He was pretty sure that nobody at the coworking center was in their line of work. Although, you never knew. . . .

"This is inconvenient," he said, bringing his attention back to the pile of folders in front of him.

"This is why we set things up this way in the first place," Dave said, for maybe the tenth time. "And yes, I know it's inconvenient, shifting everything, but it's better than having to try to reclaim anything from a crime scene, don't you agree?" Dave sighed when Ben made a face, and reached across the table to shove Ben on one arm, roughly but not without affection. "Come on. Snap out of it. We need to be on our game if we want to hit the big time. This new gig could be it, finally."

And that was another issue entirely. "You really trust her?"

"Who, Michal?" Dave laughed. "Not even remotely. She'd drop us to the cops the minute it worked in her favor, which is why we need to keep our noses clean every way we can," and he tapped the paperwork for emphasis. "But she's also our ticket to the big leagues. Mega-money, bro. But mega-risks, too. We can't have anything go wrong."

"Is that why you had Jamie killed?"

"What?" Dave swung around in his chair and glared at the other man. "What the hell are you talking about?"

"You always said he was going to be the rock around our neck. The thing that drowned us. And now he's dead and suddenly we've got an invite to the dance? You don't think that's a little coincidental on the timing?"

"Jesus." Dave visibly pulled his temper back under control. "Okay, look. First off, I didn't have Jamie killed. Yes, I thought he was going to be trouble and I was right. But killing him? You really think I'm capable of that?"

His partner stared at him. "Of having him killed? Yeah, yeah, I do. Because if you weren't a cold bastard we wouldn't be here in the first place." He didn't mean the conference room, or the small apartment they'd just leased under a fake identity, to replace the workspace they'd lost with the other man's death, or even the paperwork they were having to deal with, setting up new contacts to replace ones that might have been tainted by association with the dead man, but the entire thing, the whole business that had gotten them to all those places. And it had all started with Dave.

Making fake driver's licenses, no problem. Falsifying entire people? It made his stomach hurt a little, thinking about the risks. But Dave was right, this was the mega-money. This was every dream he'd ever had, on a platter.

"Well, I didn't do it, all right?" his partner said. "I'm not going to mourn the guy, but I didn't kill him *or* arrange to have him offed. Jesus. Did you?"

Ben felt his eyes go wide, staring at Dave. "No." He'd been tempted once or twice to deck the guy, but kill him?

"Great. We're both in the clear. Now can we focus on the details, and not what's in the past? All right?"

Dave was pushing, he knew he was pushing, but they didn't have time for Ben to have a crisis of whatever. Michal had been blunt: everything they'd done for her until now had been a test run, a trial. They would get this one chance to prove that they could handle a larger project, and once chance only. Positive results would take them to the next level, the big leagues. A failure would drop them back into the minors, back to peddling fake identification cards to underage teenagers. That was fine when they were still in college, but not now.

"Come on, Ben. Are you in or not?" Dave shoved his hands into his pockets and stared at the other man. Ten years they'd been working this angle, making sure their product was better than anyone else's, keeping their noses clean—and then Jamie had to be an ass, and if he hadn't been so damn good a salesman, Dave would have kicked the bastard's ass out the door the day after he walked in. But he had been that good, bringing in customers and keeping them happy, and so they'd overlooked his bad habits. And they were being rewarded now. Ben couldn't get cold feet: their skills complemented each other, design and implementation. They *needed* each other.

And with the better revenue stream, they could afford to hire the best photographers out there, and pay them enough to not ask any questions.

"Ben." He stood up and stepped forward, reaching out to grab the other man by the lapel of his jacket, hauling him out of his own chair. "Come on, man, where's your head, huh? Because I need it to be here."

"Hey, come on." Ben tried to back away, loosen from Dave's grip, but ended up backing himself up against one of the bare walls, Dave following up in his face. "Dave, quit it, okay? I'm here, all right? I'm in the game."

Dave uncurled his fingers from the fabric, smoothing it down and stepping back. "Good. That's good. Because we need you here. In the game." He took a deep breath, then smiled crookedly. "When we go big we're going to go big together, right, brother?"

"That was always the plan, brother." Ben's smile wasn't quite as cheerful as his partner's, but it passed muster. And if his doubts about Jamie's death weren't entirely erased, he now knew better than to voice them.

Whoever had killed Jamie, it was over and done. They had new business to consider.

Ginny liked to think that she was the face-forward, deal-with-things-immediately kind of person. Avoidance never made a problem go away, procrastination never got things done, et cetera et cetera. So when she'd said good-bye to Tonica, she'd walked Georgie long enough to tire the dog out, then set her up in the room, double-checked the information the cop who'd taken her statement had given her, and gone to the police station. Her experience dealing with bureaucracies had taught her that showing up on their doorstep would be more effective than getting handed around a phone-tree line.

The building itself was an almost-bland, brick-face structure that could have been a library, except for the lettering over the main doors and the extreme number of squad cars parked around it.

Effective was a relative term, thought. She had to wait

nearly an hour, but she was able to get decent signal inside the building, allowing her to respond to email, including several potential new clients, on her tablet. But the vending machine was broken, the coffee tasted like watered-down ashes, and the plastic seat was starting to make her backside hurt.

After a moment's thought, she added a request for references—not optional—to those potential client emails and sent them off, before tackling the harder-to-answer mail from her mother, who wanted to know why she was canceling out on dinner that weekend.

Somehow she didn't think "Hey, Mom, I'm writing this from the waiting room of the Portland PD and I'm not sure when they'll let me go home" would go over well. They already thought her actual freelance job was sketchy enough; add in the cops and they'd stage an intervention to get her back to a nice, safe, stable desk job working for someone else.

Ginny looked around at the waiting room, considered the bad coffee and the plastic seats, and shook her head. She'd still take this, boring paint and cinder-block walls, over more time served in a cubicle.

"Ms. Mallard?"

"That's me." She looked up to see a young, dark-skinned man in a uniform eyeing her dubiously. She smiled as harmlessly as she could and stood up. "So what's the verdict?" All right, maybe not the best word choice ever, but the guy smiled back at her, showing reassuringly crooked teeth.

"Sorry for the delay in sorting things out, but I'm afraid you're rather low priority."

"And that's good, right?"

"That's good," he agreed. "If you'll just confirm your contact information, in case we have need to get in touch, you're all set." His smile broadened, showing off impossibly high cheekbones that she briefly envied. "It certainly didn't hurt to have the feds vouching for you."

"I bet," she said, smiling back. More likely they were wondering why a federal agent knew her name at all, why was she known to the feds in the first place, and why was she in their town. All answers she had no inclination of giving them, if Asuri hadn't already.

"I don't suppose that you could tell me anything about the situation—do we know why the poor guy got killed?"

Whoops. She could see the pullback in his eyes, even though the smile didn't lose an inch of professional sincerity. She was about to get hit with the standard "no, they could not tell her anything about a pending investigation, ma'am, time for you to go, now."

And yep, there it came, textbook perfect. She supposed that they couldn't all be as helpful—or as friendly—as the cop she'd met on Wednesday. Pity she hadn't thought to get the woman's name. She—grumpily—suspected Tonica would have remembered. Working alone was harder, and she wished, briefly, that he'd been able to come down the moment the shit first hit the fan.

But wishes weren't horses. So she smiled back at the uniform, equally professionally sincere, and went to collect her car from the parking lot, surrounded by squad cars and unmarked sedans.

She stared at one of those sedans thoughtfully, something tingling in the back of her brain, but it didn't come forward, and finally she shrugged and got into her car. The best way to coax a thought out of hiding was to ignore it for a while.

The drive back was mostly on autopilot, her eyes on the road but her brain a jumble of what-ifs and should-haves. Teddy was right, the smart thing to do would be to hit the hotel, pack up Georgie and their gear, and point the rental car north to Seattle, putting this entire thing in the box labeled "fool me once" and filing it under "learning experience."

That would be the smart thing to do.

So when she pulled into the hotel's parking lot, she went to the front desk and extended her stay another night. Then she went upstairs and collected her partner in not-crime. Well, her four-legged one, anyway.

"Hey, Georgie," she said, as she opened the room door to the expected enthusiastic greeting. "Tired of these walls? Wanna go for another ride?"

Georgie was down with that.

Ginny was starting to think that by now she knew the drive from her hotel to the scene of the crime as well as she knew the walk from her apartment to Mary's. Three days of walking Georgie on that street, and either she'd be arrested for sure this time, on suspicion of casing the neighborhood, or the locals would start to think she belonged there.

It was an early Thursday afternoon, not quite the start of the weekend, but she had taken the measure of the neighborhood now: thirty-something homeowners, and teenagers, and retirees meant that every day there was a chance of different people being out and about. Hitting the neighborhood a few hours earlier than when she'd found the body increased the odds that she'd run into someone who had been out and about at the same time on Tuesday. Right?

It was the only logic she had, so she was going for it. When they arrived in the neighborhood, she sent off a quick text to Tonica, telling him she was in the clear and on the case, and then got Georgie out of the car, snapping on her leash and shoving a few poo bags in her pocket. Just because they were visiting didn't mean she couldn't be polite, although she hadn't seen any trash cans around where she could dump the bags, if it came to that. . . .

Her phone vibrated, telling her she'd gotten a return text: *b crfl*. It took her a minute to puzzle that out as "be careful."

Always, she sent back, and was pretty sure she could hear the snort all the way from Mary's.

They moseyed down the street, giving Georgie plenty of time to investigate every interesting blade of grass, tree root, and rock, until they'd reached their destination. If you didn't know what had happened there, the house looked like every other house on the block, quiet but pleasant, even welcoming, as if the owner had just gone for the day and would be back that evening. The house to the left felt more "closed up," as though the owners had packed up and gone on a long vacation, with the porch light still on and the curtains all drawn, and the only person at the house on the right was a sour-faced old man visible in back moving the lawn with an old-fashioned push mower. She decided, even at that distance, that he looked more likely to bite than talk, but if he ended up being her only option, she'd take the chance.

Fortunately, the house across the street was more lively: there were two adults sitting on their front porch, and one leaning against the pillar, indulgently listening to a preteen read something off at a rattling rate, while a small white dog lounged at the girl's feet. Dog people: perfect.

Then she took a closer look at the person leaning against the porch, and Ginny wondered if there was time to turn around, get back in her car, and drive back to Seattle. Then the standing figure turned and saw her.

Georgie whined, and pulled against the leash. "Yeah, okay, girl," Ginny said, and started across the street, never taking her eyes off the people on the front porch.

"Ah, Mallard, there you are." Agent Asuri was nearly unrecognizable in jeans and a long-sleeved pullover rather than her usual crisp suits, her black hair pulled away from her face in a short ponytail. It was almost like she was an actual person, instead of a fed.

"Here I am." She smiled at the preteen and—presumably— her parents, then dropped the leash and let Georgie do her thing with the little white dog, going nose to butt and then butt to nose until all the formalities had been exchanged, wondering all the while how much trouble she was in and what had happened to the businesslike suit she'd been pretty sure Asuri had been born in.

"This is Angel and Marco," the agent said, indicating the adults, "and that's Sally."

"And that's Fife and Drum," Sally announced, in turn.

Ginny assumed she was referring to the dog, until a small black cat appeared out of nowhere and rubbed against the girl's leg, eyeing Georgie with suspicion. One was Fife and the other was Drum, then. Cute. "I'm Ginny, and that's Georgie."

"That's an . . . unusual-looking dog," Angel said, her smile warm and honest, her hand resting on her daughter's hair. They should have been in the ad for a planned community, multicultural middle-class happiness. Except, of course, for the dead guy across the street.

"She's a shar-pei. Mostly shar-pei, anyway." Ginny shrugged, a "what can you do" motion. "She was a shelter adoption, so no papers. And as you can see, she's almost painfully friendly." The cat—Fife, she guessed—had moved on from suspicion to sniffing at Georgie, who was an old hand at cats and curiosity. After some mutual investigation, the three animals settled on the walkway with their heads together, as though they too were enjoying a bit of neighborhood gossip.

"We were discussing what might have happened to Mr. Penalta across the street," Asuri said, as casual as though she hadn't already told Ginny to back off the entire investigation, as though they were partners or something. What game was she playing?

"A shame, really," Marco said. He was older than his wife, his black hair starting to gray around the temples, hipster-frame glasses tucked into the V-neck of his T-shirt. "Jamie was a nice guy. And not in the 'gee he always seemed nice enough' way, either. Like I was telling you," and he nodded to Asuri, "he bought the house about a year ago—it was going into foreclosure and we were all worried, but he kept the place in shape, never threw loud parties, always had everything shut down by eleven when he did have people over."

"He was good with kids," Angel added. "I guess because he worked with them, knew how to talk to them. He set up a pretty sweet patio in his backyard, let them hang out there. Even put up a heat lamp in the winter. Better than hanging out at the mall, the way we used to."

"He was pretty cool," Sally said. "For an old guy."

Ginny smiled. Jamie Penalta, according to her research, had been in his mid-thirties. She supposed that was old when you were eleven or twelve. And Sally was too young to even think about a fake ID yet, so she wouldn't know how "cool" he could be to teenagers. Or did she? Did Sally have older siblings? There wasn't any polite way to ask.

"I wish there'd been someone like that when I was a kid," Ginny said. "Everyone was so scared of 'stranger danger,' though, I don't think my folks would ever allow it."

"Oh, we checked him out thoroughly," Marco said, shaking his head. "I freely admit to being an overprotective parent. I even had a friend who's a cop run his driver's license, just to make sure nothing popped up."

Asuri pursed her lips and nodded approvingly, although Ginny was pretty sure that that wasn't fed-approved procedure. Or maybe it was? "Boy Scout?"

"I don't trust Boy Scouts," Marco said with a grin. "Anyone who squeaks probably had a cleanup on aisle three at some point. He had some scuffles when he was a kid—drunk and disorderly when he was in college, that kind of thing. But I wasn't too worried about speeding tickets or shoplifting—although if you ever decide to try either of those things, missy"—he glared at his daughter—"you're going to be grounded until you're thirty, you hear me?"

Only child, then. Ginny could relate. She'd often wished for a sibling to take the heat off her when she was a kid.

"So he was a nice guy with a slightly shady past who made good?" Asuri asked, as if she didn't have the entire federal machine—or at least a few overworked file clerks—at her beck and call.

Ginny bent down to pet Georgie, listening intently. She was starting to get it, now: Asuri was doing her own digging, officially unofficial. Why? Who knew, but Ginny saw no reason not to take advantage of the lesson—although it would probably be tacky to pull out her tablet and start making notes. Or maybe not, considering Asuri's greeting—what had the agent told them, that she was waiting for Ginny? Why?

Her thoughts were doing the squirrelly thing again. Not good. She really needed Tonica around, to bounce things off of. Until then, she had to stay focused.

"Pretty much," Marco was saying. "He bought the

house on the cheap, fixed it up, works hard—he ran a photography studio out of the house, low-level advertising stuff, I guess, but he said he was building a portfolio, to get to the next level. He did a lot of freebie work for the kids, too. You know, profile photos, stuff for the yearbooks, that kind of thing."

Ginny nodded thoughtfully. That matched up with what she'd found, and would explain why nobody had mentioned the studio setup, or people going in and out of the house. Mr. Penalta sounded like a smart guy—so who did he piss off enough to get his head bashed in and shoved under his kitchen table? Was the fake driver's license business that cutthroat? Or was something else going on, maybe a jealous boyfriend or girlfriend in the picture? No, a regular sweetie would have gotten mention, if Marco had done that much recon on the guy.

She wished now she'd had more of a chance to snoop around, maybe check out the bedroom or bathroom, but odds are if she had, she'd still be getting side-eyed. So, yeah, better not.

"A shame," Asuri said, shaking her head again. "Do the cops have any idea what happened?"

Whoa, wait? Ginny's head came up and she stared at Asuri, not even trying to hide the confusion that had to be on her face. The woman hadn't shown them her badge, hadn't told them she was a fed? Ginny was pretty sure that was against regulations or something, that she was supposed to identify herself? Although that explained the casual clothing. . . .

Unofficially unofficial digging, then. Something was up—and something that sent Asuri into the field without identification and asking, however roundabout, for Ginny's help. Why? Ginny was *sure* that wasn't standard procedure.

"Not that they've told us," Angel said, after a quick glance at Sally, as though unsure if she wanted to keep talking with her daughter around. "That's normal, though, right? I mean, not telling us anything specific, while it's still being investigated? We have a neighborhood watch meeting scheduled for the end of the week, though, so we'll find out then, if they know anything." The woman Ginny had spoken to that first day had said the same. Angel didn't seem optimistic that there would be any news, though.

Sally made a face while her mother was talking, just a quick burst of expression that could have been annoyance or frustration, and then it was gone.

"And you didn't hear anything, that day? Didn't see anyone lurking around?" Ginny looked at Sally when she asked, not her parents. There was something that had caused that flash of emotion, and based on the reaction the teenage girls had had yesterday, and the news that teenagers apparently hung around there all the time . . .

Maybe eleven *wasn't* too young to know something about Jamie Penalta?

"I told the cop what I saw." Sally's tone was injured, as though she were assuming that people weren't believing her. Ginny could see where that might happen: her parents were protective, probably tried to keep her from "getting involved," and Asuri was smooth with the parents, but she'd not bothered to introduce Sally when Ginny came over, which means she was probably treating her as adjunct-to-parent, not a person in her own right.

Mistake, that.

"Sally was home that morning," Angel said, taking over. Clearly she didn't want to get into whatever it was that had pissed her daughter off, lending support to Ginny's theory. "She thought that she saw someone with him, on the front porch."

"Two someones," Sally said, not willing to let her mother take the presumed glory of the telling. "Maybe."

"One person for certain, possibly two," Angel said, reaching out to touch her daughter's braids in apology. "But she never saw their face, couldn't even say if they were male or female, from across the street. We told the police that."

"But it sounds like it was someone he knew," Asuri said, shoving her hands in her jacket pockets and leaning back against the porch support again. Clearly this wasn't a story she'd heard before, and Ginny would have patted herself on the back if she hadn't been sure she'd get odd looks from everyone. The expression on Asuri's face also, if you knew her, did not bode well for whatever cop hadn't put that information in her report.

"I guess that's more comforting than the thought that it was a home invasion of some sort?" Ginny said. "I mean, it's still horrifying, but less random?"

Marco made a face, but nodded. "They say most violent

crimes are committed by someone you know. But yeah, as much as I'd never wish that on anyone, I'd rather it was Jamie who was the target, not just a random house on the street."

Asuri nodded again. Ginny knew that expression, too, had seen it before: whatever the agent had come around looking for, she'd gotten it. "Well, I'm sure that the cops will get it squared away. Mallard, you ready to go?"

She said it like they had plans, so Ginny picked up Georgie's leash, letting the dog know it was time to say good-bye to her new friends, and lifted a hand in farewell. "Nice meeting you folk."

"You, too," Marco said, while Sally waved in return but ducked her head away from speaking, suddenly shy.

Ginny and Asuri walked back to the sidewalk together, Georgie ranging ahead, and when she judged that they were far enough away not to be overheard, tilted her face toward the agent and, cautious, said, "So what was that all about?"

"You can learn more talking to people than you can reading their words. And sometimes, after they've had a chance to sleep on it, things look different. The girl trusted you, more than me. I should bring a dog next time."

"Or a cat. You'd look good with a cat perched on your shoulder." She caught the edge of the look Asuri gave her, and marked up a point on her side, without letting a smirk escape. "But I meant, the whole expecting-me thing. First you tell me to butt out, then you invite me in. I'm getting mixed messages here. Are we dating, or not?"

The snark slipped out without intent, that time, but

fortunately Asuri laughed. "I'm informed that your partner has been doing some asking around about the situation that you're not poking your noses into."

"He did," she said, cautiously. "When we were still concerned that I might get caught up in a murder investigation. Now, like I said, I just want to find out why someone wanted me down here badly enough to make up a client." And pay out two thousand dollars for the privilege. "Unless you've found Mrs. Adaowsky hidden somewhere under the rosebushes?" The moment she said that, Ginny felt her heart drop about six inches. What if they *had*?

"No, your mysterious client is still just a collection of recently manipulated phosphors. There are a few theories about what purpose she may have served, but for now that's relatively low priority. But that could change at any moment, which is why you need to be careful."

"Careful, like you not identifying yourself as a federal agent? Isn't that illegal, Agent Asuri?" If you're going to poke the anthill, might as well start with the queen. Or was that only bees?

The agent hesitated, as though she was sorting through what she could say, for what she *should*. "There's more going on here than what's on the surface; you've already figured that out. Jamie Penalta might not have been a big fish, but he *was* a crack in a much larger investigation, and he died within twenty-four hours of a file being opened on him. Someone's scared—and violent. So it's even more important that you fly so far under the radar, you learn how to burrow, *capiche*?"

Ginny almost swallowed her tongue, biting back on every question that immediately came to mind. An informant within the Bureau? Penalta had been a snitch? What was the larger investigation? Was that the national ring Tonica's contact had mentioned, or was something else going on?

"*Capiche?*" Asuri asked again, the snap back in her voice.

"*Capisco.*" Ginny shoved her curiosity back into its box and slammed the lid shut. Not her case, not her questions, not her nose that was going to get chopped off, right.

"Excellent. Best to your partner, lovely seeing you, let's not do it again for at least another year."

Asuri might be able to turn it on and off at will, but there had been *way* too much shoved into Ginny's brain in the past half hour for her to process all at once, and suddenly she was starving, even though a glance at her watch said it was barely lunchtime by her usual schedule.

Then again, not much about this had been her usual, and she'd always heard that stress burned calories faster than routine. She aimed Georgie down the street, walking until they came to a small parking lot filled with food trucks that Ginny had seen on their way in. There were only a few other people there: three young men in suits, and an older woman in jeans and a sweatshirt, all of whom took their orders and left.

Ginny ordered a fish taco and a Diet Coke, then found a quiet place where she and Georgie could sit, giving the dog a stern look when she made puppy eyes at Ginny's food. "You know you don't get any of this," she said. When Georgie sighed and lay down at her feet, Ginny pulled a plastic Baggie out of her purse and gave the dog a treat. "Good pup," she said, then pulled out her phone and called Tonica.

"You got five?"

He did, and she filled him in on the salient parts of her afternoon, ending with Asuri's warning.

There was silence at the other end of the line, just long enough for her to get ready to say something, then Tonica said, "She wasn't telling us to stay out of it. Just not to get caught."

Like she hadn't already figured that out. But she bit back the immediate retort, saying only, "Yeah. We probably should send her a fruit basket or something."

Ginny licked the last bits of her taco off her fingers and, crumpling the used napkin and wrappings back into the paper bag, reconsidered her words. "Or would that constitute bribing a federal employee? Maybe just invite her to our Christmas party."

He made a noise that could have been amusement or exasperation. Or both. "We don't have a Christmas party, Mallard."

"We probably should." The thought amused her, for a moment. "We have enough former clients now, we totally could."

"Most of whom really don't want to see us again, because we gave them really bad news," he reminded her. "Or helped put them in jail."

"Details . . . Anyway, yeah." She considered tossing the bag into the nearby trash, figured the odds of her missing the trash can entirely—high—and stood up to walk it over. "That's where we stand. Although it would have been nice if she'd have told us what new news had come in that got the waters so hot. Maybe we won't send her a basket after all."

From the vague "hmmmmm" she got back, she knew he wasn't really listening to her. There was a clink of something, glass on glass, she assumed he was behind the bar, either restocking the shelves or serving an early customer. Was he on shift today? She'd thought he'd given the afternoon shifts to Stacy.

"Learn to burrow, huh?" he was saying now.

"Pretty much exactly, yeah. Low, low profile." But not "go home and don't even look at this case again." Which was interesting. Or maybe Asuri really did understand that they couldn't just back off, not until she knew why she'd been roped into this.

"Two days, Mallard. Two *days* you're on your own, and you're nose-deep in kimchee. Seriously, you're the one who should be on a leash, not Georgie."

"Three days, technically."

"Oh, that makes it *so* much better." She leaned back against the bench and let her eyes rest on the scenery. A jogger, two kids playing tag with a scruffy dog with a curled tail almost larger than it was, and two adults walking . . . no, one adult, a woman, kept walking, while the other had stopped, leaning against a tree, watching something. Her?

Unease stirred, something not-quite-paranoia, and she turned sideways to continue the conversation, moving her face away just in case the watcher happened to be able to lip-read.

"It sounds like something hotter than fake IDs is going on," Tonic was saying. "If . . . nah. If it were terrorism-related, or they even thought it was, she'd have told you flat-out to stay out of it. Right?"

Ginny swallowed a sudden lump of panic, then nodded, even though he couldn't see her. "Absolutely. I'm pretty sure she doesn't want to see either of us hauled up by Homeland Security. We haven't pissed her off *nearly* enough."

And the guy watching her wasn't wearing a suit. Or sunglasses. Not Secret Service, nope. Or did they dress them down, here in Oregon, to better fit in?

"Yeah well, let's keep it that way. Get your information and then get your ass back to Seattle, Mallard. This place isn't the same without you—Penny's sulking."

"I can't," she said. "Not just yet." She wanted to. The thought of her own bed, her own apartment, and her own stool at Mary's waiting for her made her want to turn the key in the ignition, head the car northward, and not stop until she was home. But there were still too many questions for her to relax, and the only way to get answers was to be here, on the scene.

There was a sigh, nearly as good as the ones her father let out. "Gin, Asuri just told you—"

"She told me to stay off the radar. I can do that. I have

friends in town. I'll just be visiting with them, since the job turned out to be a bust."

"I really don't think this is a good idea."

"Oh, it's a *terrible* idea," she agreed, almost cheerful with the thought. "And you probably should have bail money or something ready, just in case. But come on, Teddy." She almost never used his first name, saving it for shock value, when she needed him to really listen to her. "Do you really want me to just walk away from this?"

"Yes. Yes, I really do." He sighed again, although this one was lighter, more for effect. "And I know you're not going to. So tell me what you need me to do."

"You got a piece of paper and a pen?" Once he said yes, she started dictating a list of things she needed him to check for her, since he had access to a secure line and a laptop.

When she looked up again, the watcher was gone. Somehow that didn't make her feel better.

If he'd been there when she left, she could have told herself it was just paranoia.

11

*L*acking anything else interesting, Penny had curled up on one of the bar stools and was watching, her eyes slitted in thought, as the new girl moved through the sparse crowd of drinkers. Penny hadn't entirely understood the exchange, but Stacy had been upset that things were missing from the jar on the counter, and the new girl's paw-sweep had been over the jar, as well as the tables.

Penny understood hunting for oneself, and the mouse went to the fastest or the most patient, but Stacy had been upset.

Her whiskers twitched as an idea came to her. But before she could do anything, Theodore's pocket-phone rang, and when he answered, it was clear it was Ginny on the other end.

Penny settled back into place on the bar stool, and listened.

When they'd finished speaking, Theodore put down the phone and stared at the wall across the bar. Penny lifted her chin so she could look at it, too, but other than the occasional flashes of light reflected in the picture frames from the outside window, she didn't see anything particularly attention-worthy.

"Damn, damn, and also, damn," he muttered.

"Boss?" The new girl paused in what she was doing, tilting her head to look at him.

"Nothing. Just . . . nothing."

Penny watched her human carefully. She didn't want to admit how adrift she felt without Georgie to discuss things with—the dog wasn't always the sharpest claw on the paw, but she was a good listener, and her nose was as keen as anyone's. Plus, Ginny talked to her more than Theo talked to Penny.

She thought, doing her best to look like she was thoroughly engrossed in cleaning between her claws, that she needed to train him better. His side of the phone call hadn't given her anything new to work with, only that someone had warned Ginny, and Ginny was ignoring the warning.

Penny's whiskers twitched, this time in amusement. Ginny might be Georgie's human, but she was pleasingly catlike, in some regards.

But that didn't help her now, and Theodore had gone back to wiping down the counter, even though he'd done that just before Ginny had called. She realized, though, that he wasn't really watching what he was doing. It wasn't his hunting-look, where he was watching something somewhere else, but the thinking-look. If he were a cat, she thought, he'd be grooming his whiskers.

As though on cue, he ran a hand over the top of his head, smoothing down his fur. She used that as her cue to drop down from the top of the shelving unit and pad over to him, brushing against his legs. That served the dual purpose of marking him, because her scent faded every time he changed clothes, and getting him to pay attention to her.

"Ginny's being stubborn again," he said quietly, reaching down to pick her up. She permitted it, fitting herself to the curve of his arm. The purr that started in her chest was involuntary, but she didn't fight it, letting him rub under her chin. *"She thinks if she just stares at someone long enough, they'll tell her whatever she needs to*

know. And she's right often enough that it just encourages her. But this . . . this has me worried, cat. Someone wanted her down there, and we don't know why. We don't even know if it was the guy who got killed, or someone else."

Penny leaned her head into his hand, asking for more, to keep him talking. Out of the corner of her eye she saw the other humans moving around, and flicked her whiskers at them, warning them to stay away.

"And now, with Asuri down there . . ."

His voice changed, and the pressure of his fingers slackened, then he put her down on the floor and started polishing the counter again. It was like grooming for him, she knew: a way to occupy his body so he thoughts could work. Penny jumped up onto the counter, then onto one of the stools on the other side before he could scold her. She needed to stay out of his way, but be close enough that she could hear him clearly.

"If this is a federal investigation, not just a cop thing, we should get the hell out. Asuri should be telling Gin to get the hell out, to go home. Instead she's almost . . . encouraging her. Everything she said, from what Ginny said . . . it's like she's deliberately pushing Ginny's buttons."

Penny's ears flickered forward, hearing his tone change again. He was thinking something, planning—no, realizing something.

"Penny, I don't like this. Ginny's smart—smarter than I am, in some ways—but she's used to manipulating, not being manipulated. Not by someone she trusts."

This other person, Asuri, was a hunter, Penny gathered. Hunting the same things Theodore and Ginny sniffed out. What did a hunter need? Prey. And shelter. Ginny was away from her own home, so she couldn't offer shelter. . . .

But there was something else hunters needed, if the prey was out of reach.

Penny flexed her claws into the fabric of the stool, frustrated beyond her whiskers that she couldn't communicate with him, because it was so obvious to her, but he was being human-slow again.

Her tail thumped once, and he reached over the counter to scratch under her chin. She allowed it, because it helped him think, then pulled her head away and glared at him, willing him to see what she had.

Someone came in the front door, and they both turned to see who it was. The newcomer, a tall male, lifted a hand at them in greeting, but went to one of the tables instead of the bar, saying something to the new girl that made her laugh. But it was a fake laugh, they could both tell that; the new girl didn't really like him, but would pretend, because even Penny knew you had to be nice to customers—she wasn't allowed to hiss at them, even when they smelled wrong, or she'd get banished to the back room.

"And all right, yeah, Asuri's come through for us before," Theodore went on. "The way Gin thinks, it's logical to assume that she would again. But previously, we'd had something, some information that the agent wanted. What does Ginny have now, that Asuri wants? What trouble is my partner in?"

He stopped the motion of the cloth, leaning his upper body back as though someone had just bitten him. "Shit."

Penny allowed just a bit of smugness to creep into her tail. She knew he'd get it, eventually.

The first thing Teddy did was call Stacy, and tell her to get her ass in, pronto, and never mind that she technically had the day off. Then he made a few phone calls and waited.

Asuri was playing them. Both of them, even though it was only one set of strings she was pulling directly. Ginny was too much of a straight shooter to see it, but Teddy had grown up around politics and gamesmanship, however much he despised it himself, and he'd seen that about Agent Elizabeth Asuri from the very start.

She wasn't a bad person, or cruel, or even a casual user, but she would manipulate people to get them to do what she wanted, to get her the results she wanted. And, for some reason, she wanted Ginny—and him—to stay on the case. Not because she thought Ginny would solve it, but because she thought Ginny's poking around might flush something out that Asuri could use. Something . . . or some*one*.

It was a smart plan, actually. Clever, using someone who already had a stake in the game, who could just be wound up and pointed in a potentially useful direction, and then ignored until needed again. And no matter how much he wanted Ginny to drop it, to come home and go back to working with actual people who were paying her actual money and not dragging her into a murder investigation, he acknowledged that she was already in it, at least hip-deep.

And he was miserable up here, trying to stay out of it, trying to do *her* job of fact-checking and fact-chasing.

Screw that. He hadn't gotten anywhere except dead ends and an "I'll call you back" from his list, anyway.

He always kept a spare kit in the back office, in case he ever needed to change, or—as had happened several times in his life—things went pear-shaped enough to require him staying overnight, either in the bar itself or in the waiting room of an ER or police station. The car could stay in the parking lot overnight, no worries, and he didn't have any other obligations he had to deal with other than the ones right in front of him.

But figuring out what he needed to do was, as it turned out, the easy part. Ginny might have perpetually well-lined-up ducks, but his insisted on wandering off, quacking, just when he'd thought he had them sorted.

"Seriously, boss?" Stacy's eyes were wide, and a little panicked, when he told her what he had planned. "Seriously?"

He was uneasily certain she was about to start hyperventilating.

"You can do it," he said, putting every bit of persuasive encouragement into his voice as he could manage. "You can totally do it."

"I know I can do it," Stacy said, but her expression wasn't as confident as her words. She glanced around the bar, empty save for the man who'd come in earlier and his just-arrived companion, sitting quietly at a back table, talking over nearly untouched beers. "I just . . . What if something goes wrong? What if Patrick shows up?"

"Nothing's going to suddenly go wrong that you haven't already handled or seen me handle," he said. "And if Patrick shows up, you wow him with your ability to wrangle a crowd and he gives you a much-deserved raise. But he's not going to show up, Stace. It's a weekday, and he never shows up on a weekday." Not since he'd started working on his "expansion bar" downtown and made Teddy the manager of Mary's. Life had been better for everyone all around, he thought, even if the job did give him more headaches. . . .

"Look, I'll be gone twenty-four hours, two days, tops." He didn't try the soothing smile or any of his other "compassionate bartending" tricks, just a steady meeting of her eyes. "You've worked weekends before, and those are way worse; you know you can handle this. It's not like I'm abandoning you during Trivia Night or anything."

That didn't even get a smile out of her.

"This is your court," he said. "You know everyone, everyone knows you. And if anything goes seriously upside down, Seth will be here, and don't give me that face, you know he'll back you up, and nobody wants to give him trouble."

The man in question, leaning against the doorway with his arms crossed over his chest, gave a dour nod of agreement. Seth might be old, but he'd kept his boxing skills reasonably fresh, and Teddy had seen him lay out a drunk half his age with one swift hit. More, he actually liked Stacy, as much as the old man liked anyone. They'd be fine.

"I hate you," she said. "You need a ride to the train station?"

"Please." It was either that or call a cab, and he'd rather

not have to wait around on someone else's schedule. Bad enough to be taking the train, but Ginny already had a car down in Portland; they wouldn't need two. Probably.

He picked up his bag, handed Stacy the bar keys with as much formality as he could muster, making her, reluctantly, smile, and then stopped at the stare Penny was giving him.

"Oh. No, Penny. No," he said.

The cat didn't blink.

"I'm taking the train, cat. You can't come with me."

Stacy didn't have the decency not to laugh, while he lost a staring match with a seven-pound cat. "I don't think she believes you."

"Just because I'm leaving you in charge for now doesn't mean I can't put you on the shit shift for the rest of your life," he warned her.

The tabby followed them out the back, and watched while Teddy threw his bag into the backseat of Stacy's rinky-dink little car. "Look, you gotta keep an eye on the place, Penny," he told the cat, as seriously as he could manage. "Okay?"

He felt more than a little like an idiot, but on the other hand, the cat had responded to him enough times; who was he to say how much she did or didn't understand?

"I'll be home tomorrow. And hopefully I'll bring Georgie back, too, okay?"

"Let's go, boss," Stacy said. "If we hit traffic you're going to be cutting it tight."

He watched the tabby intently, looking for . . . what? A

sign? An all-clear thumbs-up? He sighed and shook his head. "I'm spending too much time with Ginny," he said, and got in the car. That cat would be *fine*. He needed to focus on what he was going to do once he got down to Portland.

As Stacy drove downtown, Teddy picked up his phone and rubbed his thumb across the display, then tapped Ginny's contact info. It rang three times, then went into voice mail.

"Hey, it's me. Look, I'm coming down. Meet me at the Amtrak station? I'll call you when we cross the river." He hesitated, then added, "Be careful," and hung up.

"Watch the place while I'm gone," he told her, before getting into the car and leaving her behind.

Penny thought she'd behaved with an impressive level of grace and calm in the face of his abandonment, only the minute twitching of the tip of her tail betraying her annoyance. She couldn't expect him to take her everywhere, after all—she wasn't a trained cat at the end of a string, and she did not enjoy being hauled around in a moving vehicle. But she couldn't be blamed if her ears went back in annoyance, and the entire length of her tail swished as they drove off, leaving her in the parking lot, alone.

"Watch the place while I'm gone." He'd gone and he'd taken Stacy with him, and he was right, the old man couldn't be trusted to deal with things, not properly. And the new girl . . . She'd sort the new girl out, once and for all, if nobody else would.

She stalked inside through her usual entrance, and took up

*residence in the darkest alcove she could find, watching. And
plotting.*

Ginny hadn't heard her phone ring. She sat in the rental
car in the hotel parking lot, absently petting Georgie's
head, and listened to Tonica's message, a slight frown
crossing her face. She thought about calling him back, telling him he didn't need to come down, but based on the
time stamp, he was probably already en route.

And part of her, she admitted, was glad. The moment this
had become a researchtigation—no, an *investigation*—she'd
needed her partner, and only pride had kept her from saying
so immediately. It wasn't a lack of competence that made
them better together; it was doubling the competence.

"At least he probably won't say 'I told you so.' Probably."

She checked her watch again: she had a few hours to
kill before picking him up at the station. And—her brain
suddenly clicking on all cylinders—she knew where she
should spend them.

After dropping Georgie off back at the hotel and pacify-
ing her with a treat and one of the dog toys from her bag,
Ginny headed back downtown, refining her plan.

First step, one she should already have taken: find out
the dance steps to the music being played, so she could
avoid stepping on toes. For that she needed to talk to
someone who knew all the dancers in town. She picked up
a paper bag of chocolate chip cookies from a corner bakery
and headed for her prey.

Ron was hunched over a cramped desk that, clearly, wasn't his alone from the number of coffee mugs and Post-its stacked at every angle, and the second chair shoved up against the other side of the desk. A power strip was duct-taped down the center like some kind of no-man's-land divider. He was the only one currently there, though, a laptop charging from the strip, his phone charging off that, and Ron himself rummaging in the desk for something, his attention focused entirely on that.

Ginny made her way to his desk and sat down on the empty wooden chair on the opposite side, placed the cookies just beyond easy reach, and waited. And waited.

"It's awfully quiet in here," she said finally.

He didn't give her the satisfaction of being startled, or even looking surprised. "What did you expect, someone running through the room yelling 'stop the press!' or 'everyone go cover the wreck on the docks?'"

"No." She made a face. "Maybe?"

"Yeah well, those days are gone, with the four-drink lunch and the two-drink breakfast. A-ha, there you are, you little bastard!" He triumphantly pulled out a memory card, still in its plastic case, and used his thumbnail to pop it out and insert it into the side of the laptop.

"I miss the drinks but I don't miss typewriters, let me tell you. Give me modern, portable technology and I'll get the job done in a third the time. Okay, sorry. You said on the phone that you were free to go. Congratulations. So why're you still hanging around? Not that it wasn't good to see you, kid."

"Yeah, I'm feeling the love. This entire town loves me. They're going to throw me a parade. I'm still here because I still have questions. What do you know about any federal investigations that might be happening in town?" She pushed the cookies closer toward him.

That got a bark of laughter out of him. "New or pending, and if pending, how far back do you want to go?"

She opened her mouth to say something, couldn't think of what it had been, and closed her mouth again, thinking. "New, or only going back about . . . six months? It might or might not have something to do with money."

"In the end, doll, it all comes down to money. But I take your point. If you have a line on something, you're going to tell Uncle Ron, right?" He reached over and unfolded the bag, pulling one of the thumbnail-sized cookies out and making it disappear.

"If I can," she hedged, and he sighed. "Yeah, that's as good as I ever seem to get. My friends are all utterly useless." Another cookie disappeared. "This has to do with your little run-in with the law?"

"Maybe. Maybe not. Once I know that—"

"You'll know how much trouble you just dunked yourself in?" He shook his head. "You missed your calling, kid. You should have been a reporter."

"I couldn't take the pay cut," she said dryly, and watched him mime a blow to the heart.

"Just for that, young woman, you're buying dinner. Somewhere with real napkins."

"If you come up with something by dinnertime, sure."

"Oh ye of no faith whatsoever." He leaned back in his chair, crossed his arms over his chest, and looked down his nose at her. "Assuming I kept track of such things, there are currently two federal investigations of which I am hypothetically aware that were opened within the past six months and are still active. One of them involves some hinky behavior that may or may not qualify as sex crimes, so I'm presuming that's not yours because rumor has it it's about to go to plea bargain, and the other has to do with a certain nonelected government official who may or may not have been raking in a little side financial action involving access to federal project bids. That your puppy?"

"I don't know. Maybe." She couldn't imagine *how* that could tie back to the death of an identity forger, but she'd seen a lot of stuff in the past few years she wouldn't have been able to predict before it happened, so . . . "Wait, sex crimes? In Portland?"

"Yep." He made the *p* sound pop with satisfaction. "What, you think just because we're crunchy granola we can't be just as horrible as any other city?"

There really wasn't any way to answer that, so she didn't.

"I don't suppose you could find out who's assigned to either of those cases?" The latter sounded more like Asuri's "where the money stinks, there sniff I" style, but . . .

That got her a sharp look. "Virginia Mallard, what's really going on?"

"I wish to hell I knew, Ron. I wish to hell I knew. Right now I'm still trying to gather all the shards and figure out what kind of window they came from."

"Hrm. You sure it's a window you're looking into, and not a mirror?"

She looked at him, her confusion clear, and he shrugged. "A window lets you look at things, but a mirror just reflects what you already know. The worst way to write a story is going in with the ending already decided. Can't imagine your thing's much different."

Ginny chewed on her lower lip, drumming her fingers on the edge of the desk. "A mirror." Same shards, but a different view. A reflecting view. Something about that idea tugged at her, and she tried to quiet everything else in her brain, following that thread.

Ron looked at her with narrowed eyes, then shook his head and turned back to his laptop, leaving her to sort her own thoughts out.

Crime might pay better, but it didn't pay enough to quit the legit side. Not yet, anyway. After their meeting, Dave had gone off to handle his own side of things. Ben was supposed to be doing the same, had even settled himself in front of his monitors in his home office, the work lights turned on, tools at the ready, when an alert pinged on one of the monitors and caught his eye like a red cape waved in front of a bull. It was from a search he'd set up for any mention of Jamie's death; perfectly normal behavior when someone you worked for was murdered, nothing the cops could hold against him, if they ever got interested enough to probe his Internet use.

He clicked on the link and skimmed the article, then licked his lips and reread it, feeling his adrenaline surge.

He reached up to grab a piece of paper tacked to the corkboard and compared it to the article, then bolted out of his chair, out of his office, and down the hallway of his apartment, the slip of paper gripped too tightly in one fist.

"Fuck. Fuck fuck fuck."

It was just a name, a URL, and an email address, nothing particularly upsetting or disturbing. He'd written it down himself, after Jamie had shown them the article, for a laugh. "Look," he'd said. "Our eternal opposite!"

They'd laughed, but then Ben had thought, what could it hurt to keep the information? Might be useful to know about an off-the-books, off-license PI someday. He'd been half amused by the thought.

He wasn't amused now. No matter what Dave said about compartmentalizing the business to protect themselves, so no one piece could topple the other, the truth was that it was all one messy knot of strings, and you couldn't tug on one without the others feeling it. He knew that. They'd all known that, it was part of—hell, it was probably the *only* thing that had allowed them to work together, to trust each other.

And now it was all a mess. A mess that—somehow—had that PI in the middle of it.

Ben's palms were sweating like they hadn't since the sixth-grade dance, slick and kind of gross, and his stomach felt like he'd swallowed helium, all tight and sick, and the piece of paper he held in one hand, already creased and crumpled, was starting to look worn and grubby, like the trash it should have been, weeks ago.

He'd tried to feel guilt, or sorrow, or something beyond concern for what Jamie's death meant to them. He really had. But Dave had been right about that much: it wasn't like Jamie had been a friend or anything. He was just a guy they did business with. Ben hadn't even liked him, particularly. So yeah, no. No guilt, just a shitload of worry. Because when a guy you did business with ends up beaten to death, you worry.

And when the person who finds the body is an amateur detective? You worry some more. Especially since it wasn't just any PI, but *that* PI.

He reached the end of the long hallway, then turned and strode down the other end, making a full circuit of the living area and pausing by the oversized windows. Unlike his high-tech, nearly pristine office, the rest of his apartment was homey, comfortable, soothing. But he didn't feel soothed. He felt like he needed to get out of his skin somehow.

It was just one line in a two-paragraph follow-up that probably all of ten people in the entire city had read. Dave wouldn't be worried. Dave would wave his hand and say, "Be cool, man," like it was that easy.

Ben took a deep breath, exhaling through his mouth, trying to shove the tension in his stomach out that way. Maybe it was that easy. Maybe Dave was right. So Jamie got himself killed. And a PI he'd read about, had clipped an article about, shared with them, suddenly shows up on his doorstep right after that. So what? There was no reason to think that it had anything to do with them. What they did, it was harmless, mostly.

"Okay, not harmless but not the kind of thing that gets you beaten to death." The words had a solid ring of truth about them. The late afternoon sunlight was warm on his face, and he closed his eyes, letting that bit of grace soothe him for a moment.

"Probably some side deal he had going, or an outraged daddy. And when the cops—or the PI—poked around, that's what would come up."

And hell, odds were Jamie had called the PI himself . . . but why? The adrenaline was replaced by a cold ball of dread. To poke around at them? Had Jamie been planning on selling them out?

No. That made no sense: Jamie'd had more to lose than any of them if this went sour. He'd had more bad habits, and they'd all known it.

Ben started pacing again, down the hallway, feeling the ache in his calves matching the ache in his neck and shoulders.

"And Dave had nothing to do with it." He believed that. He had to believe that. Dave wasn't that stupid, for one. And two . . . yeah, he had a killer instinct but there was a difference between seeing a chance and taking it no matter what, and actually killing someone. He'd seen Dave mad, and he got cold, not hot. If he'd thought Jamie was a real risk to the business, he would have come to Ben and talked about cutting him out carefully, shifting the work to other photographers until enough time had gone by that Jamie would just shrug and find other work. Purely business.

"And I had nothing to do with it." He'd wished Jamie dead once or twice, maybe. Had cursed him out over the phone a few times, sure. Told him to clean up his act, or else. But that was all. He hadn't done anything. He hadn't caused anything.

Everything had been fine, more or less, until Michal showed up. It all came back to Michal. She'd come out of nowhere, approached them with the golden ticket, gotten them bigger jobs, more money, and now, with Jamie dead, another jump . . . big leagues. International clients. And that was when Ben had thought it might be a good idea to spook Jamie with the PI they'd read about, make him clean up his act.

But he hadn't done it. Hadn't called the PI, hadn't said anything to anyone. Because you couldn't do that, couldn't pull one thread and not expect everything to unravel.

Ben rubbed his stomach as though that might make it feel better. He'd known what they were getting into, when Michal made his offer. Nobody had said it, but he knew. They weren't going to be selling their new product to nineteen-year-olds who wanted to drink, or battered housewives looking for a new identity.

There were some things he could live with, and some things he couldn't. This . . . He thought about the money they'd be making, and knew he could live with it.

And the current investigation? Dave was right. He hadn't killed Jamie. Dave hadn't killed Jamie. Jamie's own idiocy had gotten him killed. It had nothing to do with them. Nothing could be traced back to them.

PI or no PI.

With a sigh, he paused by the counter and dropped the small rectangle of paper into the trash, then got a beer from the fridge, taking a long drink.

All they had to do is wait it out, let the cops come to the obvious conclusions, and they'd be home free. They just needed to not fuck it up.

12

Teddy had meant to work on the train, had even bought a notebook and pen for the sole purpose of writing out everything he knew so far, in hopes that it would turn up something new, spark some connection he hadn't seen before. Instead, he'd settled into his seat on the train, plugged his phone into the outlet to charge, and promptly fallen asleep, waking up only when the train chugged its way into the Portland station and stopped, the conductors making enough noise to rouse even the dead.

Which meant that he'd not called Ginny when they crossed the Columbia River, the way he'd promised. Shit. Teddy grabbed his bag in one hand and scrambled to unplug his phone with the other, waiting until he picked up signal again before hitting her contact. He strode through the crowds at Union Station, crossing the tracks and into the building itself, only to stop dead and hang up the phone when he saw a familiar head of blond curls, standing next to an older black guy with long gray hair. The friend she'd been planning to visit with while she was down here, he supposed.

"Lucky for you, I thought to check the schedule," Ginny said. "Teddy, this is my friend Ron. Tom, this is—"

"Yeah, I got it," the older man said, reaching forward to shake Teddy's hand. His eyes were a surprising blue. "Glad to meet you, wish it were in less complicated circumstances. Come on, Ginny's buying dinner."

"Not for both of you, I'm not!" she protested, already turning to walk out of the station, the two men trailing in her wake.

"Yes, she is," the older man—Ron—said in an aside, and Teddy grinned, already liking the guy.

They ended up in a tiny restaurant where the menu was printed on sheets of paper and the kitchen was visible over a low wall, the seven tables already full when they walked in a little after six thirty. Ron raised a hand to signal someone behind the low wall, and an older Asian woman came bustling out, wiping her hands on a towel at her waist, to greet them.

"So finally you show up? Please tell me these two are food reviewers from a national paper? Or NPR? NPR would be good."

"Sorry, Sandra-san. Just some hungry folks looking to buy my conversation with your excellent food."

"Nice to see you're not a cheap date. Come on, then—chef's table is all yours."

The table was tucked away out of sight, but with a clear view of both the kitchen and the dining area. The food was excellent, even if Teddy didn't have much familiarity with most of the menu, and Ron, who turned out to be a local reporter, was unsurprisingly good at helping put bits and pieces of the story together.

They paused long enough to allow the waiter to clear the dishes from the table, then Teddy shook his head. "So we've got a photographer moonlighting with fake ID, a possible federal investigation that had him as a potential person of interest in their case, and someone who hated the guy enough to bash his face in with extreme prejudice. And at least one fed with an ongoing interest in this case. And, on the side, we have a mysterious nonexisting person who hired Ginny to come down here for a nonexistent job just in time to find the very existent dead guy."

"That's hardly 'on the side,' from my point of view," Ginny said.

"Suck it up, buttercup," he retorted. "Having the feds poking around makes you secondary."

"The two cases you know they're here to investigate are none of the above, though," Ginny said. "Officially, anyway."

"Yeah, I'm not sure how either a sex scandal or payola could tie into this," Teddy agreed, having been brought up to speed on the car ride over. "And that still doesn't tell us who actually called you in, and why. Which is what we're supposed to be focusing on. Right?"

"Maybe it does," Ron said thoughtfully. "And maybe we've been looking at this all through the wrong end."

"Like a mirror, not a window?" Ginny said, and Teddy shook his head, not getting the reference.

"Exactly. We're trying too hard to figure out who might have called you in, and why, but we haven't been thinking about why they might have wanted *any* PI."

Ginny looked at Teddy, who made a face at her—it was a good point and Ron was right, they'd totally bypassed that.

"You had something going on in your head earlier, Virginia, and enough time for it to germinate. So spill for the rest of the class."

"You're mixing your metaphors again," she teased, then her expression went sober again. "What you said earlier, it made me think about that room in the house, the one he was obviously using to take photographs. About maybe someone not liking what they saw? But I couldn't get much further than that. I mean . . . it was a small room, it wasn't like the kind of setup you'd get blackmail photos out of."

"Or sex tapes," Teddy said, and lifted his hands when they both looked at him. "What? Like neither of you thought about that?"

"I hadn't, actually," Ginny said, although the reporter made a face that indicated that yeah, he had. "But no, it wasn't set up like that at all. There was one chair—a stool, really—and the supply cabinet, and that was it." She stopped to remember more carefully. "No, there wasn't any video equipment visible. I suppose he might have had something hidden, but . . . Whatever they did they'd have to do standing up. I don't think there was even enough room to lie down, not unless you moved everything out of the way. And ugh, that carpet was not nice."

"So no sexcapades that we're aware of. Or that the cops are aware of and have let us know."

"Nothing on the radar?"

"The sexual antics of ordinary citizens tends not to blip my radar," Ron said. "Not unless they're shtupping an elected official out of season."

"So . . . photographs of something unwanted?" Ginny shook her head. "I can't make it work. Head shots aren't the kind of thing that need investigation. . . . Unless someone wanted to find out if their kid was using a fake ID? But then why not approach us—or any PI, if we're going that route—directly?"

"Maybe it wasn't someone else they wanted investigated. Go back to basics." Teddy might have had the advantage, coming in more or less cold, while Ginny'd been in the thick of things, her thoughts all tangled. "Maybe they wanted the dead guy investigated, before he was dead. But they couldn't risk being involved in it, having anyone know they were having him investigated."

"That . . . might have legs," Ron said, making a notation on the palm-sized notebook he'd pulled out when they started talking. "Someone who was dirty, but not as dirty as him? Or more dirty but with more of a grudge?"

"That's almost razor-proof," Ginny said. "The simplest, most logical explanation. But it's all still theory. We'd need to know who would want him taken out, though, and why, to prove anything. And that's where we're still seriously lacking in information."

Ginny frowned down at the now-empty table, then

looked up at Teddy. "I think that's going to require another look at that studio, maybe the entire house this time. See if there's anything the cops didn't realize was important, something that predates the actual murder."

"Breaking and entering, and without Good Samaritan justification, this time," Teddy said, gloomily.

"In that case," Ron said, closing his notebook with a snap, "I think we're going to need dessert."

None of them really had much appetite for dessert, though, and after watching them push it around the plate with forks, Ron finally put them out of their misery, sending them back to her hotel, where Georgie and Tonica had a happy reunion, the shar-pei giving the human a thorough face-washing, followed by the two of them wrestling on the floor.

"Good thing you're not a pet person," she said dryly, throwing his own words, now several years old, back at him, and getting a raised finger in return.

She willingly handed the leash over to her partner, along with a few poo bags, and sent them off for Georgie to do her business while she took a hot shower. By the time they came back, she was dressed, sitting on the edge of the bed and drying her hair with a towel.

"We've got three hours to kill," she said, "and I for one—not having had the opportunity to take a four-hour snooze today like some people—intend to take a nap. Feel free to order a movie or whatever, so long as it's not from the porn channel."

Tonica gave a snort that could have done Georgie proud and dropped himself into the room's single armchair, while the dog headed for her travel crate, turning around several times before making herself comfortable on the padding. "Sounds like a plan. See you at midnight, Sleeping Beauty."

Ginny had thought it would take her a while to fall asleep, but she would have sworn she'd just put her head down where there was a beeping near her ear, and then a hand on her shoulder, shaking her awake.

"C'mon, Mallard. I walked Georgie, so all you have to do is wake up."

She batted his hand away, then sat up, rubbing the sleep from her eyes. Tonica was already dressed, his usual dark jeans and pullover shirt covered by a dark windbreaker. She didn't have anything like that with her, but she'd packed for a professional trip, so she had a dark green blouse that wouldn't catch the light, to go with her black slacks. Her shoes had enough of a heel to be impractical, so she went with her sneakers, even though they were eye-catchingly pale, and hoped for the best.

"We should have stopped at Target and bought watch caps and face paint," Tonica said, and she ha-ha-ha'd at him. "The first rule of successful breaking and entering is to never look like you're there to break and enter."

"Life isn't a caper movie, Mallard."

"And that's just more of a pity, Tonica."

They stuck their tongues out at each other at the same moment, but she started to laugh first. She'd been right: having him here made it seem more manageable.

All they needed was Penny, sitting placidly on the desk and watching them with unblinking green eyes, to make everything right again.

Her phone vibrated, and she checked it to see the expected text from Ron. "He's here. Let's go."

Ron's car was a four-year-old Toyota Camry, black and slightly battered, nothing that would attract attention or cause comment. He pulled to the first clear spot on the curb he could find and cut the engine, then reached up to shut off the automatic overhead lights.

"I'm going to stay here long as I can," he said. "Cops come by I'll tell 'em I felt too tired to risk driving the rest of the way home, and was taking a nap, but they'll probably watch to make sure I move on after a while, so if you see the map light's on, don't come back until I pull out, and then I'll meet you around the corner. If I'm not here, meet me two blocks south. Got it?"

"You sure you've never done this before?" Ginny asked, not entirely joking.

"Dear heart, I've been at this job since you were in junior high. The things I've done would match the devil's to-do list. Now go."

They both slid out of the car, Ginny from the front passenger's side, Teddy from the back, and started walking down the street. They'd waited until after midnight in the hopes that the night owls would be watching TV, or otherwise occupying themselves, not sitting outside investigating the neighbors. There was a slight risk of someone paranoid after the murders, or an impromptu neighborhood watch, but Ginny had thought that if that was a thing, Angel and Marco would have mentioned it to Agent Asuri and herself, when they talked about the neighborhood meeting to come. Or not, and they were going to have a very unpleasant surprise any minute now.

They made it to the house without seeing so much as a twitch in anyone's curtains, or being accosted by a neighborhood vigilante. Tonica took her arm at the elbow, tugging gently toward the back of the house. Thankfully there was enough light to see, and nothing left in the pathway one of them might have stumbled over.

"Gloves," she said, and they paused a minute to pull on the thin latex gloves Ron had given them in the car. She resisted the urge to snap them into place, rubbing her fingers together and grimacing at the feel. "Finger condoms."

"Not leaving fingerprints," Tonica said. "C'mon."

There was a brief scuffle over who was going to pick the lock, which Tonica won by dint of actually being able to maneuver his credit card and a piece of wire to do the job. Ginny made a mental note to add her lock-pick kit to her always-take-with list, after this.

And then they were inside the kitchen, and she had to force herself to look at the table where she'd seen the body. The space was empty, the floor clean, and she let out a breath she hadn't realized she'd been holding.

"You okay?" Tonica's voice was low, somewhere between his normal voice and a whisper.

"Yeah. I wasn't sure but . . . yeah." Whispers carried more than normal voices, she'd read that somewhere, and kept her own voice as close to normal as possible. "C'mon, through here." Ron had given them each a tiny flashlight in addition to the latex gloves, and she switched hers on now, letting the powerful beam sweep over the doorway, keeping the illumination below any window. "I feel like Dana Scully."

"If anything with fangs or ectoplasm jumps out at us, I'm going to make a new door out of here," Tonica warned her. "And none of that ladies-first crap. You're on your own."

"So noted."

The room was pretty much exactly the way she remembered it, except most of the equipment was gone—police evidence locker, probably. She bent down and pulled open the cabinet door, flicking the flashlight's beam over the insides.

"Empty," she said, unable to hide her disappointment, even though she really hadn't expected anything else. "You got anything?"

"File cabinets are empty, too," he said. "Hang on. . . ." There was a faint metallic noise, and she turned to see him pulling the drawer out, and checking the sides. "A-ha."

"What is it?"

"Old trick a friend of my dad's used. He wasn't much for computers, didn't trust his housekeeper, so he kept his list of passwords taped to the underside of his filing cabinet drawer. Most people only look on the side." He tucked his own penlight under his chin and carefully peeled the piece of paper away. "Huh."

"What?"

"Hang on." He repeated the exercise on the other side, then pushed the drawer back in and shut off the light. "That's it, here." He looked around the room, then at her. "You want to risk tossing the rest of the house, or are we ready to go?"

"There were computers out front. Think they're still there?"

"Unlikely. But let's check."

The computers were gone, the table barren of the paperwork that had been there, and Ginny felt a twinge of regret that she hadn't snooped harder, her first visit. But if he'd been hiding a guilty secret, something dirty enough to warrant calling in a PI, it wouldn't be down here. The dirtier a secret, the closer people held it, she'd learned.

"I'm going to check upstairs," she said. "Keep watch."

"Yeah, 'cause if someone walks in the front door, me warning you is going to do a lot of good."

"Well, I can go out the window while you're distracting them by getting arrested," she said, already halfway up the stairs. Humor was a good way to keep her nerves from biting her on the ass, even if their banter might not be up to their usual standards.

Upstairs wasn't much: two small bedrooms and a bathroom between them. One bedroom had clearly been used for just that: a queen-sized bed filling most of the space, no nightstands, and a single dresser. It looked like he'd slept in there, but not much more.

The second room held a love seat and a large-screen television mounted on the wall. "He lived up here, worked downstairs. Nice separation of personal and private space."

But that meant they probably wouldn't find anything useful up here: no computers, desks, or filing cabinets to be seen. And absolutely no sign of the alleged but very much unreal Mrs. Adaowsky.

"A cop car just drove by," Tonica's voice said, low on the stair. "Let's get gone, okay?"

"Yeah." She looked around one last time, thinking that it was a sad residue left behind, and wondering if hers would be any better. "Yeah, okay."

The cop car—or another one—drove by again as they were walking away from the house. Tonica grabbed her hand so they looked like any couple out for a late-night stroll home from the bar. She let her eyes rest on the car, an ordinarily curious citizen, and something about it bothered her, but she couldn't quite figure out what. Paranoia, probably.

The sedan was where they'd left it, the overhead light dark, so they walked up to the car and slid inside, even as Ron was starting the car. "You weren't in there long," he said.

"Not much left to see," Ginny said. "Cops didn't give you a blink?"

"I slid down enough so they probably didn't notice—any extra patrols they put on were just a community song and dance to make taxpayers feel better. Like you said, if your boy was into some dirty things, they're going to assume it was related to that, and not a neighborhood-general attack. And contrary to rumor, murderers don't often come back to the scene of the crime, especially if they're pros. They're already on to the next job. You find anything?"

"Maybe. I don't know." She turned around in her seat to look at Tonica, who still had the papers. "Did we?"

"Two sheets of paper tucked away where paranoid people normally keep passwords." He was squinting at the writing, and Ginny pulled out her microlight again and trained it on the paper. "Thanks. First one's just two names, first names only, and phone numbers. Second one's a list of names. First only, again, no phone numbers." He frowned, then looked up at her. "The second list's all female."

"You think that's important?"

"Call me a protective paranoid bastard, but when a guy has a list of women's names hidden away somewhere? It's usually not a good thing."

"Oh. Yeah." And now she felt like an idiot for not thinking of that first.

"He's not wrong," Ron said. "Give me the names, I'll run a search, see if anything in recent news comes up. And yes, missy, I know you can do a search almost as well as I can, but it's nearly two a.m. and right now all you're doing is going back to your hotel and getting some shut-eye. Let the professional insomniac handle this."

She wanted to argue, but with the adrenaline from the

break-in fading, her body felt like it was made out of lead, and the idea of going to sleep for about six hours—or until Georgie woke her up—sounded too good to pass up.

"I got a queen," she said to Tonica. "So long as you don't kick while you sleep, we can share."

"At this point, I'd be okay with the floor, so long as Georgie didn't object." He folded the papers in half, the way they'd been taped up, and passed them over to Ron. "I don't know about you, but my nerves are shot. I'm not cut out to be a cat burglar."

"Should have brought Penny," she told him, and it was a measure of how tired they both were that they found that funny.

"There's a coffee place nearby, the Toot," Ron said. "I'll meet you guys there in the morning, seven thirty?"

Tonica groaned, but nodded, and Ginny added her agreement. "All right, then. Here's your stop," he said as he pulled into the hotel's driveway.

Ginny noticed that Ron waited until they were past the doors, and nearly to the elevator, before he pulled away. "He's worried," she said quietly, not wanting to catch the attention of the sleepy clerk behind the counter, although the man hadn't done more than lift his head and nod when they walked in.

"You're not?" he replied.

"About being accosted in my own hotel? Not until this moment, no, honestly. No more than usual, anyway." The elevator came, and they stepped on, Ginny punching the button for their floor. "Right now, I'm tired, and I'm annoyed, and I'm more than a little skeeved out by what that list might mean. That's about it."

And tired was winning over annoyed and skeeved. There would be time enough for all that in the morning. Later in the morning, she corrected herself, and prayed that Georgie wouldn't need to go out before then.

13

The queen-sized bed was large enough for both of them, although Teddy woke up Friday morning without a pillow, and with a dog licking his face anxiously. He may or may not have yelped loudly enough to send Georgie scurrying across the room, forcing Ginny to spend five minutes reassuring the dog that big mean uncle Teddy hadn't meant to scare her.

"Now I need someone to reassure me," she said, finally. "Or prescribe a tranquilizer."

"You're too tightly wound for pharmaceuticals," he said. "If you got that loose, you'd fall apart entirely."

"Gee, thanks." Her sarcastic voice wasn't up to par, though, and he let his hand rest on her shoulder. "Just don't think," he told her. "You try to figure things out now, before we know anything else, and you'll just chase your tail until you bite it, and—don't look at me like that. You know what I mean."

"But—"

"Wait until we've talked to Ron," he said. "And had coffee."

It was too early to deal with any of this. He went and

took a shower and, thankfully, by the time he got out, she'd managed to calm herself down again, with an obvious assist from the dog curled asleep half on her lap.

The coffee shop Ron had suggested was actually more of a diner, six booths on either side of an aisle, the kitchen running the length of one wall, the splatter and hiss of the griddles running under the low clatter of conversation. There was a small grassy area in front of the diner where two other dogs were already tied up, clearly waiting on patrons inside. Georgie settled in quickly, clearly not the least bit stressed about being left in unfamiliar surroundings.

"Do you ever worry about leaving her, after . . ." After one of their jobs turned up details of how often dogs were stolen off the street, for illegal labs or dog-fighting rings, he meant.

"Always. But we worked on it with her trainer," Ginny said. "Georgie won't willingly go with anyone who isn't familiar, or doesn't know the right command." She gave Georgie a treat and turned away. "And besides, anyone who tried to pick her up and run would get a hernia for their effort."

Since he'd had to haul the dog in and out of his car more than once, he couldn't argue that point. She wasn't that large, but what was there was solid muscle under plush, wrinkled skin.

Ron was already there, and had ordered them a carafe of coffee, much appreciated after Ginny had warned Teddy off the free coffee in the hotel lobby. He was pretty sure that, despite a hot shower and a brisk walk to the diner, even a vat of coffee wasn't going to wake him up all the way. But he was willing to try.

"Any luck?" Ginny asked, sliding in next to Ron, while Teddy took the opposite bench. She was still—if you knew to look for it—twitchier than usual, her air of bright cheer only a façade, but neither of them called her on it.

"Depends on what you mean by luck," Ron said. "The list of girls' names turned out to be a bust—no hits on any missing-persons reports or recent crimes. Which is a relief on the one hand, and a worry on the other. I mean, if it's not a bad thing, why hide the list?"

"No reports just means nothing's been reported. They still could be in trouble or causing trouble." Off their look, Ginny shrugged. "Don't assume just because the names are all female that they're innocent. Trust me, women can be just as deadly as the male, and you both should know that."

Ron paused with his coffee cup halfway to his mouth, considered her words, then saluted her with the mug before taking a sip. "You're not wrong. But since the dead guy's dead by means most foul, doubt is called for. Since you said the guy did a lot of work with teenagers, yearbook pictures and whatnot, it might just be a client list, totally innocent, if weirdly stashed. Or maybe it's women he's slept with, and he's keeping it secret from his main partner. Or hell, maybe your vic was just trying to come up with names for his next Pretty Pony."

"His what?" Teddy frowned.

"Don't ask," Ginny advised him. "Trust me. What about the other two names, the guys?"

"There, I had luck. Back-traced the phone numbers, did a little deeper digging past the unlisted part, matched the first names to two gentlemen. David Collins, and Benjamin Lee. Went to high school together, local boys, roomed together three of their four years at Lewis and Clark. Lee moved here right after college, started working for a small architecture and restoration firm, Collins showed up a year ago, got a job at Candle Creek Brewery. They're both considered promising newcomers, thirty-two and ambitious without being obnoxious. Have a sideline doing design work for start-ups—no real money to it, but their work looks competent enough."

"So, was our guy a friend of theirs?"

"Not on paper, anyway."

The waitress came by, and they paused to order off the blackboard menu, then Ron continued. "Nothing in common—no school, no friends, no career crossover."

"So . . . you think our two golden boys are involved in the fake ID gig the victim was running?"

"Based solely on the fact that their names were in his secret place, I'd say that's a good guess, yeah. But they were clean—no connections I could find. You have better sources; you might want to check with them."

"Yeah, no," Teddy said, shaking his head. "I'd like to stay out of her way as much as possible."

Ginny wadded her napkin and threw it at him. "She's been helpful!"

"She's been setting us up to dig for her, Gin. And I wouldn't put it past her to use you as bait for whatever she wanted dug up."

She frowned at him, as though suspecting that was why he'd rushed down here, that he thought she was going to do something stupid, or needed rescuing. "We were going to dig anyway, Theodore. And if she wants us to dig successfully . . ."

"You said yourself she admitted our competence, and *then* told you to stay low, that the stakes were too high for us. Is there a better way to get you to do something on the QT, than raise a challenge like that?"

They had a stare-down that Teddy won, but only barely.

"Fine. We won't call her. Unless we have to," she said, glaring at Teddy. He raised his hands in surrender, willing to concede that point. He didn't know for *certain* Asuri was using them as bait; it was just a strong and supported suspicion.

"So how do we actually get to talk to these boys?" Teddy asked, moving the conversation away from the question of Asuri. "I mean, a reporter showing up might flip them out a little, and we've got even less reason."

"When in doubt, do the time-honored reporter thing," the other man said, pouring himself more coffee.

"Which is?"

"Lie," Ron said.

Joke aside, dancing around the truth—what Ron referred to as "prevarication in the pursuit of truth" and Tonica called "bullshitting the mark," meant that getting in to see one of their suspects turned out to be almost embarrassingly easy.

"We're terribly sorry to bother you, and thank you so much for taking time out of your day."

"No, that's quite all right. Please, sit down."

David Collins had a broad, open face, his sandy brown hair falling into his face, frequently swiped back with an exasperated hand, and a quick smile that not only reached his eyes but seemed to fill his entire body. Ginny smiled back at him, and resisted the urge to check for an alligator tail.

The brewery was hopping out front, but they'd been escorted to a small room to the side, with a long wooden table and chairs and not much else. "We have group tastings here," he said, noting their curiosity. "Décor's less important when we want them focusing on what's in their mouths."

"You're a brewer, too?" Tonica asked, gesturing to the stained apron he was wearing over his khakis.

"No, not yet. Someday. Right now I'm sort of jack of all trades, mainly, as we discussed, working the sales angle. I'm rather disgustingly good at schmoozing."

Fortunately, so was Tonica. Ginny leaned back in the chair, aware that Collins had already checked her out, read her "not here to flirt" body language, and—wonders of wonders—respected it. She supposed that was part of what made him good at schmoozing: reading and paying attention to body language.

"It's all part of the trade, isn't it?" Tonica said. "Making, selling . . . and straddling the bar, so to speak, gives an excellent view of the larger picture. There's certainly far more to running a bar than I ever thought when I was just tending one!"

That was their story, their excuse for being here—that Tonica had heard about the work the brewery was doing, and wanted to see if they could work a deal with Mary's. It was enough to get them in the door. . . .

What happened now, she didn't know. They were pretty much winging it. Her job was to take notes, smile occasionally, frown every now and again, and if she saw an opening, take it. So while the two men went on to discuss various beers and ales they were making, and a young woman came in with a tray of one-ounce sample glasses, Ginny waited, watched, and after a few different ales had been tasted—Ginny abstaining, as the designated driver—she said, "This seems more like a labor of love to you, than something you do for money. Or did you manage to luck out and land both in one job?"

"It doesn't pay all that well, no," Collins admitted. "But I do all right."

"You must," she said, with as much admiration as she could. "That's a Diva Noir shirt, isn't it?"

"Um. Yes." He clearly wasn't sure if he should be flattered or wary. Tonica wouldn't know Diva Noir from Nike, but she did—and so did Collins. And he knew she knew how much one of those button-down shirts cost, and you didn't wear it under an apron unless you had more than one.

Hah. Take that, Mister I-can-read-people-better-than-you, you-need-to-be-rescued-from-your-own-impulses Theodore Tonica. Their target was slightly suspicious now, but she saw no indication that he had recognized their names, no flash of hesitation that you got used to seeing when someone knew they were being questioned. This guy had no idea who they were, other than their cover story. She hid a vicious-feeling grin. Time to up the pressure a little.

"Nice." She leaned back a little and looked down, as though checking him out without wanting to be obvious about it. She might not have had much opportunity to flirt recently, but that didn't mean she'd forgotten how to do it. "The brewery must be doing well, or do you manage to juggle even more than all this?" A little surprise, a little awe, and she saw his eyelids flicker, shifting to glance back at Tonica before focusing on her again. Not that Ginny believed she was any kind of femme fatale, but very few people could resist the urge to humble-brag. And Collins seemed like the type who wouldn't enjoy working for other people, from what she'd heard already—and she knew the type from looking in the mirror every morning.

"I've got my fingers in a few pies, here and there," he said casually. "You know how it is: you can't assume any one particular thing's going to work out, so you spread your chances."

"Oh, I know how that goes, yes," she said, smiling. "A little here, a little more there, and if one pays out, you put more there."

"Exactly. And if one of those things pushes the envelope a little, well hey . . ."

His face froze mid-smile, making him look a little like a chipmunk caught stuffing his pouches. She, on the other hand, kept smiling, even as she could practically hear in her head Tonica asking her what the hell she was doing.

Ginny shook her head. "Hey, business is business, right? I don't judge."

His face relaxed, but his eyes were steady on hers, cold and thoughtful. Yeah, she'd gotten him right. Come on, she thought, take the bait just a little more. . . . "This isn't about setting up any kind of deal, is it?"

"It is, actually," Tonica said, picking up the conversation again. "Everything I said is completely true." It wasn't the entire story, no, but Tonica hadn't had to lie at all, despite Ron's advice. "You'd got good product here, but no national distribution yet, so showcasing it in another city can't hurt you, and it would be a nice shout for my place, promotion-wise. Everyone likes to think they're getting some special deal, right?"

"And any other product I might be involved in?" The way he said it made Ginny wonder what else he was involved in, and where he thought this was going. They had to be really careful now. Or they could go all in.

Ginny was tired of creeping around the edges, playing it safe. She wanted this done, so she could go *home*.

"Truthfully? We're really not interested in whatever else you're doing," she said. "We're not in the market. We're only interested in what—if any—connection you might have had with Jamie Penalta."

Someday, no lie, he was going to die of a heart attack, and the cause was going to be one Virginia Mallard. But the past few years had taught him a little about how her brain worked, so he was able to recover without too much gaping like an idiot. Thankfully, Collins's attention had been on her, not him, while he recovered.

They had learned how to be a damned effective team, actually, he thought: one of them reassured and the other set things to spin. Although it would be easier if they actually planned this out, rather than a vague "let's see where it goes" and then winging it. And Ginny claimed to be the logical one?

"Jamie." Collins—on the verge of a conniption fit—seemed to deflate. "Is that what this is about? Poor Jamie."

Time for him to step in again. He put on his very best Sympathetic Listening face and leaned in again. "You two were friends?"

"No." Collins laughed at that. "No, we weren't friends. Bluntly, Jamie wasn't someone I'd associate with, outside of business purposes." He leaned back in his own chair, the previous façade of friendly sales manager evaporating into something more wary-eyed and cynical. "You're not cops. I recognize cops. And his murder, while tragic, wasn't enough to warrant a follow-up article. So . . . what's the story?"

"That's what we'd like to know," Teddy said, pulling the man's attention back to him. "Someone pulled us into this mess without our consent, and we want to know why. Which means knowing why Jamie's dead."

"Yeah, seems there are a lot of people who'd like to know that. But I'm not one of them. I mean, I don't care, and I don't know." He looked around the room, then held up a finger to indicate they should wait a moment, then got up and left the room.

"Nice way to spring that on me," Teddy said.

"Yeah, sorry." She didn't sound sorry.

Collins came back before they could get into it further and took his seat again. "Wanted to make sure this conversation wasn't going on the tape," he said, indicating a small camera in the corner of the room neither of them had noticed before. "It's just there for legal reasons, when we've got tastings going on, so nobody will stress about it being off for a few minutes."

Teddy nodded. He'd asked Patrick to install closed-circuit cameras, for the parking lot if nothing else, but the bastard was putting him off until Teddy was about ready to call in some favors and get it done himself.

"So. Jamie," he prompted. "Not a friend, but you did know him."

"Jamie's a photographer. Was, I guess. And he was dependable—you always knew exactly what you were going to get from him, and you'd get it in a timely manner. And—hell, I'll give him credit, he was an artist. Didn't have to use Photoshop to get the results we needed; it always looked perfect."

"He used a physical backdrop instead of adding digital effects in later?" Ginny asked, remembering the fake ID artists from her college days. "That's old-school."

"I know, really? But he made it work. And the things he could do with film? God, I wish we could have . . ." Collins stopped. "But you don't care about that."

"We really don't," Ginny agreed. "Like you said, we're not cops. Or lawyers."

"So what are you?"

"Interested parties," Teddy said, with a new flatness in his voice that would hopefully convince the other man that it wasn't a thread he wanted to yank. Let the guy look them up after the fact, if he wanted, not get distracted now.

"In why Jamie died. Yeah. You know, I couldn't tell you, because like I said, I didn't pal around with the guy."

"For a reason. What was the reason?"

That, for the first time, seemed to put a stutter in Collins's smooth routine. "Okay. I don't have any proof, okay? I don't know anything for certain, and anything I do know is hearsay and gut, really." Collins looked up, away from them, staring at the wall behind them although Teddy would bet that's not what he was seeing. "But if I'd had a younger sister? I wouldn't have let him get within ten feet of her."

Ginny's jaw twitched, but Teddy beat her to the punch. "But you were okay with him taking photographs of teenage girls?"

Collins shrugged, not denying the implied accusation. "Business was business. Besides, like I said, I didn't have any proof. Jamie would joke about things but he never . . . Just being a sleaze isn't a crime, right?"

They sat in Ginny's rental car, after their meeting ended rather abruptly, with Collins showing them the door with a charming, if forced smile for anyone who might have been watching them, and very carefully didn't look at each other.

"Those lists of girls' names?"

"Maybe. Maybe not."

"Probably, though."

"Yeah. Probably. But it could just be his version of a little black book. Sleazy, but . . ."

"He was decent-looking," Ginny said. "And he had access to something they wanted—fake ID."

"That could be the good reason we were looking for, for someone to sic you on him, indirectly," Teddy said. "A teenage girl, knowing that she'd get in trouble if she tried to report him directly, or maybe couldn't risk . . . his word against hers, and her only point of contact is buying something illegal from him, that gets complicated. But if someone else pokes their nose in . . . ?"

"And a teenager wouldn't, probably, have thought through how the hell I would go from 'huh, you're not my client' to discovering he's scummy. . . . " She checked that thought. "No, a teenage girl would know exactly how I'd start poking around, because guys like that give off vibes. And if this guy gave off vibes even another *guy* could pick up after a while . . . But that doesn't explain why he had my info on him, though, if someone else—especially a teenage girl who wanted nothing to do with him—called me in."

"Yeah. I got nothing there. But at least that gives us an age range of possible impersonators. If they needed fake ID, they were under twenty-one, and probably over

seventeen—below that and most kids can't afford the level
he was probably charging."

Ginny was already on her phone. "Ron, hey. Any luck
on your side? Uh-huh. Yeah, all right, sorry. Sheesh. Look,
can you run a check on something for me? Uh-huh. Okay,
then just scan the list of girls' names and send it to me?
No, we—we might have something but I don't know for
certain yet. Yes. Yes, you get the scoop, Jesus, seriously?"
She looked at Teddy and rolled her eyes, and he bit his lip
to keep from laughing. "Yeah, all right, thanks."

"He's sending the list?" Teddy asked.

"With the proviso that he gets all the dirty details as soon
as we, and I quote, 'break the case open,' yeah. But he can't
get to it right away—something about him having an actual
job he has to do, too. This isn't enough of a story—yet—
for him to dump everything else."

"I don't suppose you've come up with some brilliant
plan on how to approach the other guy on the list, while
you were improvising? Because he might be able to give
us specifics—or something that contradicts Mr. Collins's
soul-bearing, but I don't think the Seattle bar card is going
to get us in the door there."

"Sorry, no. Unless his architecture firm has a sudden
strange need for a party planner, I'm out of ideas on that
one. And if they are partners, I bet Collins was calling or
texting him the minute we walked out of the brewery,"
Ginny said.

He sighed in agreement. "And they've both shut the
barn doors and nailed them closed for good measure. You

think we should have pushed more? If they're part of the fake ID gig . . ."

"If we'd pushed more, we'd be pushing right into the local cops'—and Asuri's—turf," she reminded him. "National-level stuff, meaning higher chance of visibility. You were the one who was all against that, remember?"

"Right." He hated when he was right, almost as much as he hated when she was right. "So far under the radar we're burrowing."

"Gophers are us," she said. "C'mon. It's lunchtime, and you know I don't think well on an empty stomach. And we can't do anything more until Ron sends me that list anyway."

She pulled out her tablet and opened the LocalEats app. "What're you in the mood for?"

Inside the brewery, in his tiny closet of an office with a door that actually shut, Collins sat on the old wooden table that passed for his desk—having to move a pile of sales binders out of the way to do so—and pulled out his cell phone. He didn't want to make this call—he *really* didn't want to make a call—but not calling would be worse.

He was good with names; it was part of the job, to remember someone he'd only met once in passing, to remember the name of a dozen beers, to keep a hundred different facts straight in his head, and they'd talked about it—laughed about it—long enough that the name stuck in his head. Tonica was an odd enough name, and connected with a female partner, it had only taken a little while for him to remember the article Jamie had showed them.

Private investigators.

"It's Dave. Yeah, I know, but look, we may have a problem. I don't think it's serious, but . . ." He waited for the go-ahead, then picked his words carefully. There was a difference between admitting a problem and hanging yourself with it. "Someone—not cops—came by, asking questions about Jamie. No, they—no, they knew about the fakes. Didn't seem to care, either. I don't know. No. Ben wouldn't—look, he wouldn't, okay?"

He'd go to the grave convinced Ben wouldn't sell him out, no matter how freaked out he got. Jamie might have, but Jamie was dead, and if he'd called them they wouldn't be asking about him. Right?

"Yeah, um . . . Theodore Tonica was the guy. I didn't get the girl's name, Virginia something. They're from Seattle, guy claims he manages a bar up there, called Mary's . . . yeah. Yeah, it's legit, do I look like an idiot? No, they came in asking about our beer, but then everything took a weird left turn. No, no, I don't think so but—all right. Okay."

He ended the call and ran a hand over his face hard enough to push the stress out. Michal hadn't sounded pissed, but you couldn't tell with her. Still, he hadn't let anything slip they didn't already know, and he'd done damage control the moment he could. That was all anyone could ask for, right?

"Yeah. Yeah, everything's going to be fine." He slipped his phone back into his pocket and strode back into the main room. That was the bennie of being part of a larger organization—not just more money. Support. He'd put the camera back on, finish the orders he'd been writing up, yell at Marco for screwing around with the menu. Life as normal, like nothing was wrong, let other people clean up the mess outside. He could do that.

14

Georgie was used to being left alone for long periods of time. She didn't mind. Mostly. She slept, and chewed on her bone, and listened to the birds outside, and waited. Dogs were good at waiting, although Penny said that cats were better. Ginny didn't believe that; Penny was always twitching, either her tail or her ears, wanting something to happen.

It had been forever since Ginny and Teddy left her in the room. It was a nice room, with a window low enough she could look out of it, and fresh water, and her toys, and a comfortable den, but Things Were Happening outside the room, Georgie knew it.

She sniffed once, taking in the lingering, comforting smell of Ginny's Things in the room, of Ginny herself. Smells were important. Smells told you who was there, who had been there; reassured you that those smells would come back, if you were only patient.

Georgie was a good dog; she could be patient.

But she also wanted something to happen. No, she didn't. She didn't want something to happen without her, that was it. She was supposed to be with Ginny, to find out what was happening; Penny had said so.

Georgie sniffed again, and something tugged at her, like a leash that wasn't there. Something about a smell she was supposed to

*remember. Supposed to do something about? No. But there were
no bad smells here, only Ginny and Teddy, and the human who
had come to visit who had visited before, and smelled of something
smoky and nice, and underneath all that smelled of something sharp
but not unpleasant, deep in the carpet.*

*But there was a smell, yes. She had smelled it on the girls, the
unhappy-scolded girls, and she had smelled it before. But where?
And why did it feel important?*

*She wanted to talk to Penny, to know what was going on, what
smell she was supposed to remember. Penny would know. Penny
always knew.*

*Penny was in the box. No, not in the box, Georgie wasn't
a puppy anymore; Penny was back home, but she could talk
through the box. But Ginny had left the box on the desk, and
Georgie wasn't supposed to ever touch the box. Ginny had made
that clear.*

*Georgie knew this was a bad idea, probably the worst idea she'd
ever had. But she still found herself with her paws on the chair,
sniffing at the box, trying to figure out how to make it show Penny
again. . . .*

"Huh."

That was either a good "huh" or a bad "huh"; he
couldn't quite tell from context. Once Ron had sent over
the list, they'd settled in at a little coffee shop that was
empty enough not to care if they sat there all afternoon,
so long as they occasionally refreshed their coffee. Ginny
had been scrolling through her tablet while he worked on a

scratch pad they'd picked up after lunch and his cell phone. But they hadn't been getting anywhere, even with the annotations the reporter had added.

And then that quite contemplative "huh."

"What?" he asked, when Ginny didn't say anything more.

"Kimberly."

"What?"

"On the list. The second-to-last name is Kimberly."

"Yeah, so?"

They'd been at this for two hours, and from the way Tonica was rubbing at his eyes, he had a headache but was too stubborn to admit it and take a break. She reached for her bag and pulled out a pill case, tossing it to him.

"Kimberly—Kim. We're idiots. Kim's a nickname."

He shook some aspirin into his palm, then looked at her blank-eyed. He could see from her expression when she realized that he needed more context than that. "One of the girls I spoke to, the one Georgie tracked down. Her name was Kim."

The penny dropped, and his eyes widened. "Oh."

"Yeah. Oh. I mean, it might not mean anything, it might not be her, it might be coincidence, the list might not even be related."

"Or it could all be connected, and tugging on it will get us some answers."

She nodded, her need to keep those two girls out of trouble at odds with the probability that one of them, at least, already *was* in trouble. "The young girl I spoke with,

with Asuri, she said she saw two people on the porch the morning that Jamie was killed." Ginny drank the last sip of coffee in her mug, even though it was cold, because her throat had suddenly gone dry. "She couldn't tell if they were male or female."

"You think it was Kim and her friend?"

"I think it might have been, yeah. Maybe?"

"They're what, seventeen?"

"Thereabouts. They were seniors, they said." Ginny kicked herself, mentally, for being off her game. She had first names, ages, and geographic location. That was enough, unless the girls went to a private school out of the area, and she was betting that they didn't, if they'd been cutting on their own front porch. "High schools, seniors, class lists . . ."

Ten minutes to track down the local high school, another few to find and skim the senior class list and find Kim on it, and another few minutes to cross-check the name with photos to confirm it was her.

It shouldn't be that easy, but if Ginny was more comfortable online than her parents, teenagers were even more so, and with less clue about privacy concerns. Photos, check-ins, the ability to scream "here I am, look at me!" across the Internet sky was too much temptation to resist, even if you knew better, at seventeen. And even if you could resist, your friends would tag you in their photos. . . .

"Kimberly Joan Siddig, age seventeen. About to head off to the University of Tennessee at Knoxville, where her father also went. Plays soccer, and likes to hang out at IHOP with some friends who like to Instagram."

He got up to look over her shoulder. "Have I ever said how thankful I was to have gone to school before Facebook and YouTube were things?"

"A few times, yeah," she said. "Me, too. Negatives might be hard to burn, but at least you had a chance then."

"You know we're way the hell off the map, figuring out who hired you and why, right?"

She tapped the list of names with her finger and nodded. "Yeah, I know." Nobody else was looking, though. And they couldn't take the list to anyone, not without admitting where they got it, which meant admitting to breaking and entering . . . and without proof, without the list, they had nothing.

"Maybe we should just let it go?" Tonica suggested gently. "I mean, he's dead. That's all the justice they're going to get."

"The articles are calling him a victim. Whoever called me wanted to have him exposed. I took the money, Tonica. I have to do the job."

"All right. But if we go have a chat with Ms. Kimberly, is this going to open a larger can of worms than you're ready to deal with?"

She tilted her head and looked at him. "What do you mean?"

"Do you think they killed him?"

"No." Her response was instant. "They were shocked when they heard he was dead, I'd bet Georgie on it."

"Okay, if not killers, then possibly witnesses. If she—

with or without her friend—was there that morning, which would explain Georgie following them home."

Ginny blinked a few times, letting his words sink in. "If she was there, the killer might have seen her, too. He might think she saw him! Teddy, we've got to—"

"Let's not borrow trouble, Mallard," Tonica said, but she could tell from the way his forehead creased that he'd been thinking the same thing. "Let's just talk to the girl, see what we can get from that. And if she or her friend did see someone, that's when we call Asuri, and get her some kind of protection, and let *them* spill the beans."

It was a good plan, a practical, sensible plan. Ginny could get behind that. And maybe the girl knew who had hired her, maybe *she* had hired her, her or her friend. Maybe she should have been straight with them up front, and they would have told her that?

"I don't suppose her phone number's listed online, too?"

He sounded so dourly disapproving, she sniffed back at him. "No, but her chatcatch is."

"Her what?"

"Her chatcatch. It's like texting, only it's not hooked up to your phone number, so it gives you a little more privacy. Apparently all the high school kids are using it."

"And you have an account . . . why?"

She gave him a sideways look. "Because I had a job setting up a surprise birthday party thrown by three teenagers last December. Chatcatch was the one sure way of talking to them that their dad couldn't overhear."

Thankfully, she remembered her password.

★ ★ ★

Georgie met them at the hotel room door as though she'd been alone for weeks, not several hours. Ginny let Tonica handle the ear-pulling and chin-scratching, and went to grab her laptop where she'd left it on the desk.

It wasn't on the desk.

There was a moment of panic before she realized it had fallen onto the floor, then another moment of panic until the screen woke up and she determined that it hadn't been damaged. She righted it, then frowned, eyes narrowed as she looked at the desk, the laptop, and the chair that she was pretty damn sure she'd left pushed in, not shoved away from the desk. She'd left the do-not-disturb sign on the door, and the bed hadn't been remade. . . .

"Georgie?" Her tone was half question, half accusation, but the dog responded to the last part, dropping away from Tonica's greeting to go belly-down on the floor, ears drooping even more than usual.

"Damn it, Georgie." The laptop wasn't broken, but it could have been. "What got into you? If you were that bored, why couldn't you eat a towel or something, like a normal dog?"

Tonica raised an eyebrow at the dog. "Georgie, were you trying to get to puppy porn?"

"It's not funny, Tonica. She could have seriously broken it!" Ginny looked at the screen and frowned. "I thought I'd closed that application yesterday." She closed Skype again and checked for email instinctively. Her mother, some sale alerts. Nothing urgent.

"You left her alone in a hotel room, Ginny. Kids get bored."

"Shut up. For that you can take her for a walk. I'm going to see if I can track down the rest of the names on the list, while we wait for Kim to get back to me."

"And what if she doesn't?" he asked, bending down to attach Georgie's leash, despite the dog's happy wiggling the moment she'd realized a walk was in the offing.

That stumped Ginny for a minute. "I don't know," she said. "I guess we go to her house? Even if she's not a witness, if that is her name on the list, and it is more than just girls who wanted fake IDs . . . there are too many really ugly things a guy with a camera could do." Tonica nodded; they'd both danced around that idea when they talked about the list, neither one of them wanting to actually voice it. "So maybe we could convince her to go to the cops about that, and I can finish the job that way? But . . . she's got a right to not get involved, too. I'm not . . . My need to finish shit can't trump her right to stay out of it."

"You're a good kid, Mallard."

She rolled her eyes and shook her head. "Shut up and take my dog for a walk."

The room was quiet for a few seconds after Tonica and Georgie left, and Ginny sat at the desk, staring at her laptop but not actually doing anything, until her phone vibrated, indicating a new text message.

It was from Ron. "Just got shot down and shut down, kid. You're on your own. Sorry."

"Well, shit." She wondered if he'd gotten in real trouble,

or if he was being slammed with a new project. Her first instinct was to call him, to apologize, to see if she could make amends if she'd gotten him in trouble, but the fact that he'd texted her rather than calling suggested the former and if it was the latter he'd be out chasing leads or calling other people now, and her interrupting wouldn't be helpful.

It wasn't as though he hadn't already gone above and beyond, anyway. She sat down in the chair and entered the first name on the list, plus the high school, into her normal search engines, and waited to see what kicked back.

Whatever else she might be uneasy about, here she was back in familiar territory. Researching and investigating was where Ginny was comfortable, no matter what the topic.

And maybe Kim would call her back after all.

"Your dog is a flirt," Teddy said when he came in the door half an hour later, Georgie already off leash. "Totally tried to chat up both of the dogs in the run, at the same time."

"Mmmhmmmm."

That was Mallardese for "I'm working; don't actually expect an answer to anything you say."

"And a Hollywood talent scout thinks she's got real potential, gave me his card. You may have to give it all up to become a stage mom."

"Mmmmmhmmmmmm."

He gave up, sitting on the edge of the bed while Georgie

sniffed her owner's leg and then went to the corner and curled up on her blanket, turning her muzzle under her paws. He was so used to seeing Penny curled between those paws, it gave him an odd twinge that the cat *wasn't* there. He shook his head, refusing to admit that he might be missing the tabby's company, and lay back on the bed, arms crossed behind his head, waiting patiently for Ginny to resurface.

"I managed to track down nine of the eleven names," she said, about ten minutes later. Teddy had almost managed to zonk himself into a meditative state—or maybe it was closer to a catnap—and so her words didn't register at first.

"Only nine?"

"Only? Excuse me?" She turned in the chair, giving him a Look from under arched blond eyebrows. "That's damn good work, than you very much. What do you have?"

"Not a thing," he admitted, sitting up. "Now that you're herding the information superhighway, I'm just here for charm and intimidation factors. But I can tell you that our boy isn't on any of the sexual predator lists, nor is he pending or under investigation for anything of the sort."

She raised her eyebrows even higher, and he held up his cell phone. "You're not the only one who can make a few phone calls, even if I can't make the Internet sit up and beg. Friend of a friend has access to the stuff the general public, even ones as talented as yourself, can't get into. Called him while I was walking your dog." He owed Corky for that— the other man had emailed him the contact info. The conversation had taken ten minutes, and while he couldn't say if Penalta had been under investigation for anything, he could say what the guy *hadn't* been. And sexual deviancy of any sort was on that list.

"Yeah, the neighbor said the same thing. That he didn't have a record, anyway. Doesn't mean he's not, just that he hasn't been caught."

"Yeah well, I'd say someone caught him doing *something*." Innocent people get killed every day, but getting beaten to death when you're already involved in something illegal, and the feds are sniffing at your tail, upped the odds of not-a-sad-coincidence significantly. And Teddy might never have met the guy but he knew he didn't like the company he kept.

She nodded. Her shoulders were tight, and her fingers were still on the desk, not drumming the way they usually did when she was brain-deep in figuring something out. Everything about her screamed *stress*, and he could feel his own body reacting to it.

"Mallard." He said it softly, but it got her attention; she looked up at him. "You know, we don't have to keep digging. We've got a reasonable guess why you were called in, even if not *who*, and if we're not actually investigating his murder because the cops seem to actually be on that . . ."

"We could just close up shop and go home? Forget about reaching Kim, getting her to talk?"

"Yeah."

"And the girls on that list? Seven of the nine are seniors this year; the other two graduated last year. They don't deserve to have their attacker exposed for the sleaze he was?"

"He might not have . . . We don't know for certain. It might have been a client list, maybe he was running a side deal, not cutting his partners in? That's a real good way to get your neck broken and your face punched in, and Collins looked strong enough to do it."

"Maybe. But Collins . . . He's a jerk but he didn't seem like the brutal killer type."

"From what I've read, you don't know who's the type or not until they're beating your head in. Sorry," he added when she winced. "But all we know so far is that his neighbors called him a nice guy—and that's *always* a warning sign—and his erstwhile business partner didn't seem all that broken up that he's dead. Maybe something else went wrong—he might just have been a small cog in a larger disaster, and Asuri was doing us a solid, warning us away from it."

"But she didn't, did she? Not really. You're the one who pointed it out, that she said just enough to make me jump for it."

He exhaled, unable to argue with that, since yeah, he had been the one to say it first.

He realized that he'd clenched his hands and forced them to relax. Ginny angry was terrifying but exhilarating. Seeing her furious with guilt—he could have lived his entire life without that. But going into overprotective mode in response wasn't going to help.

"This entire shitstorm, it's been me being manipulated. Someone wanted me down here, and Asuri took advantage of that, played me, and I dragged Ron into it, dragged you down, too, and . . ."

"I dragged my own self down here," he said sharply.

"Okay, yeah." She wasn't so guilty that suddenly the entire world was her fault, and he was thankful for that, at least. "But you wouldn't have if I hadn't gotten so tangled up in this, like Penny when she can't get her claws out of something and ends up doing a faceplant."

"Gin, stop it. If we're right, this guy was at the very least a sexual user, and nobody knew about it, because nobody was talking. Whatever Asuri's using us for, whatever game she's playing with her own case, none of that matters. You said the girls were scared, but not unhappy that he was dead, right? If we're right, we've got the chance to expose him for being a sleaze."

Because if the feds were looking at him for identity theft and crap like that, they weren't going to care about what he did on the side. Not enough to dig into it. Not if none of his victims could make a difference in their case. And they sure as hell wouldn't be able to get the girls to talk.

He didn't say any of that to Ginny. He didn't have to: she was smarter than he was, she already knew it.

"All right." Her body untensed, just enough. "All right. So you don't think I was supposed to find the body?" He could see her turning that idea around in his head, reslotting the puzzle pieces until the picture made sense again.

"Maybe not. Maybe that was just the worst possible timing in the history of bad luck? Maybe you were supposed to arrive when he was harassing Kim?" The timing was too uncertain, the case too flimsy, but for once in all this mess, it felt right.

"Maybe it was one of the girls on this list," she said, finally. "Or a friend of theirs, or a parent who didn't want their daughter to have to step forward, not if they could protect her. That makes sense. All right."

"You good?"

"No," she said. "But it's going to have to do. Poking further is liable to run us into the murder investigation, and I'm not going to count on Asuri bailing me out again, no matter what game she's playing. And I don't feel like doing the feds' dirty work, not without a please and thank-you and maybe a tax break out of it.

"I'm tired of being someone else's puppet, Teddy. If Kim doesn't get in touch with me . . . it's time to go home."

He must have betrayed his surprise, because she smiled at him, a wry curl of her lip. "Ron texted me while you were out. Either he got in trouble or he got assigned something else big, because we're on our own. So that door's shut and . . . short of going to Asuri, I don't know what else to do. This isn't a matter of public records I can search out, or witnesses you can schmooze, not if Kim won't talk to us." She frowned. "And the younger girl, Sally, I think her name was. I should have pushed more to see what she remembered, but I didn't want to challenge Asuri without knowing what she was up to, and now . . . if Sally's folks are smart, and I'm betting they are, they won't let me talk to her without some kind of official notice and identification."

"Her memory's not worth it now, anyway," Teddy said. "Even trained witnesses have memory degradation after a few days. A kid? Between what she actually saw and what she's heard since then, there's gonna be a lot of gray."

"Like I said, there's not much more we can do. And it's not like we have a case, or a client, anyway. I just wish I'd—" A sound came from her phone, and they both jumped. Georgie, reacting more to the movement than the sound, opened one eye, then, seeing there was nothing going on, went back to sleep. "It's Kim."

"Damn it, cat, what is with you? You feel the need to make my life *more* difficult?"

The tabby stared at her, those unblinking eyes still unnerving, and flicked her tail once as though to say "you idiot human, I'm trying to *tell* you something."

"Yeah well, I'm not the boss, Mistress Penny. I don't speak cat, fluent or otherwise. So please leave the damn tip jar—and my arms—alone, okay?"

She righted the jar for the third time and glared back at the cat, daring her to tip it over again.

"Seriously. What's with you?"

The bar phone, an old-fashioned landline, rang just then, interrupting their staring match.

"Mary's Place, how can we—hey, boss. No, everything's fine, you were right, I humbly apologize for even doubting you an instant, all right?" Stacy rolled her eyes, although there was nobody at the bar just then to see it. They'd opened late, her morning gig running overtime, but there was no need to tell Teddy that, not if nobody was around to hear it. Fridays started slow—Thursday nights were busy but the afternoon after was the calm before the storm. "Yeah, no, no, I—"

There was an ungodly noise, like a car engine stalling, and Stacy looked up to see Penny stalking toward her, tail erect and whiskers quivering, demanding—and there was no other way to describe it—to be heard.

"That? Is your cat, boss. I think she's pissed at you."

She laughed at his response. "Nuh-uh. Let me put you on speakerphone."

"Hey, Penny," Tonica's voice came through. "You keeping everyone in line up there?"

Stacy was pretty sure Penny said something rude in reply, and a deep woof came from the background on the other end of the line.

"I'm sorry, did you want to say something?" she heard Teddy say, muffled enough to be turning away from the phone, and she could imagine Georgie looking up at the boss, asking where Penny was, why she could hear her but not see her.

Penny let out another meow, this one less insistent if still as loud, then came up to the phone and butted her head against Stacy's hand, a rare signal of affection. Or, possibly, asking for control of the phone held in that hand.

"No," she told the cat. "Not until you grow opposable thumbs. And start paying for your share of the phone bill."

Teddy came back on the line. "All right, I accept that the place hasn't burned down in my absence. And Seth hasn't given you any backtalk?"

"I think he's actually better behaved than when you're here, honestly," she said. "He likes being the sole rooster."

That got her a snort, and she heard Ginny saying something in the background.

"Well, he's got the chicken legs for it," Teddy said, and he had to speak loudly to be heard over Georgie's woofs, and that was odd, because Georgie was usually quiet, not like Parsifal, who still yipped like a crazy thing every time he saw her. "Damn it, dog, hush."

Penny was sitting on the bar in front of her, ears pricked up, eyes wide and staring at the phone like she expected it to turn into a mouse at any moment.

"We're going to be here another day, looks like," Teddy said, "but I'll be back in time for tomorrow night, promise."

"You'd better," she said. Friday nights were bad, but Saturdays were when things could get iffy, if they picked up overflow from other bars, and she was already going to be exhausted working double shifts today. "I'm going to make Seth bus tables tonight, because there's no way we can keep up." They'd managed last night, but only because their regulars weren't drunk assholes, and started clearing up after themselves. She couldn't count on that over the weekend.

"Call in Allison to work the floor," he said. "Off the books."

That would help. Allison was a retired career waitress who could still handle the average drunk with a quip and a touch on the shoulder, and she never minded picking up an under-the-table shift over the weekend, to help pay off her tab.

"Seriously, kid, how's it going? You going to be okay working double shifts today?"

She wasn't, really, but he'd never asked her to do this before and she knew it was because Ginny needed help, so she'd suck it up and hold it over him later. And like Allison, she wasn't going to turn down the extra paycheck. Being an artists' model—her other job—meant less time on her feet, but the tips were for crap and there was only so much posing she could stand before the need to talk to someone got overwhelming.

"You guys just finish up whatever you're doing and come home safe," she said. "If you leave me here alone much longer, though, I'm gonna redecorate. I think a nice retro eighties look would really bring in the crowds, don't you?"

She hung up before he could reply, and grinned triumphantly at the cat. "That'll get him back here, don't worry."

Penny could feel her tail lashing back and forth, and she stalked the length of the bar, aware that one careless flick could send something breakable to the floor but not caring a bit. Just then, if there had been something she knew Theodore cared about, she would have happily pushed it to the floor while he watched, just to say "so there."

But he wasn't there. He was Elsewhere, and Georgie needed her help, they all needed her help, and she was stuck here. They were sniffing out something, and she wasn't part of it, and meanwhile there was a threat here, and while Stacy was kind, and good-

tempered, she wasn't up to Theodore's or even Ginny's level. Yet. There might be hope for her, but Penny couldn't wait for that to happen now.

Penny swatted at the girl's paw in annoyance, careful to keep her nails sheathed, but the girl tried to scoop her off the bar anyway. She hissed, ears back and tail flat.

"Hey!" The girl sounded outraged and hurt and Penny felt a little bad but not enough to apologize. Some moods, humans should just know to keep their hands to themselves. If she wanted Penny to get down—

"Penny, off the bar."

She waited a minute just to show that it was her idea, not just following orders, then leapt down to the floor, her tail a warning to anyone else that she was not in the mood to be admired today.

There was a ledge at the back wall, high enough above that no-body could reach her, and most people never looked up to even see her. Only Theo, and Theo wasn't here today.

Three leaps and she was invisible, blending into the shadows near the ceiling. It was quiet, the girl moving behind the bar, the old man in the back, his muttering a soothing, familiar sound, and no other humans had come into her domain yet. She curled her tail around her flanks, unable to keep the tip from twitching irritably, even here.

The new girl had upset the proper order of things, with her taking of things out of the jar. That had to be dealt with first. Once she had made sure the Noisy Place was running smoothly, she'd get back to solving Theodore's other problem, now that Georgie had— finally—checked in.

A rumble of irritation rattled in her throat. Georgie said that they were about to go meet with someone, the girl they'd talked to before, because the girl might be in trouble, but that was all the dog knew. Georgie had been stressed, unhappy. Georgie wasn't good going into situations she didn't know; she needed Penny to explain things. And she. Wasn't. There.

Penny intensely disliked not being in the middle of things. Georgie and the humans were good, but they weren't good enough. Not without her.

14

It had been an awkward-as-hell conversation, but Kim had agreed, very reluctantly, to meet with them after school, in the gym. Ginny figured that meeting on school grounds—Kim's turf, as it were—might make the girl feel more in control of the situation. The point here was to get information from the girl, not scare her. If they were right, she'd had enough of that already. God, if she could just lay hands on that bastard, and he wasn't dead already . . .

"Ease up, Mallard."

"What?"

"You look like you're about to go in like an avenging angel. Ease up. So maybe the guy traded sexual favors for fake IDs. Maybe. Your yelling at her isn't going to—"

"Is that what you think?" She turned to face him, her eyes wide with a mix of shock and irritation. "Is that what you think I'm . . . You think that's what happened?"

"You can't assume worst-case scenario off the bat, Mallard."

She made a sound of disgust. "Only a male would say that. Didn't any one of your sisters ever explain the facts of life to you, Tonica? Always assume the worst-case scenario is going to happen. Because you're right more often than not, and that assumption's what might keep you safe. So, no, I'm not going to assume it was consensual until she says so." And maybe not even then. Seventeen was about as dumb as you got, from her memory.

"Shit."

"You really didn't—" She stopped herself from saying it. He was a guy, however good a guy he was, however well his sisters might have taught him not to be a jerk. His brain wouldn't automatically go to the same place hers did.

"I hope you're right," she said, instead. That would be bad enough, but not as bad as it might be.

Bu somehow, Ginny didn't think it was going to be only bad. Only bad didn't end up on a hidden list of underage girls, or have someone hiring a PI to poke around, without telling them why or what they should be looking for.

"This might all still just be tied into the identity theft stuff," he said. "Maybe one of his partners . . ."

"When was the last time someone got beaten to death for identity theft, Tonica? Collins is a sleaze, but can you see him actually taking a tire iron to someone else's face? Or spending money hiring someone to do it?"

He didn't have an answer to that.

The school was a large, gray stone building, and the halls echoed the way buildings that are normally filled with people do when they're empty. It wasn't that long after 3 p.m., but Ginny thought final exams might have started already, and anyone who didn't have to be here wouldn't be.

Kim was waiting for them in the gymnasium, sitting on the second-to-bottom step of the risers. She was wearing running pants and a tank top with her school's name on the front, her dark red hair pulled back in a ponytail and her skin flushed, as though she'd just finished a hard work-out and cool-down. Ginny was uncomfortably reminded that she'd let her own exercise routine slack off in the past week, and that she wasn't a teenager anymore.

"All right, I'm here. What do you want?" Kim was, if possible, even less comfortable talking to them now than she'd been before.

Ginny looked at Tonica, and he shrugged. They'd discussed their approach, briefly, on the way over. If Ginny's worries were true, he needed to back off, project his nice-guy-only-here-as-support aura, and not seem even remotely threatening. He might be the people-schmoozer, but she was the one who had talked to the girl before, and odds were she'd open up to a woman more than she would a guy, especially a stranger. The problem was, Ginny had absolutely no clue how to begin. "Did the guy who died touch you in bad places?" was a crappy opener.

Georgie, obviously recognizing the girl from their previous meeting, came to the rescue, settling herself at Kim's feet and pressing against her leg with the "please pet me my life will be incomplete if you don't pet me" expression that nobody could resist. Kim was no exception. She started rubbing George's ears, and they could see her shoulders ease out of their tight hold.

They joined her on the bleachers, Tonica on the bench below with Georgie, and Ginny sitting next to the girl, careful to leave enough room that she didn't feel pressured.

"Thank you for meeting with us," she said finally. "I have a few questions I'm hoping that you could help answer?"

"About Jamie? Mr. Penalta, I mean?"

"Yes." Interesting slip, using his first name, but not unexpected, based on what they knew. But it didn't incriminate, one way or the other: everyone said he spent a lot of time with the neighborhood kids, and in her experience that meant you either went full-on formal to maintain respect, or encouraged informality to improve communications. It didn't curse or exonerate him, either way.

Kim stopped petting Georgie for a moment, and then nodded. "Okay, yeah. I figured. What questions?"

Ginny decided, on the spot, that the only way this was going to work was if they didn't go in the direction Kim was clearly bracing herself for, if they kept her in her comfort zone and didn't freak her out. So the obvious questions were out, at least at first.

"You called him Jamie? Makes sense—not that much older than you, really." Ginny wasn't all that much older than the dead man, but she knew that the difference between mid-twenties and early thirties would be huge to a seventeen-year-old.

"Yeah, I guess. It was . . ." She toyed with the lace of one sneaker, picking at the plastic end. "Stupid. It made us feel older, I guess. Important. Like we were on the same level, or something."

Ginny flicked a glance at Tonica, who was frowning, his arms crossed over his chest, and for a minute she saw him the way a teenager might: a large older guy with a military-style haircut, muscled and slightly fierce, with that frown on his face. She widened her eyes at him and shook her head slightly, trying to tell him to ease up a little. He was supposed to be stern, not scary.

"Being seventeen sucks," Ginny said in response to the girl's words, less to Kim directly than a memory of her own, and the girl scoffed bitterly, like Ginny had no idea what she was talking about. "Yeah, it really does. You're supposed to know everything, what you want, who you are, but nobody lets you actually *do* anything. And please, don't tell me 'it gets better,' because when? When does it get better?"

"My mom says around forty," Ginny said, so dryly that it broke through Kim's quiet rant, and she looked up in surprise, then laughed—only a little, barely a huff, but it was a real laugh. "Yeah. My mom said that, too. That sucks."

"So you thought getting a fake ID would make things better?"

Kim looked like she was going to deny it, then all the air went out of her, and any defiance with it. "Maybe not better, but different. All my friends were getting into clubs . . . It wasn't about drinking, we just wanted to dance. And I'm going to college in the fall, and everyone has fake IDs there. . . ."

"Not everyone," Tonica said, and when she looked at

him he smiled at her, and shrugged, the charm turning on again, if powered down enough that it wasn't even remotely flirtatious. "I'm a bartender. I check a lot of ID. And we're pretty good about spotting fakes."

"Oh." Kim looked a little taken aback by that, more than anything else. Ginny hid a smile. She hadn't been a big drinker when she was a teenager, either, but the lure of being able to go where they weren't supposed to, to pass as adults . . . she remembered that. She thought, though, that reassuring the girl that there would still be bars she could get into, especially in a college town, wouldn't be the most responsible thing to say just then.

"Guess I spent a lot of money for nothing, then. He wasn't cheap." Bravado shone on her face, even though she kept her tone even, a little irritated but not too put out. She was good, Ginny would give her that, trying to be an Adult talking to Adults while her body was practically curled over Georgie, asking for reassurance. "But I'd heard from everyone how good his work was, all year, and I'd saved up enough money for my own, finally."

Ginny nodded, and let her own hand rest on Georgie's backside, a nonverbal reminder to the girl that the dog trusted Ginny, and she could, too. "So you got your ID from him, before he died?"

"Yeah. I'd gone over the week before and had my photo taken, and he'd texted me the day before to say that it was ready." She looked at Ginny quickly, then dropped her gaze again. "That was the day before he . . . before he died, I guess."

"And you went over to pick it up that morning?" That was their guess, that she'd been at least one of the people Sally claimed to have seen on the porch. "Did you go alone?"

"Yeah. I brought him the cash—he never made you pay up front, just when he delivered—and . . ." She stopped talking and rubbed Georgie's ears again, frowning at the planked floor of the gym like it held an answer to whatever question she was asking herself. Tonica looked at Ginny and she shook her head slightly. They should wait the girl out, not push her, or ask if anyone else had been there. It was the longest few minutes Ginny could ever remember, waiting to see if the dam would break, or get reinforced.

"He was always such a nice guy, you know? I mean, he wasn't creepy-nice. He didn't give us booze or anything or act weird, he was just . . . nice. He didn't talk down to us, and he didn't try to pretend we were anything other than dumb kids, you know what I mean? It was just . . . it was like he remembered what it was like, having everyone shouting at you to figure things out and at the same time telling you that you couldn't do anything." Once she started talking, Kim didn't seem capable of stopping. "So I guess we trusted him?"

Ginny noted the past tense, and didn't think it had anything to do with the guy being dead. Damn it, she hadn't wanted to be right, she really hadn't. She wanted to look at Tonica, to see what his reaction to that was, but she was afraid to take her attention off Kim, as though that would be an insult or betrayal.

"So you went over there, alone."

"Yeah. That was one of his rules; that any business had to be done solo. He said if you weren't able to do things on your own, you weren't old enough to have a fake ID. And I didn't think anything about it, until . . ." She was still petting Georgie, still focused down, but still talking. "Until he'd taken my money, and given me the ID, and then he was up in my face, trying to push me against the wall." She swallowed audibly, and the hand on Georgie's head was trembling. "He said it was a bonus, just a little bonus, he said, and his hands were everywhere and I freaked. I totally panicked and forgot everything we'd ever been told about self-defense, or anything. I couldn't get him off me no matter how hard I shoved, and he just kept talking like it was okay, like I wanted it, and I didn't."

Even without looking, Ginny would tell when Tonica tensed up. She didn't know much about his childhood, or even his life before he came to Mary's, but she did know he'd been surrounded by sisters and female cousins, and she knew enough about him to know that right now all he wanted to do was a) beat the dead guy to a pulp and b) comfort Kim, and neither one of those things was going to be useful right now because a) dead guy was dead and b) another guy touching her right now was not going to make it better.

She was really, really sorry she'd been right, and Tonica had been wrong.

"Did he—?" She stopped, not able to get the words out of her throat.

"He got his hands under my shirt, and he was grabbing

at me, and he kept *talking*. And then he tried to give me a hickey. On my neck. It was so gross, I started to cry, and I sneezed on him 'cause my nose runs when I cry, then the doorbell rang and I guess that freaked him out enough that he let go, and I grabbed my stuff and I ran."

Ginny let out a sigh of relief. But at the same time, her brain was shuffling the pieces around, trying to make room for this new information. "Kim did he ever . . . Did you ever hear of him trying that on anyone else?" Because if there was one thing you learned it was that creepers rarely creeped on only one person. Especially if their preferred target was teenagers And if they were in a position of having something said teenagers wanted.

"I don't know." She shook her head, but didn't seem certain. "Maybe? I mean . . . guys like that, it's not about me, right? That's what Nancy says, it's not me that set him off, it's them?"

If it wouldn't have freaked Kim out more, Ginny would have hugged her, and then and found her friend Nancy and hugged her, too. "Yeah. Yeah, you're a hundred percent right. They . . . But you never heard anything?"

Kim shook her head, her ponytail swishing gently. "Nancy said we should ask around, but even if he was . . . he was the only source for decent ID, you know? Nobody'd want to hear it. We'd be the ones making the problem, not him." She swallowed. "And then . . ."

Oh Christ, there was more?

"And then you came by, and we found out that he was dead."

Ginny inhaled, then nodded slowly. No wonder they'd looked so shocked, and also, yeah, she could see it now, relieved. She'd basically just told them that the monster was dead, that they didn't have to decide what to do because someone else had taken care of the problem for them.

Except there was still a monster out there: the guy who'd done it.

"And you didn't see anyone else there that morning?"

"No. Oh, wait." Kim frowned, and Ginny could see dots connecting in the girl's head. "When I left, I ran out the front door and there was a woman there. She'd rung the doorbell, I guess, it was all kind of a blur then, and . . . she made him let me go. Or he let me go because she was there?"

The two people the little girl said she had seen on the porch with Penalta. Kim, and the unknown woman. Ginny felt a stir of excitement, the way she felt when she was *this close* to figuring out a problem, or cracking a case.

"Did he know her? Did he mention a name?"

Kim shook her head, face still down and intent on Georgie's back. "If he did, I don't remember. But . . . he was killed just after that, wasn't he? That's what they're saying, that he died mid-morning, and I was there before school, and . . . oh my God, was she the killer? She touched me!" She was shuddering now, her eyes tearing, and from the way she kept sniffling, her nose was probably starting to run, too.

"Ease up," Tonica said, his hand gentle on her shoulder. "Breathe out, then in, slowly."

Kim shuddered, and Georgie pressed harder against

her knee, doggie breath a comforting miasma against her cheek. "Breathing, right." But she followed his instructions, until she could speak easily again. She glanced at the clock up on the wall, then stared at the wall itself.

"He was alive when I left, I swear it." She didn't look at either one of them, her eyes steady on the wall, her jaw tight. "I was scared, and I was angry, but I didn't kill him. But if that woman did . . . I'm going to have to go to the cops, aren't I?"

That had been their best-case scenario, that Kim raised that option herself, rather than their mentioning it.

"You probably need to talk to them," Ginny said, keeping her voice soft. "Don't worry, they're not going to think you did it. I saw the body, Kim. I'm pretty sure even if you were in a rage, you couldn't have done that."

She looked at Ginny then, and the confusion on her tear-streaked face solidified Ginny's thought that Kim couldn't have murdered the guy; she had no idea how he'd been killed, and hadn't even *thought* that the cops might suspect her.

"Whoever it was, they beat him to death, Kim. They beat him so badly his face was . . . It was ugly." And that was why she'd assumed the killer as male, to show that kind of rage. . . . If a guy had done that, she'd have been pissed at the assumption that a woman couldn't kill just as easily as a man. They'd been idiots.

Ginny shook it off. They had a suspect now, and if they could get a description out of Kim, maybe the cops would have a good chance at catching her.

But that only solved the cops' problem, not hers: they still had no idea who had actually hired her—Kim hadn't, obviously, and the thought of trying to track down every other girl on that list, knowing they'd probably have the same story . . .

Maybe it didn't matter, after all. Maybe it was enough that she was here, and he'd never hurt anyone again.

Not that she was condoning murder . . .

The chorus of "He Had It Coming" from that musical earwormed into her brain, and Ginny winced. Now she'd have that in her head all day.

"Oh God. Poor—no, he deserved it. But—"

There was the sound of a door squeaking open, and they all stilled, suddenly aware that they were discussing this in a semi-public place, but the footsteps echoed into the gym from the hallway, someone walking away. Ginny was worried that the interruption would make Kim freeze up again, but having decided to unburden herself, she was going to go all the way.

"Yeah. Maybe I should, yeah, I should tell you, because maybe that explains—"

She could *see* Tonica's ears prick up, the way Penny's did sometimes. "Explains what?"

Kim took a deep breath, trying to settle herself, not at all weirded out by the fact that the until-now-quiet guy had asked the question. "I didn't think anything about it at first, because, well, I didn't notice, honestly. But when I got home that day, the day he . . . I emptied my bag out, because I was going to switch bags—I use one for school and one for after," and Ginny nodded, although that was a level of teenager she didn't remember at all, "and there was a thumb drive in there. I mean, who uses thumb drives anymore?"

Ginny didn't respond to that. Tonica, who probably still used Zip drives, wisely stayed quiet, too.

"It was his, it had to be. I thought at first it must have fallen into my bag when he . . . But then I remembered something catching at my bag when I tried to leave the house, and I didn't stop because I was just so glad to get out of there, but what if Jamie dropped it there when he saw the woman waiting for him? What if she wanted it, and when it wasn't there, she killed him?"

From the look on Tonica's face, he thought the girl was reaching with that theory. Ginny couldn't disagree, but she wasn't going to dismiss the girl out of hand, either.

"You're sure it came from his house?" Tonica asked.

She nodded. "It was silver, and I'd never seen it before, and that was the only place I could have gotten it."

"What was on it?"

Kim shrugged, and wiped her nose on the back of her hand, then pressed the heels of her hands against her eyes, to try to stop the tears that were still leaking, turning her eyes bloodshot. "I don't know."

"You never plugged it in, tried to use it?" That, Ginny didn't believe.

The girl shrugged, as though Ginny had asked a stupid-adult question. "I did, and it was protected, password encryption something-or-other. And I . . . Then he was dead, and I didn't really want to know? I guess."

"Fair enough," Tonica said. "What did you do with it?"

"I threw it in my drawer, figured maybe I'd need it someday, I don't know. It felt good, knowing I had something of his, after what he tried to do, which is weird but—"

"No, that makes perfect sense," Ginny said. She got it: the guy'd made Kim feel weak, helpless. Having something of his, something that he'd maybe valued . . . It was a quiet, safe kind of payback.

"But then after you came by I started to think maybe . . . something was going on. And maybe . . . maybe I should have given the drive to the cops?"

"Ya think?" Tonica said, not quite quietly enough, and Kim flushed angrily. "All right, yeah. I was dumb. I get it. That's . . . that's why I agreed to meet you. I mean, in the real world, who cares about fake IDs? It's no big deal. But the way you were talking, and that other woman who was asking questions, and all the cops, obviously *something* was going on."

Kim might be seventeen and oblivious, but she wasn't dumb.

"And let's face it," she went on. "Him being a creeper isn't enough to get everyone so worried about him being dead. And the way you said he died . . . That's someone who was pissed-off. Really pissed-off."

"Probably, yeah," Tonica said.

Ginny patted the girl's arm, caught between feeling glad that the girl was talking, and mildly frustrated because great, they were solving her problem, but they still had no idea who had dragged them into this in the first place. And how did you put "helped expose a sexual predator after he was dead" on your resume, anyway?

"I need to give the drive to the cops. Even if it's nothing, it might not be something. It could be . . ." Her imagination failed her, and her eyes suddenly went wide, as though she'd just thought of something horrible.

"I can't believe I have to go talk to the cops. My parents are going to kill me," Kim wailed mournfully, burying her face in the soft folds of Georgie's plush back. Ginny's own thoughts seemed somewhat less inane after that, and when Teddy caught Ginny's eye and rolled his own, she had to bite the inside of her cheek to keep from laughing. Grounding until the girl was *thirty*, at least, would be a good start.

Tonica started to say something, then checked himself and asked instead, "Did you bring the thumb drive with you, Kim?"

"I . . . Yeah." She hesitated, then dug into her pocket, pulling out a small silver object. "I've kept it on me ever since then. I was . . . If I couldn't lay hands on it, I started to get a panic attack. I know, a guy was dead and all, but if I took it to the cops, they'd know I bought a fake ID and that's a crime and my mom would kill me and there's no way there's enough extra activities to make a college overlook that, is there?"

Ginny looked at Tonica; he had more experience with that sort of thing than she did, since her experience level was pretty much zero. "Did everyone who hung out at his place buy fake IDs?"

"No . . . no I don't think so."

"Well then," Tonica said, with the air of someone disposing of a problem. "You were there hanging out, the way you guys did sometimes, and he tried to be a jerk and you ran, and the next day you discovered the drive in your bag and once you realized what it was and what it might mean, you took it to the cops, and you're a hero."

Kim looked at Ginny as though to ask if she thought that would work. "And if they . . . if they find out?"

Ginny had wanted the guy exposed but not if it meant shredding Kim's future—or even the *risk* of that. Georgie shifted, stepping on Ginny's feet, pressing against her leg, and she reached down without looking to shove the dog away. "I think, if you help catch a killer, that makes up for it, in the eyes of most colleges."

There was the sound of a floorboard creaking, and a smooth voice said, "Or, we can simply make this entire situation . . . go away."

Georgie shifted again, and Ginny realized that the sharpei had been going on guard, getting to her feet between Ginny and the newcomer. The woman in the well-cut suit was holding her high-heeled shoes in one hand, explaining how she'd managed to walk up behind the bleachers without alerting them—and there was an ugly little pistol in her other hand.

And the muzzle was pointed at Kim.

16

Once upon a not so long ago, Teddy was reasonably sure that feeling the fight-or-flight pulse of blood in his veins had been a rare experience. In the past few years, the feeling had gotten more frequent, and he was pretty sure he wasn't okay with that.

And yet, here they were again.

He shifted his upper body, getting ready to stand up—or launch himself, if needed—and the woman tipped the pistol in his direction. "Please don't. I have no desire to make this messy, or any messier than it's already become, and I'm sure you don't, either. So let's discuss the matter rationally before anyone does anything that can't be undone, hmmm?"

There was a look in the woman's eye that told Teddy that rational had left the station a long time ago. They stared at each other, her weapon matching up against his mass and greater relative strength. Out of the corner of his eye Teddy saw Ginny reached out to place a hand on Georgie's collar, just in case the dog suddenly decided that the newcomer was a threat, and didn't wait for a command.

He might refer to the dog as the world's largest marshmallow, but he'd seen how fierce she could get. Forty pounds of muscle and teeth was nothing to underestimate. But no dog was fiercer than a bullet.

And that went for human mass, too.

Teddy could hear noises in the distance, people walking and talking in the hallway outside the gymnasium, and he prayed that nobody came in, almost as hard as he was praying that someone *would*. The woman's eyes were brown, her hair almost black with a scattering of silver, and the hand holding the weapon didn't shake, not even a little.

She'd beaten a man's face in.

Kim, almost forgotten, broke the silent stalemate. "You killed Jamie?"

The woman in the suit didn't look at Kim; the girl was fourth in her concerns, apparently, after the two adults and the dog. Just once, Teddy wished they could come across one of those fabled idiot criminals, who were easily distracted and never planned anything out ahead of time.

"Ah, Mr. Penalta. He was a very talented forger, but he had become a risk factor. I manage my risk factors very carefully." The stranger pursed her lips, as though she was considering smiling. She was in her mid-forties, and good-looking in an utterly ordinary way, Teddy thought. The kind of person you'd pass on the street—or the steps—without even noticing. "I was perfectly willing to settle this in a businesslike manner. He refused to accept his dismissal gracefully, however. In the ensuing discussion, it turned out that his little hobby with young girls had given the local authorities a handle with which to turn him.

"After that revelation, I thought that it might be best if he was removed from the equation entirely. And, truthfully, he was no loss at all to society." The potential smile became a very definite frown. "He should have been put down long before."

Ginny let out an ill-timed but understandable snort, and Teddy couldn't blame her; agreeing with killers left a bad taste in his mouth, too. But Penalta's skeeviness wasn't the point. The point they needed to focus on was the fact that the woman in the suit still had a gun pointed at them. And in front of three witnesses she'd just admitted to killing a man.

That fact didn't seem to bother her at all.

Sociopath, his brain whispered. She doesn't even seem to realize that killing someone is a not-good thing to do, talking about it like admitting she took the last cookies on the plate.

Teddy shook his head, huffing a laugh like he couldn't believe what his life had turned into. Probably a year or two too late for that, but whatever. "So, what, you followed us?"

"Her, actually." The gun didn't waver, but her chin tilted in Kim's direction. "As she told you, she had the misfortune of being the last of Penalta's . . . hobbies, the morning I had a conversation with him. I was going to leave her be . . . and then she spoke with Ms. Mallard here, and, well, that suggested a risk."

"You were watching me?" Kim shuddered, like someone had walked over her grave.

"She was watching the house," Ginny said suddenly. "That was you in front of it that morning. . . . I thought you were a cop, but the car wasn't quite right, not the same model the police force actually uses for their unmarked cars."

The woman smiled tightly. "And then you came back, and led me to Kim here. And I've had my eye on her ever since. I told you, I manage my risks carefully."

Oh, keep talking, Teddy thought, keep talking, and give us time to figure out how to get out of this. "So that was you lurking outside the door earlier, too, waiting to make the perfect entrance?"

"As a matter of fact . . ." The stranger smiled, and shrugged. "I was actually listening to see if the girl was stupid enough to incriminate herself as a thief as well as an idiot. Which, indeed, she was."

"Wait, what? I didn't steal anything!" Kim said, her body jerking forward as though she needed to make her protest physical as well.

"Shut up," Ginny muttered, although it wasn't clear if she was talking to the girl or Teddy, or the woman with the gun. Probably all three. She put her free hand on Kim's wrist, keeping her still. "So you killed him—not premeditated, maybe, but definitely manslaughter at the least, am I right?"

The woman shrugged. "In front of a court of law, perhaps. It was a business decision, perhaps tempered with a little annoyance of my own. I dislike predators. And I needed his former partners focused on our mutual interests, not distracted by a possible police investigation. Using violence allowed his . . . infelicitous behavior to be considered a reason why he might be so brutally murdered, and made it all too easy for everyone to look down that rabbit hole, rather than dig deeper into his professional dealings."

Either the woman didn't know about the feds being in town, or she thought she was smarter than they were. Or maybe the feds were here about something entirely different. Because if Asuri had set them up as bait for this psycho, he was going to have serious words with her afterward. Assuming he was still alive to do so.

"And why me?" Ginny asked. "Why did I get dragged into this?"

"I have no idea," the woman said. "He had a great many people who disliked him, I'm gathering. It could have been any of them, no? And bad timing, to be caught up in the middle of it all. But once here, I could not ignore such a useful tool. I needed to be sure that the body was discovered in such a way that the investigation would head *away* from my area of interest."

"Okay, but why use *me*?" Ginny could be worse than her dog sometimes, when she got something between her teeth.

"After we encountered each other outside the house, I did some research," the woman said, her smile oddly and disturbingly warm. "And I was intrigued by your dedication, above and beyond the financial aspect of things, the both of you. And your curiosity, of course. I tend to see alternative uses for traditional things, you see, and I thought certain that, in the right place at the wrong time, you would not be able to resist checking the house, and thus discovering the body. And then, once intrigued—and possibly fearing that you had been implicated—you would dig just enough to redirect the police investigation elsewhere. As, in fact, you have. Quite impressive."

"A fan club among criminals? Oh no, that's not creepy at *all*." Ginny shook her head. "And you didn't think our poking around would lead back to you? I mean, with your connection to the . . . operation he was part of?"

Ginny also had a really bad habit of poking bears with very short sticks. But while the woman's attention was on her, Teddy had been able to shift just enough that—given a distraction—he could probably hit her at the knees, and take her off balance enough that even if she managed to get off a shot, it wouldn't hit anyone.

Probably. With a distraction. But the next shot—and Teddy wasn't going to kid himself that the woman was good enough to recover in time to take that next shot—*would* hit someone. Ginny was brave, but the few self-defense classes she'd taken weren't going to make her bulletproof, and Georgie could be checked by a hard kick, if you were determined and nasty enough.

This woman seemed both, in spades. But she also seemed . . . weirdly calm, even considering she was the one with the gun. Almost as though they were having a nice chat over the bar. Probable sociopath. Right.

"None of this needs to end badly." The woman was still focused on Ginny's question. "You certainly have no need to fear me, so long as you do nothing ill-advised."

Like try to jump her, he assumed. Or go to the cops with a description, assuming she left them alive.

"Shooting you would be pointless bloodshed, further complicating a situation that should have been simple. I fully expected the police to spend the next few weeks chasing some unknown, faceless irate father or boyfriend—or, not to dismiss the female of the species—mother or irate victim.

"If, however, they did follow the track of his illicit activities, all they would find would be his former associates, who have nothing whatsoever to do with the crime, are in fact horrified by what happened, and therefore would not be able to shed any light on the situation. And I, by then, intended to be holding the reins from a very long, and untraceable, distance, as usual. Getting hands-on was never the plan."

Teddy was pretty much done for the rest of his life with sociopathic bad guys who needed to tell everyone how smart they were. Hell, he was tired of heroes who had to do that, too, but they were less prone to pointing guns at him. But the ego-blabbering could be useful—and if she was talking, she probably wasn't going to be shooting.

Probably.

"So what went wrong?" he asked, putting as much of a taunt into it as he could.

Unfortunately, that also moved the woman's attention to him, so any element of surprise his attack might have had was lost. "Ah. Yes, something does always go wrong, does it not? As I said, the local authorities had a handle on

Mr. Penalta—but his bad habits did not include stupidity, and he informed me that he had recorded information that could, indeed, link me to his actions." She sighed, the noise of a disappointed teacher. "He threatened me with that, told me to sweeten the severance deal, or he would give all of it to the authorities." She shook her head. "It really was a shame he couldn't keep everything in his pants; the boy could have gone far."

Teddy wasn't sure if she knew how creepy she sounded. He was betting on not.

"The thumb drive." Kim got it now, a little late. Her eyes were wide, and she was biting her lower lip hard enough to probably hurt. Great, the kid had taken—intentionally or otherwise—something that tied the killer to the victim.

"Yes, my dear. A rather nasty little potential blackmail package. He used his last breath to taunt me with that fact." She tilted his head to the side, and as though admitting a slightly amusing foible, said, "that may have been when I lost my temper with him."

And beat the guy to death for it. Whatever the definition of sanity was these days, she didn't fit it.

"Unfortunately, once he told me what to look for, I could not find it. It has been a vexation, forcing me to linger . . . until you returned it to me, my dear. I thank you for that, and for the knowledge that it is encrypted, and therefore was not copied, while it was in your hands."

"So you come in and, what, kill us? All three of us?" Teddy pretended to do the math in his head, then pursed his lips and shook his head. "Not going to work. You shoot one of us, sure. But that leaves the rest of us to rush you, and even if you're fast, you're not going to be able to get off three shots well enough to stop all of us." Plus Georgie, but he didn't think now was the time to mention how strong the dog's jaws were.

"Oh, no," she said, seemingly genuinely insulted. "As I said earlier, I'm a practical women, and dead bodies, especially when they pile up, are deeply impractical. You have no—what is the phrase? No skin in the game, that's correct. I go my way and you go yours, and everything works out best for everyone."

"Lady, you're not playing with a full duck. Or even half a duck. Maybe a duck wing."

Ginny's outburst made Teddy want to slap her. Was she *trying* to upset the sociopath?

"Perhaps not." Sociopath lady seemed amused by the thought. "But I don't believe in waste, and you two are far too interesting to waste. Although I will without hesitation if I am threatened, you should be aware of that." She gestured toward Kim with her gun. "Now, we all know that the young lady there has something that belongs to me. I'd like it back."

"Oh, is this yours?" The girl held up the thumb drive, her eyebrows raised. The scared, hesitant girl of just minutes ago was gone, and in her place there was a sassy, sarcastic teenager. Knowing it was a façade, Teddy decided, only made it all the more awesome, even as he wanted to tell her to sit down and shut up before she got herself—and them—killed.

"Jamie was an idiot," Kim went on, tilting the drive back and forth in her hand. "I mean, sure, it looks cool and all, but the cloud is way more portable: you just access it wherever you set up shop. He could have totally screwed you over with a dead man's drop."

Teddy was pretty sure she had no idea how macabre that term sounded, in context. Or maybe she did.

"Well then, I am fortunate that he was not as wise as you—and that you may yet learn that attempting to blackmail people rarely leads to a happy ending for the blackmailer." The woman tilted the muzzle of the gun up, an emphasis that was not lost on anyone. "Now, if you will give me that drive, and come with me—"

"Hey, no, wait a minute," Teddy started, and stopped when the pistol was turned on him again.

"Please don't make this difficult. Things have gotten slightly off plan, but that's easily correctable." She gave Kim a look that might almost have been fond. "The girl has been foolish, but not stupid . . . yet. For now, she is merely insurance." She paused, her free hand reaching out for Kim. "Come on, then. And you two—you three, stay here."

Teddy couldn't help it, he calculated the new distance between them, how fast he could build up speed with a burst start, swing the arm so to take her down, cut her legs out from under her. . . .

And she had a gun. The first thing you learned when you started breaking up fights professionally was that a gun changes everything.

"All right." Kim stood up, pulling her shirt down when it rode up and squaring her shoulders when she met the woman in the suit's eyes. "All right, I'll go with you." The sass broke just long enough for uncertainty to show through. "You're not going to kill me and toss my body by the side of the road, are you?"

That weirdly fond smile showed up again. "I am not going to kill you if you—and your friends here—don't do anything stupid. As I said, you're my insurance out of town, in case your two would-be protectors call the cops once we're gone. After that, I may leave you by the side of the road, but all in one piece." She smiled. "After you give me the thumb drive, of course." She held out the gun-free hand expectantly.

Kim snorted, and tightened her grip. "I'll give you the drive after I'm out of your car, in one piece."

If the girl lived to see eighteen, Teddy thought, she might actually be one hell of an adult.

The woman in the suit considered it for about eleven seconds. "Deal."

Kim nodded once, then looked back at Ginny. "I'm sorry. We should have gone to the cops the moment you told us he was dead."

"Yeah. You should have. Be careful, Kim."

She grinned, more a grimace than anything else. "You, too."

The woman in the suit jerked the pistol impatiently, bored with the farewells. Kim stepped forward, moving ahead of her as they walked out of the gym, the woman's attention evenly split between the girl and the three of them still sitting on the bleachers.

"Well, fuck," Ginny said as the door closed behind them, and she was already pulling out her phone and hitting a number.

"You have the Portland cops on speed dial?"

"Better," she said, and then was speaking to whoever picked up. "Agent Asuri? I hope to hell your people are as good as you say. . . ."

17

The moment the door slammed shut behind Kim and the crazy psycho bitch who'd taken her, Ginny had her phone out. She could feel her hand shaking as she hit the emergency contact number she'd programmed a few days ago; the adrenaline that had been building up throughout the entire standoff suddenly had nowhere to go except out through her pores, apparently. Someday she wouldn't break into a sweat the moment danger was over, but today was not that day.

And how sad was it, that she now had a *pattern* of post-death-threat reactions?

The other end of the call went through, and she didn't bother with a polite greeting. "Agent Asuri? I hope to hell your people are as good as you say, because your shark just bit."

Asuri didn't even bother trying to deny or create plausible deniability: she hit Ginny with a series of rapid-fire questions, even as Ginny could hear the woman's fingers flying on a keyboard.

"We're at the high school—no, I don't know what it's called—but the woman's taken Kim—a witness—as hostage. Kim's seventeen, dark red hair, I don't remember her last name—

"Siddig," Tonica said from behind her.

"Siddig," Ginny repeated. "The woman's tallish, Tonica's height but slimmer, black hair, shoulder length, and dark eyes, skin tone a medium, maybe? Wearing a suit. A pantsuit. Dark blue, white blouse. Wait, her hair was starting to go gray, not just at the temples, but throughout. No, she didn't stop to give us a name! She's a crazy person!" Ginny made an exasperated noise, then went on. "I do know that earlier this week she was driving a dark sedan, looks almost like an unmarked police car, but isn't. No, I don't know what the license plates were! Yes. Yes, all right, yes, I . . ." Ginny held the phone away from her ear, just a few inches, but she could still hear the agent's voice, loud and clear.

"Yes, what? No, I'm not holding the phone away from my ear, I wouldn't dare. Yes, we'll stay where we are. Shouldn't you be—"

Ginny made a face at the phone, then slipped it back into her pocket. "She hung up on me."

Tonica sighed, leaning back against the bleachers, the tension still obvious in his body. She could tell that he wanted to get up and race after the guy and Kim. So did she. But they both knew it would not only be pointless, but dangerous. "To be fair," he said, "she's probably kinda busy right now."

"Yeah." She thought of poor Kim, in a car with a killer, and felt that morning's coffee try to make a return visit, the acrid taste in her throat not even close to what the girl must be feeling. Oh God, what if the woman lied. What if Kim was dead now, a bullet in her brain, the thumb drive in the killer's pocket, any chance of nailing her gone forever?

"Shit," she said, and sat down again, the shaking in her hands moving to her legs, turning them into wobbly rubber stalks. Georgie whined, and pushed against her leg, either trying to give or get comfort, Ginny couldn't tell.

"It'll be okay, Gin."

"How is it gonna be okay, Teddy? Because she said she wouldn't hurt Kim? She admitted to murder, added kidnapping . . . She's a total psycho!"

"She's a sociopath probably, yeah, but that's what might keep Kim safe." He swallowed, and ran his hands through his hair. "She meant it when she said she didn't see the need to kill anyone, I think. This is . . . just business to her. The kind of thing anyone—everyone—does. It probably never even crossed her mind that we'd call the cops, because she's right, we don't have a stake in it. You did your job and now we're out."

"That's—" Ginny was about to say "crazy," then subsided. That was Tonica's point. "Fuck." She bent forward, pressing her face to the rough folds of Georgie's skin, feeling the dog press back, trying to give comfort.

"So, we're supposed to wait?" Tonica took three steps away from the bleachers, then stopped as though realizing they had nowhere to go, turned, and came back those same exact three steps.

"Like disobedient children in a time-out, end quote. Yeah." Ginny rubbed Georgie's ear and reached into her pocket for a treat. Positive reinforcement after a stressful situation, their trainer had told her. "She's sending someone over to take our statements and yell at us some more."

Knowing Asuri, every *t* would be crossed and every *i* dotted before they were allowed to go home. "She apparently thinks that confronting a killer was all part of our mad plan to get ourselves—and a witness—killed." Ginny paused. "She did say congratulations on finding both a witness and evidence, though. So yay us."

Georgie let out a sharp bark, as though to say "excuse me, *who* found the witness?" and Ginny, reminded, gave her the treat. "Yes, and you helped, you absolutely did, because you're the best dog ever."

Tonica sighed, and it looked like the adrenaline rush had ended for him, too—she could practically see his muscles untense. "So we still don't know who hired you."

"Nope." She poked at that sore cautiously, to see how much it hurt. "But if Penalta was planning to turn state's evidence, and was willing to blackmail her into giving him more money to go away, or whatever it was he wanted . . . I'm not sure I would put it past him to call me in, too. Cover his tracks with the fake client, then ask me to do something for him on the QT once I was here, maybe play himself as a concerned citizen, I don't know." She shrugged. "And he called me and not you because you would have seen through his bullshit?"

"I think you did pretty good on the bullshit detecting, Mallard."

"Yeah, maybe. I'm glad you were here, anyway."

"Me, too. So I suppose we should go outside and wait for our police minders, rather than force them to come find us?"

"I guess." Ginny rested her hand on Georgie's head and hauled herself to her feet. "C'mon, Georgie, let's . . . huh." She bent down and picked up the piece of plastic that had just fallen from under Georgie's collar.

"What is it?"

"A micro SD card."

"A what?"

"A memory chip," she said, showing it to him. "It fell out of . . ." She stared at the small blue square in her palm.

"One of yours?"

"No, I don't use these." She could feel his impatience, and held up her other hand to slow him down. "It was tucked under Georgie's collar."

Tonica might not be technologically apt, but he was fast. "You think Kim put it there." When she was petting Georgie. Not only for comfort, but looking for a hiding place.

"I think Kim is a very smart young woman." Smart enough to know that encrypted files from a dead guy's house might be bad news. Smart enough to make a copy—it would still be encrypted, but Ginny was pretty sure that, oh, the FBI might have someone who could crack it open like a walnut.

"Smart girl," Tonica said, and she closed her palm around the card, and smiled down at Georgie. "Very smart girl," she said. "C'mon. I want to give this to Asuri myself."

They headed out of the gym and she turned to look at him. "Were you really going to try rushing her, even with a gun?"

". . . probably not. You?"

She shook her head. "Hell no. Does that make us cowards?"

"It makes us not-idiots." He put an arm around her shoulders, something he rarely did; neither of them was much on hugging. "C'mon, Gin. We're not the heroes today. If anyone is, it's Kim. Our job now is to give them enough detail to put the bastard away. Okay?"

"Yeah. Okay."

Whoever had been hanging around when they arrived had gone now; even the echoes had faded. They went out through the front doors, passing a single janitor mopping the floor, without anyone stopping them or asking them what they were doing there. They were sitting on the cement stoop and soaking up what was left of the afternoon sun when a car pulled around the side of the building and took up two parking spaces, the cops inside getting out and walking toward them. No sirens, no guns, just a pair of middle-aged uniforms, one male, one female, both white, and both clearly already briefed on the situation.

"Mallard and Tonica?" The woman glanced them over and didn't seem impressed.

"That's us," Teddy said. "I'm Tonica, that's Mallard. The one with the fur coat is Georgie."

The female cop bent at the knees slightly, and gave Georgie the back of her hand to sniff. "Hello, Georgie. My name's Jennie, that's almost the same sound, isn't it? Mind if I take your humans' statements?"

Georgie got to her feet and gave the hand a polite sniff, then settled back onto the asphalt with a soft groan, clearly prepared to wait.

"I already gave a description—" Ginny started, and stopped when the guy raised a hand.

"Humor us," he said. "It's simpler if we don't have to go through the feds to get the details."

Joint investigations looked to be about as much fun for the locals in real life as they were on TV. He glanced at Ginny, who shook her head slightly. She was still going to hold out for Asuri, not the local cops. He could see the logic: the cops would take it and pat them on the head, at best. Asuri would acknowledge the debt.

"I got this, Shawn," the woman, whose name tag read J. MACK, said. "You check in."

"Best two out of three?" he asked, and she gave him a Look. "Yeah, all right." He took off his hat and headed into the building, Teddy guessed to see if there was anyone at the front desk, although he didn't know what answers they might give: Wouldn't the cops be able to get Kim's personal info directly?

Or maybe they were going to check the gym. Had Ginny told Asuri where they were? Maybe there was evidence there that they'd missed, or . . . well. There had been, only they hadn't missed it.

"No, she never gave a name. I really didn't think it was the time and place to exchange business cards."

Teddy came back to the conversation in a hurry, hearing That Tone in Ginny's voice.

"It's been a long couple of days," he said, trying to soothe things over, but both women shot him glares, and he decided to stay out of it unless asked a direct question.

For all her tone, Ginny seemed perfectly willing to recount everything that had happened, and the cop just nodded, or occasionally asked Teddy if he had anything to add.

They had just about finished when her partner came back, shaking his head, so whatever he'd gone in for, he hadn't found. He looked like he was about to say something when a call came in on his radio. He held up a finger and stepped off to the side to answer it.

"Got that." He turned back, and the lines on his face had eased slightly. "They found your girl just before the I-5 bridge. She's fine. A little shaken up, but they're bringing her back to the station and her folks."

"And being grounded for the next decade," Teddy said, and the guy cop widened his eyes and nodded.

"Oh yeah. You got kids?" the cop asked.

"Seven nieces and nephews."

"Ouch."

"All right, now that you boys have finished bonding . . . ?" Officer Mack tilted her head, indicating that she thought she and her partner should get back to it, and not stand around chitchatting.

"What else do you need from us?"

Shawn—S. WITLOCK, as per his name tag—shook his head. "Nothing."

"That's it? We're done?" Ginny frowned, looking at them. "But what about—"

"Your mystery woman's got hounds on her tail," Witlock said. "She was smart enough not to take an underage hostage across state lines, but the feds were already in the loop, so it's just a matter of time before someone rolls over on her. You might get called back to testify, but if the feds manage to work up a half-decent case, they may not need you." He shrugged, indicating that he really didn't give a damn either way.

"So we're free to leave?" Teddy asked. Translation, in his own mind, at least: He could take Ginny back to Seattle, where they both belonged?

"Please," the male cop said, with considerable feeling. "Go home. Leave town. Don't come back."

That was a little harsh, considering they'd helped crack the case, but Teddy could see the guy's point of view. He could also see, though, that Ginny was hesitating: after all this, the stress and the frustration and yeah, the fear—she didn't want to let go. Not until she'd handed that chip to Asuri directly, anyway.

"Gin. The girl's safe, we know who the killer is, and they're right, Asuri'll put the full fear of the federal government on everyone involved—Collins and the other guy, they're not that tough, and they'll roll. They'll get her. We can send Asuri her fruit basket later."

She looked at him, confused, then her expression

cleared when she understood what he meant—no need to tell the cops what they had; if they gave it to Asuri directly, she'd owe them. Again.

He put a hand on her arm and tugged Georgie's leash gently out of her hand. "C'mon. Let's go home."

"I got her voice mail," Ginny said, with a tone of distinct annoyance from the passenger seat of the car, phone held to her ear.

"So leave her a message." He grinned at her, and the mischief in that smile sparked an imp of her own.

"Agent Asuri. As per the nice folk at the Portland PD, I am on my way home. But before you head back to wherever it is they have you stationed, you might want to swing by Mary's and buy us a drink. And pick up a memory card that you may find of interest."

She ended the call and leaned back against the upholstery. "If there's nothing on that card, or it's just Kim's homework assignments, we're going to look like idiots."

"We might," he agreed.

There was silence for a few miles, Georgie half asleep in the back, when Ginny started to laugh, a choking kind of noise. "A killer used me as a cover-up."

"Tried to use you. Failed." He reached over and patted her knee, with overtly mock patronization. "Because you're just that awesome."

"Shut up. I'm pissed-off." She stared out the window, then looked back at him, finally. "We did a pretty good job, though. Even Asuri said so, even before the chip. In her own, really brusque way."

"Maybe she'll send us the fruit basket."

Ginny gave that comment the respect it deserved, and he batted at her upraised finger, laughing. "Kim's okay, the murder was solved, and okay, we still don't know who called you in on this, but we're pretty sure we know *why*. And we're heading home. Why are you still so bitchy?"

Ginny folded her arms across her chest and found a new thing to worry about. "I'm going to have to vet every single damn client from now on, to make sure they're for real. I'll be too paranoid not to."

"Probably."

"And everyone who tries to hire us. Which we should have been doing anyway. No more taking whatever jobs come our way because they tug our heartstrings."

"Uh-huh." She glanced sideways at him. He was staring at the road, but there was just enough of a smile at the corner of his otherwise deadpan expression that she knew he was laughing at her.

"I'm serious."

"I know you are. I also know that the next time someone comes and tugs our heartstrings, we're going to leap before we look. But it's nice that you're worrying about it."

She resisted the urge to stick her tongue out at him, and instead went back to looking out the window, watching the landscape go by. She should be driving—it was her rental car, after all—but she was so damn tired, she hadn't bothered to argue when he held out his hands for the keys, back in the school parking lot. She'd grumble at his pushy alpha-male car-owning behavior some other time.

"We really need to start taking this seriously," she said. "The investigations side, I mean. More seriously. Because obviously other people are. And Asuri said she was bragging on us to other agents. Okay, she didn't exactly say bragging but she was. Said that we were higher visibility than we knew. So we need to up our game."

"Yeah. Yeah, okay." He wasn't agreeing to anything, much less her not-yet-voiced plan to actually get them both licensed, but it was a start.

She frowned. "And we never got paid for this."

"Yeah, I know. Believe me, I know. And I'm going to have to dock my own pay for the time away from the bar, which sucks."

"So you agree, at least, that we stop taking on jobs where we don't get paid?"

He glanced at her then; she could feel his attention move from the road to her, then back again before he spoke. "Giving up our amateur status?" He waited a beat, and then when she didn't say anything, went on. "You're seriously thinking about getting a license, aren't you?"

"Maybe. I don't know. Yes." She very carefully did not look at him. "We want a better class of clients, we're going to need to get official. And advertise."

"Gin." Her partner sounded pained, and she almost smiled. "Can it wait until we get home, at least?"

"Yeah. Okay."

Home sounded pretty damn good right then.

★ ★ ★

They were almost at the Seattle city limits when Tonica's phone rang. She answered it for him, then put it on speakerphone.

Stacy's voice came through, slightly muffled by the background noise of the bar. "You're on your way home? Both—all three of you?"

"Yes. We should be there in less than an hour, assuming traffic isn't too screwed up."

"Yeah, good luck with that. But good. Because I'm about to kill Seth *and* your cat."

They exchanged worried looks, and then Teddy, his voice apprehensive, asked, "What's wrong?"

"With Seth? Just the usual. But your cat . . . We're down staff, again."

"What happened?"

"I don't know what happened *exactly*," Stacy said, hedging, "but Tricia found a mouse in her apron pocket. Well, half a mouse, anyway. And quit, on the spot."

"I would, too," Ginny said, sotto voce.

"Curiously," Stacy went on, "the next night, tips were back up to the usual level. Interesting, huh?"

"Interesting," Teddy agreed, frowning.

"So, yeah, before you get all warm and fuzzy about Miss Penny's hearth-guarding skills, you should be aware that she was pissed about all three of you gone on your little getaway." Stacy laughed a little, and there was a touch of malicious humor that made Teddy cringe in anticipation.

"And I mean that literally. You're going to need a new keyboard for the computer. Also a new chair, because that's where the other half of the mouse landed. I assume it was a mouse, anyway."

Ginny covered her mouth, either from shock or to keep from laughing, he couldn't tell. "Oh, she didn't."

"She did." Stacy was *definitely* laughing. "Seriously, man. Your cat does not like being abandoned."

There was a noise from the backseat, a weird sort of hurmmphing snort. Teddy said good-bye, heard the click on the speaker that indicated Stacy had hung up, then turned to squint at Ginny.

"Mallard, did your dog just snicker at me?"

In the back, Georgie shoved her muzzle under her paws to hide her grin, and pretended to be asleep.

Coda

"Are you insane? Yes, you are. No, not insane, you're bat-shit crazy."

Ginny's back went up, and her hackles rose, even though she knew he didn't mean it—not entirely, anyway. "Thanks for the vote of confidence, there, partner."

"Don't call me partner. You're not dragging me into this—not any deeper than you already have, anyway." Tonica glared at her like she'd just announced her intention to swim naked through shark-infested waters, then turned on his heel and stalked into the back of the bar, muttering under his breath.

"Well, that went well," Stacy said cheerfully. "You want a refill?"

"Thanks, yeah." Ginny pushed her mug forward across the bar, watching as Stacy poured coffee into it. Mary's had been open for about an hour, but it was a lazy Monday afternoon, and they were the only ones there yet.

Her phone was pushed the side, the sound set to mute, in case one of her clients had an emergency, but her attention was focused on the forms she had been looking over for the past half hour, until Tonica had come out and seen what she was doing. A private investigator's license application, and an employment form for Oxendine Security and Investigations.

"You're really gonna do it, huh?"

Stacy leaned across the bar, elbows folded, and Ginny made wide eyes at the other woman. "Have I ever not done something I said I was going to do?"

She'd gotten the four hours of training already, courtesy of a friend of Asuri's, and a letter of recommendation from both him and Asuri, to Arthur Oxendine himself.

"It's only part-time. Not even part-time. And mostly I'm going to be sitting behind a desk." Oxendine had seen her resume and lit up like a Christmas tree. She'd always known the research part of researchtigations was the most important part.

"Going back to work for someone else, how the mighty have fallen."

"Shut up, Seth," they both said in unison, and the old man walked by, cackling.

"It's more like an apprenticeship," Ginny said, probably for the hundredth time since she'd told them what she'd decided to do. "To learn the stuff we've been making up as we go along."

"And then you'll be official? Mallard Personal Services, Security, and Investigations?" Stacy pursed her lips and nodded, seemingly impressed.

"Well, more official, anyway. But no security work. Tonica's the ex-bouncer here, not me."

"Well, I think it's cool that you're getting officialized and everything," the bartender said. "And I bet Teddy'll do it next year, just because you did."

Ginny smiled into her cup. She wasn't going to take that bet. Especially since, once she was on her own, she could sign off on his application directly. He'd gripe and he'd drag his heels, but in the end, he wouldn't be able to resist.

She felt something butt up against her ankles, and looked down at the cat, smiling. "And maybe we'll get a license for you, too, Mistress Penny. And Georgie, too."

"You'd better," Stacy said, "since they're basically the brains of your operation."

"I'd be offended, except some days I think you're right." She reached down to pet the cat, and smiled fondly at the dog half dozing in her corner, curled under a table.

Then Stacy was looking up, over Ginny's shoulder, and her expression changed from amused to stern. "I'm going to have to ask for some ID, please," she said.

"Yeah, I don't have any," a vaguely familiar voice said. "Not anymore, and it wasn't anything Tonica said he couldn't see through, anyway."

"Kim?" Ginny swiveled on the bar stool, and sure enough, Kim Siddig stood in front of her. Her hair was shorter than it had been three months ago, down in Portland, and she was wearing a skirt and jacket instead of jeans, but the face and the voice were familiar enough to recognize.

"Hi. I hope you don't mind . . . Agent Asuri said . . ."

"It's okay, Stace," Ginny said, telling the bartender to stand down from ID inspection. "She's not here to drink. Go get Tonica out of the storeroom, will ya?"

"She's still too young to be in here," Stacy muttered, but she went to the end of the bar and yelled—quietly—for Tonica to come up front.

"How've you been?"

"Okay." Kim shuffled her feet, and looked up from under the bangs across her forehead. "Well, yeah, okay, I guess. I decided to go to U Wash after all; that's why I'm up here. Orientation started this week. My folks were kinda freaked about me going far from home after . . . everything, but it'll be okay."

Ginny nodded. "That's great, you're going to do great. And staying close to home's not so bad, after all."

They didn't mention the figure shadowing their conversation, the woman who'd kidnapped her—and still hadn't been caught. Asuri had told Ginny—and she presumed had told Kim, too—that they had very little to worry about, that the woman would have larger problems than doubling back to bother them. But Ginny still sometimes had nightmares about watching Kim led off, and then *not* getting word that she was okay. She could only imagine what Kim—and her parents—went through.

"Kim?" Tonica came forward and took Kim's hands in his own, a subtle kind of hug. "How are you doing?"

Penny head-butted Ginny, so she reached down and picked the cat up, holding her on her lap so the cat could see what was going on. From her corner, Georgie lifted her head, then when she saw that it was nothing exciting or relating to food, put her head back down.

"Anyway, my mom and I were in Seattle, and I asked agent Asuri if it would be okay if I . . . I thought about sending a letter but it didn't seem right. So here I am." She shrugged, and half smiled, as though she were gauging her welcome.

"You're not hiring her, boss," Stacy warned. "Not until she's twenty-one. She shouldn't even be *in* here. Sheesh, when did I become the grown-up here?"

"Yeah, yeah, give us fifteen minutes, and I'll toss her out myself," Tonica said, and pointed Kim at a stool. "You want a soda? What classes are you taking? You know not to drink anything at frat parties you didn't open yourself, right?"

Kim's gaze met Ginny's, and they both started to laugh.

"Georgie?"

Mmmmm? The shar-pei looked up, and then lowered her head again. "Mmmmsleepy, Penny. Ginny made me go for a long walk this morning."

"Who are they talking to?"

Georgie snuffled the air once, then her ear twitched, and her tail flicked once. "I know her. Who is she?"

Penny twitched her tail once in annoyance. "That's what I was *asking."*

"Oh." The shar-pei sniffed again, then gave a canine shrug. The

smell was familiar, and good, but lots of people petted her and told her she was a good girl. People came and went in the Noisy Place. The only ones who mattered were Ginny and Teddy. And the bar-girl and old man who smelled of food and smoke. And Penny. Always Penny.

Georgie put her head back down on her paws and went back to sleep.

So long as they were all here, everything was all right.

ACKNOWLEDGMENTS

Acknowledgments, as ever, to the Fab Four: Barbara Ferrer, Kat Richardson, Aynjel Kaye, and Janna Silverstein, who from the very first worked so hard to get this New Yorker to fall in love with Seattle that now they're stuck with me . . .

Also to Jennifer Heddle, Micki Nuding, Kiele Raymond, and Natasha Simons, who kept things moving even when I was stuck.

If it takes a village to raise a child, it takes a team to raise a series. And that's been mine.